As for

IRELAND

As for IRELAND

M. MALLACE

SAKONNET PRESS, INC.

The decision to create this book was made five years ago. During the past five years I have done a great deal of research and travel. This text is the result of that research and represents my honest evaluation of what has value and interest to a tourist like myself.

Since the archeological research in Ireland is an ongoing process, new materials are being discovered and old theories may be negated or expanded. This book is not about Northern Ireland although it includes major sites there when they relate to the Irish art and culture I discuss.

ACKNOWLEDGEMENTS

This work would not have been possible without the support of many people. I want first to thank the Irish. They have been helpful, kind and cordial. Particular thanks go to the National Museum in Dublin, which allowed me to photograph many significant items in their collection. I am most indebted to the Dúchas, The Heritage Service of the Department of Arts, Heritage, Gaeltacht and the Islands, who have provided me with information and material, granted me permission to quote their texts, AND are an outstanding resource for all tourists in Ireland. Their publications are updated each year and provide the visitor information that is not included here.

I also want to thank the following publishers for permission to cite from the various texts:
Thames and Hudson, *Irish Art and Architecture* and *Houses of Ireland*; Ulster Archeological Society, *Navan Fort, The Ancient Capital of Ulster*; Gandon Editions, *Barrycourt Castle and the Irish Tower-House*; Academic Press, *Guide of Irish Mythology*; TownHouse and CountryHouse, *Megalithic Art in Ireland* and *Irish Archeology, Illustrated*; Farrar, Strauss and Giroux, *Over Nine Waves*; Claire O'Kelly, *Illustrated Guide to Lough Gur*; and Methuen Publishers' *In Search of Ireland* by H.V. Morton. This book has been quoted extensively as this author's tales and sense of Ireland are important for gaining a perspective of Ireland.

Published by SakonnetPress, Inc.
ISBN 0-9709333-0-4

FRONTISPIECE: Dublin Castle, Dublin

With special thanks to

my husband, Peter Freeman,
without whom this book would not be possible

✦

Jennie, Nathan, Abbie and Pamela
for their encouragement and support

✦

Janice Clark whose unlimited confidence
in this project carried it through

✦

Frank Robinson for his advice,
encouragement and most valuable time

✦

Gilbert Design Associates, who have provided the expertise
and ideas to make this a creative publication

CONTENTS

1. *Introduction*

T HIS TRAVEL GUIDE is for a tourist like me. I like to
know about things, what they are and what they mean. I
am curious. On the road, we all need a good map and an
easy-to-read and easy-to-carry book which provides an inventory
of the important historical sites and a sketch of the history, culture, art, literature and government. It needs to include only the
important information that you can understand and will remember. More is not always better. Since a travel guide like this was
not available, I made the decision to create one. Here it is.

We see things differently when we know what to look for. So
it is my endeavor to be your guide through Ireland. To give you
the information you need to see, enjoy and have fun, as well as to
come away with the sense of the pleasure of having visited Ireland.

Not only is Ireland a playground for the
sportsman and a country of great scenic beauty,
it is unique in its wealth of historical monuments. It is one of the few countries which has
well preserved Stone Age field monuments in
abundance. The gold jewelry and ornaments in
the National Museum of Ireland attest to a way

of life and skill of craftsmanship in Ancient Ireland which often
is not noticed. The monasteries were seats of learning which
achieved great heights of sophistication and talent as exemplified
in the *Book of Kells*. The Vikings, Anglo-Norman invaders, the
Irish chieftains and subsequent planters from England and
Scotland all contributed to the upheavals throughout the centuries which are a part of the Irish Heritage.

The history divides naturally into six chapters: Stone Age,
Ancient Ireland, Early Christianity, Monasteries of Ireland,
Anglo-Norman Invasion and 18th Century Through Independence. In this book, the historical sites are sorted on this basis in
chapters that are color-coded for easy reference. The interesting
features of the art and architecture – the features that make them
what they are – are described and illustrated with photographs
and drawings. The best examples are highlighted in the text.

Since there is too much to see and do in Ireland, I have
included Chapter 3, "Highlights of Ireland: Best of the East and

Courtesy of
Hedley Park
Montessori
School, Merrion
Square Dublin.

Best of the West." These are my choices of what you might like to see because they are the history and heritage of Ireland. These sites are described in the text. Please make use of the index for cross referencing.

Chapter 4, "The Land," describes areas that are naturally picturesque and provide superior opportunities for photographers and artists. The planted gardens are extraordinary, for this climate is warm and wet enough to sustain a great variety of tropical plants. Many of these gardens are open to the public.

Other chapters include: "Irish Heritage," a summary of the important trends which affected the course of Ireland's history; "Mythology," a sampling of the tales of early history as told by the druids and the bards and transcribed by the early Christian monks; "Modern Ireland," the key to understanding the process by which this country achieved independence and "The City of Dublin," an inventory of historic sites as well as information on Ireland's literary figures and fine arts.

The chapter, "Counties of Ireland," includes a description of each of the twenty-six counties, with a map showing approximate locations.

Once you know where you want to go and what you want to see, it's time to turn back to Chapter 2, "Fundamentals." Not only to plan when and where you want to go, but you also need to decide where to stay. Food and lodging are plentiful in Ireland. From the simplest Bed and Breakfast to the most elegant Relais Chateau, the Irish Tourist Board certifies their credibility and provides listings. Many of these have formed affiliations within specific price ranges. You'll find this information in this chapter.

The text is indexed and there is a bibliography for follow-up reading.

2. *Fundamentals*

Why Ireland

ALTHOUGH THIS BOOK is **primarily** concerned with the Irish heritage, there are other reasons to visit Ireland. Before you plan your itinerary, decide: why do you want to visit Ireland? what are your interests? how do you want to get about? and where do you want to stay? Wherever you are or whatever you do, this handbook will be of use. If you prefer more in-depth explanations, references are included.

Ireland is a beautiful country with fantastic scenery – the kind of scenery you see in the landscape paintings in art galleries. Perhaps your roots are in Ireland and you wish to see the Old Country or research your family – there are about 8 million Irish in Ireland and about 40 million Irish in the United States. Perhaps you're curious about its history, art or why so many people emigrated to the United States; or perhaps you're a sportsman after sea fishing or angling, hiking, horseback riding, and golf; or perhaps you're a horticulturist eager to visit the spectacular gardens; or perhaps you're a person interested in horse breeding or racing. **There is so much to see and do that a visit to Ireland will always be a delight.**

Let this reference handbook be your guide to understanding Ireland.

When to Go

Ireland has a temperate, rainy climate. A set of silk long-johns, raincoat, umbrella and an extra pair of shoes makes one all cozy and comfortable. If you should experience inclement weather, photographs on gray days have interesting atmospheric and color tones. In any weather, it is a place to relax and enjoy.

The high tourist season is May through November. The weather in the summer is at its warmest and the days are at their longest. However, it is at that time that Ireland can be beset with many tourists. Although the weather is cooler, the spring and autumn are less crowded. Winter is also acceptable, although some sites are closed and lodging is limited. Many of the country houses which serve as guest houses in the high season are closed

The high tourist season is now May through November.

during the winter. Country inns as well as the hotels are open and often offer off-season rates.

The key to visiting any country is having access to what interests you. Golfers want the courses open and playable; fishermen want the fish biting; and gardeners want flowers in bloom. For those interested in the heritage of Ireland it is important to know when the sites are open. Dúchas, The Heritage Service (formerly the Office of Public Works or OPW), 6 Ely Place Upper, Dublin 2, Ireland, is an excellent source for this information. If the site merely requires a hike across a pasture, there is no problem, but if it is staffed, it may be operated on a seasonal basis. Much of this information is also available through your guest house or hotel.

Dúchas
The Heritage Service
6 Ely Place Upper
Dublin 2, Ireland
Tel. 01 647-2461
www.heritage
ireland.ie

How to Get About

When you look at a map of Ireland, it seems small — about the same size as Massachusetts, Vermont and New Hampshire together, or one half of Florida or one fifth of California. Why not see everything? Ireland may not be large but there are well over a thousand sites and sights. You need to be selective. An ideal, if you have the time and the interest, is one week in each province. Relax and enjoy. Do not spend all your time in a car traversing the narrow main highways at high speed while driving on the left side of the road. Make a preliminary list of what you would like to see and what aspect of Ireland you prefer to emphasize.

I cannot recommend the Irish Tourist Board (1 800 223-6470) too highly. They have collected and organized material on all the specialties in Ireland: transportation, car rentals, general tour operators, special interest tour operators which include angling, culture and historic sites, cruising the inland waterways, cycling, horses, gardens and golf, Tracing Your Ancestors and more. **If you would like to take a tour,** request the Irish Travel Magazine or specific information from the Irish Tourist Board. If you have already scheduled a tour, proceed to the section on the Irish landscape. If you are a serious enthusiast in a specific area, contact the Irish Tourist Board. They are an excellent resource.

Irish Tourist
Board
1 800 223-6470

If you decide to rent a car and do this tour on your own, you must be relaxed about the **road maps.** There are many wonderful maps of Ireland: Michelin, Rand McNally, Ordnance Survey and others. However, many of the roads are not signposted. You often are not able to find the road you want. You do get lost. It is an excellent idea to take a small compass attached to a suction cup which can stick to your windshield. It will not solve everything but it helps. Sites in this text are listed with route numbers (when available) and/or roads (for example, between Dublin and Limerick). BUT there is no problem being lost in Ireland. It is rather fun – just leave a little extra time when planning your day for exploring. You find the most delightful roads and meet the wonderful Irish, who are always helpful. Of course, they may not know where your site is either, even though they will tell you how to get there. Relax and have a wonderful time.

I was told by an Irishman that the Irish never like to say 'no' or 'I don't know.' They will always give you the answer they think you want to hear. I then asked this same gentleman about their license plates. Most have black letters and numbers on a white background: there are two numbers at the left, in the middle of the plate are some letters and another number is at the right. But, there are some plates which are bright yellow or bright red with perhaps a combination of six letters and numbers. He replied, after

It is an excellent idea to take a small compass attached to a suction cup which can stick to your windshield.

Signs in Gaelic – mostly in the west

barely a moment of hesitation, that the "European Community is standardizing all the plates and Ireland is the first to adopt the new system"!!!

I felt quite knowledgeable with my new information until I realized that there were not enough letters or numbers to ever accommodate the whole of the European Community. I asked someone else a few days later and learned that a license plate is issued when the car is bought and stays with the car forever. The two numbers at the left reflect when the car was purchased and the letters in the middle represent the county. This system was initiated in '87. Those cars which are older have the old plates which were yellow or red. Perhaps?

Another day we were driving about in circles looking for a particular hotel where we had reservations for the evening. Finally, we stopped and inquired directions of two gentlemen. They were rather reticent at first but then made a sweeping gesture and replied "up and around." Well, it was indeed up and around. It was in the city through which we had passed 45 miles back.

Entrance to Shannon Airport

Where to Stay

The best resource for lodging on a trip to Ireland is the Irish Tourist Board. They have a toll-free number and are willing to send you their publications. These accommodations are all approved by the Irish Tourist Board. This approval rating is taken seriously and the descriptions are generally accurate. It will be rare that you will not be delighted by the wonderful Irish hospitality. When you do book your rooms, be sure to request the price for your specific accommodations. Some quotes are per person, others per room and there is often a supplement for single occupancy. Unanticipated expenses are not a pleasant surprise when traveling.

But wait before picking up the telephone! Which of the following publications do you want?

Accommodation Guide includes everything with a brief description and pricing. There are at least 3750 places to stay, from large chain hotels to many bed and breakfast establishments. This is beneficial as a cross-reference.

Town and Country Homes Association "Guest Accommodations" provides a listing (over 1500 entries) of bed and breakfast homes with description and photographs of the facilities. These are primarily private homes which tend to be less expensive and more intimate.

Irish Hotels Federation: "Be Our Guest" lists hotels and guest houses (over 600 entries) with ★★★ classifications, gives descriptions of facilities and photographs of the premises. This publication includes a large range of accommodations and pricing from private B&B's to hotel chains to luxury hotels.

Irish Farm Holidays Association: Farmhouse Accommodation is a listing (over 500 entries) of working farms in agricultural Ireland. These are bed and breakfast homes with fresh foods. The listing includes descriptions of facilities with a photograph of each.

Village Inn Hotels includes a group of small village inns with home cooking and local fare. The brochure includes descriptions, photographs, prices and directions.

Coast and Country Hotels lists a group of family hotels which have been selected for their settings. The listing includes photographs, descriptions, pricing and driving directions.

Manor House Hotels is a group of hotels which range from hunting lodges, castles, or manors with 'luxurious accommodation.' The brochure includes photographs and a listing of facilities.

Friendly Homes of Ireland is a collection (about 125 entries) of private family homes and small hotels, with a wide range of facilities and prices. Most entries include a brief description and a photograph.

Hidden Ireland: Accommodation in Private Heritage Houses is a listing of privately owned country houses which the owners are prepared to share with you. A set dinner menu is often available which is not included in the price. There are sketches of the houses and detailed descriptions in the brochure. The prices span a wide range that reflects the amenities and locations.

Ireland's Blue Book of Irish Country Houses & Restaurants is a listing of owner-managed gourmet country houses and restaurants. There is a photograph and description of each facility. As a rule these are private homes with wonderful Irish hospitality as well as being quite stylish.

Elegant Ireland provides a listing of houses and castles which may be rented, with or without staff, and which provide a family or business group with elegant surroundings and accommodations. Prices are not available in the brochure but inquiry will generate more information.

Relais & Chateau Guides have information on some excellent hotels in Ireland under the auspices of the Relais Chateau Organization. These hotels are expensive and very comfortable with many amenities. (This publication is not available through the Irish Tourist Board but may be procured through Relais Chateaux, 11 East 44th Street, New York, NY, 10017. Tel: 212 856-0115.)

Other Accommodations: For information on self-catering facilities, utilize the Irish Tourist Board publications *Travel Weekly*, *Visitor* or *Choose Your Own Ireland*. More facilities can be found in *Gardens of Ireland. Golfing Ireland: Forty Shades of Greens* lists courses, clubs and golf packages.

Notes: Since the pricing continues to change, the above list is presented from less to more expensive. High season prices are no longer for summer months only but now apply from May to November. It is less crowded in the spring and fall, but not by much. There is also the old adage that "you get what you pay for" which only means that the amenities in a less expensive accommodation will be less, or not as "American." I have tried a sampling from most categories, found the photographs and descriptions helpful and the 'hosts' welcoming. In this way you see a side of Ireland that you will not witness or share in the big city hotels.

THERE IS AN excellent Michelin guide to dining in Ireland which includes restaurants of all price ranges. It is also a good idea to take the recommendations of the hotel or guest house where you are staying. The Country Houses may provide dinner, although it is a set menu with at least three courses. The Irish breakfast is normally available at all B&B's and should be tried as a new experience.

Irish Tourist Board Office: 1 800 223-6470 (New York)
Toll Free access to AT&T direct from Ireland: 1 800 550000

Where to Go

If you are determined to see every single historic marker in Ireland, this reference is not for you. The Michelin Green Guide and the Eyewitness Travel Guides are excellent. The Dúchas: The Heritage Service has issued maps of nearly a thousand sites. Heritage Island Properties has issued a guide to their properties and the Irish Tourist Board has published a visitor's guide of superior quality. There are also publications in many areas of interest and activity.

This handbook explains and recommends the more significant sites. A limited set of road directions are included. There is also a chapter on the counties. Each **County** is described; all of its important sites are numbered and a 'casual' map with major roads and the approximate location of the sites are included. These maps help you, generally, to know where things are located, to complement an official road map. All official road maps highlight particularly beautiful scenic roads. It is always delightful to drive through the countryside. Many counties have published a "Touring Guide" which provides detailed information: itineraries, maps and shopping. All queries for information of a special nature can be answered by the Irish Tourist Board, Dúchas or any Irishman you happen to meet.

Northern Ireland is a part of another country, the United Kingdom. It is on the northeast border of the Republic of Ireland and in ancient times they shared a culture. I include a map of Northern Ireland indicating the sites that relate to Ireland. It also is a scenic land, but is not a part of this guidebook because its culture is based to a great extent on the immigration of Scots over the centuries and must be viewed from a different perspective.

My most important recommendation is to relax and enjoy as you travel.

Many counties have published a "Touring Guide" which provides detailed information.

3. The Highlights

THE BEST OF the East and the Best of the West list the most significant sites from a historical perspective. Since there are over a thousand sites in Ireland, these lists, with accompanying maps, can help you sort them out. They are especially for the traveler who prefers an agenda, or is short on time or doesn't like to miss anything important. However, travel in Ireland should not be a Marathon. Be sure to take the time to smell the roses, enjoy the scenery and savor the ambience of Ireland. You can return.

The Best of the East

Dublin (1) is a great city for the arts and should not be missed. I recommend a stay of three days (without jet lag). Although it is

not an old Irish city, it reflects many aspects of Ireland's history. Make your reservations for one or more of the theater productions immediately. The Abbey Theatre is not the same old historic building of Lady Gregory and William Butler Yeats, but they produce, nevertheless, some wonderful Irish plays. Look in the paper for what's playing, check the section on literature (chapter 12) and choose the play that appeals to you. You will not be disappointed.

Wander the streets to see the wonderful Classical architecture of the **Four Courts**, the **Custom House** and the **General Post Office** on O'Connell Street, where the Easter Rising occurred. There are some wonderful sculptures: Deirdre of the Sorrows, the Parnell Monument and the Children of Lir in the Garden of Remembrance in Parnell Square. The River Liffey divides Dublin on the east/west axis while O'Connell Street divides it on the north/south axis. While on O'Connell Street near the Parnell Monument, stop in the **Rotunda Hospital Chapel**. The architecture and stucco work are delightful. The theme is angelic babies, appropriate for a maternity hospital.

Pass by the majestic **Leinster House**, the seat of government, and visit the **National Museum of Ireland** and the **National Gallery of Ireland**. **Trinity College** is most famous for the old library and the **Book of Kells**. These should be seen, but also take a stroll (or

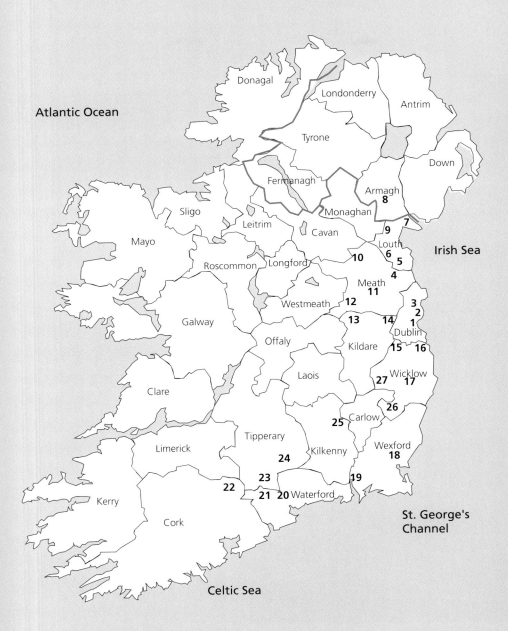

Atlantic Ocean

Irish Sea

St. George's
Channel

Celtic Sea

Donagal

Londonderry

Antrim

Tyrone

Down

Fermanagh

Armagh
8

Sligo

Leitrim

Monaghan

7

Mayo

Cavan

9

Louth
6

5

Roscommon

Longford

10

4

Westmeath

Meath
11

3
2
1

Galway

Offaly

12

13

14

Dublin

Kildare

15

16

Clare

Laois

Wicklow

27

17

26

25

Carlow

Tipperary

Kilkenny

Wexford
18

Limerick

24

23

19

Kerry

22

21 **20** Waterford

Cork

a guided tour) about the campus. The new library is modern and is offset by the Campanile, the Venetian style science building and buildings in a variety of architectural styles.

The two Anglican cathedrals in Dublin, **St. Patrick's** and **Christchurch,** are great examples of Gothic architecture. They each have salient points. Do not limit yourself to these buildings as Dublin is diverse and interesting.

North of Dublin there are several spectacular sites. In the suburbs is the **Marino Casino (2)** which is an eccentric structure. **Malahide Castle (3)** and the Talbot Botanical Gardens are also well worth a visit.

If you are restricting your visit to the east, a visit to the **Proleek Dolmen (7)** should be included. This is close to the border with Northern Ireland so you should continue north to Armagh to visit **Navan Fort (8)** or Eiman Macha. **Newgrange (4)** is an absolute must with a visit to either **St. Columba's House (10)** in Kells or **St. Mochta's Oratory (9)**. **The Hill of Tara (11)** is one of those places that you would be embarrassed to miss.

Old Mellifont (5) was a wonderful Cistercian abbey which was modified and expanded into a great Gothic structure. Little remains today except the Lavabo, or fountain house, and part of a restored cloister. It is not a necessary stop when you are limited in time. The **High Crosses at Monasterboice (6)** are exceptional. These scenes carved in stone were the teaching tools of the monks for illustrating and teaching the Scriptures. **Trim Castle (12)** is also a must: it is a Norman Castle with round towers, curtain walls and the original keep or tower house within the bawn. Be sure to walk all around to get the full sweep of this very large castle.

As you head south, a detour to the **National Irish Stud (13)** is well worth the excursion. Do not miss **Castletown House (14),** the first Palladian style house, which was the prototype for much architecture that followed in Ireland. South of Dublin are two others: the **Russborough House (15),** unique in that it houses the famous Beit Art Collection, and **Powerscourt (16)** in Blessington that burned several years ago. There is still hope that it will be repaired. Much of the structure is still there, but it is the gardens

Statuary in Powerscourt Garden

and their setting which are worth the visit. The nearby Waterfall is spectacular if there is a great deal of rain preceding your visit.

Be sure to drive through the Wicklow Mountains on your way south to **Glendalough (17)**. It is not restored although preserved; the scenery is exquisite and there is an oratory as well as a round tower. Just south of Glendalough is **Enniscorthy Castle (18)**, a 13th century tower house, which has been reconstructed according to the original plans. The stone fort of **Rathgall Stone Fort (26)** (Ancient Ireland) is the only one left in the east. It has been excavated. **Baltinglas Abbey (27)** or **Jerpoint Abbey (25)** are both Cistercian foundations with sufficient ruins to be well worth the visit.

As you travel westward, Waterford offers two wonderful gateways: the **Hindu-Gothic Gateway (20)** and **Ballysaggartmore (21)**. In the Carrick-on-Suir area is **Ormond Castle (19)**, which has an interesting history and includes the remains of a round Norman tower. On to Tipperary for **Swiss Cottage (23)** and **Cormac's Chapel (24)** on the Rock of Cashel, which represents the art and culture of the Irish stonemasons more than any other building. The blind arcades were innovative and provided stability for the thick high walls.

Not too far to the southwest is **Blarney Castle (22)**, where one feels obliged to go and kiss the Blarney Stone especially as it is done backwards and upside down from a great height.

As you head back to Dublin or continue farther west, there are many optional sites along the way.

The Best of the West

Whether you are continuing from the east or have landed at Shannon Airport, the west will be covered best by two loops from Limerick – one to the south and the other to the north. The greatest feature of the west is its wonderful and unusual scenery. **Connemara** and the **Burren** are awesome. You need only to drive or walk about the area to appreciate the rugged landscape.

Traveling southwest from Limerick, the coastal road offers some interesting sites such as the ruins of **Dromore Castle (1)**, but it is **Newcastle West (2)**, also called Desmond Castle, which is a good example of the 13th century castle. It has been restored by the Dúchas.

Two other superb scenic drives are the **Ring of Kerry (4)** and the **Dingle Peninsula (3)**. I favor the latter but feel reticent in saying that, as the tour buses may also discover its quiet charm. The **Gallerus Oratory,** a collection of **Beehive huts** and the **Blaskett Island Interpretive Center,** which has an outstanding presentation, are located on Dingle. **Ogham Stones** and **Staigue Fort** are in the Ring of Kerry. Not only are there many side roads which are fun and interesting to explore, it is mountainous and the passes open to many spectacular views. After driving through Moll's Gap you descend to Killarney, the **Killarney National Park (7)** and **Muckross House and Gardens (7).** The grounds and surrounding area are inviting.

If you go south along the coast of the **Beara Peninsula (5),** to the **Ilnacullin Gardens (6),** Garinish Island, in Bantry Bay there is an Italianate garden. The climate here is quite mild, which allows for much diverse planting. The small ferry to the island also passes by a small group of seals sunning on the rocks.

The coast of Cork is interesting and beautiful with opportunities for meandering. (If you have not seen **Blarney Castle,** do go there and be sure to take a side trip to **Cormac's Chapel,** a must.) There are many sites along the way for your leisure, but if you are limited in time, travel north to the **Dominican Friary in Kilmallock** and **Monasteranenagh Cistercian Abbey** if you haven't yet visited the ruins of a Cistercian foundation. **Lough Gur Interpretive Center (11)** includes the **Great Stone Circle.** The monuments have not been restored, only preserved, and there is no commercialization. It takes walking about.

County Clare is the home of the **Burren (14), Poulnabrone Dolmen (33),** and the **Cliffs of Moher (13).** It is possible to do a trip from Doolin to the **Aran Islands (15).** If there is sufficient time and

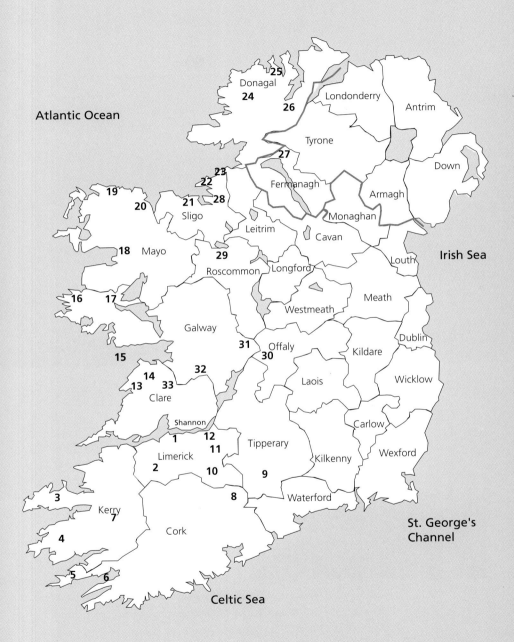

Atlantic Ocean

25
Donagal
24
26

Londonderry

Antrim

Tyrone

Down

27

19
23
22
Fermanagh

21
28
Sligo
Armagh

20

Leitrim
Monaghan

Cavan

18
Mayo
29
Longford
Louth

Irish Sea

Roscommon

16
17
Westmeath
Meath

Galway

Dublin

31
Offaly
30
Kildare

15
Wicklow

14
32
Laois

13
33
Clare

Shannon
Carlow

1
12
Tipperary

11
Kilkenny

Limerick
Wexford

2
10
9

3
8
Waterford

Kerry
St. George's
Channel

7

Cork

4

5
6

Celtic Sea

*View from
Moll's Gap*

*Portal tombs in
the Burren*

good weather, do not miss the Aran Islands with a visit either to **Dun Aengus** or **Dun Conor.** Transport to these islands is also available from Galway. At the Burren Center there is information for safe hiking – do not attempt it without checking with the center.

Take the western route by the shore north through Galway, Mayo and Sligo. This passes through **Connemara (16)** and **Joyce country (17).** There are many ruins of Franciscan monasteries such as **Rosserk (20)** as well as castles and 18th and 19th century houses. There is a wide choice which is totally dependent on individual interests. I prefer colorful history and seek out those sites connected with Grace O'Malley, which include Clare Island, Rockfleet Castle and her descendants at **Westport House (18)**, which is an interesting architectural gathering. Sligo's **Ceide Fields (19)** are for those who are interested in the culture of the Stone Age farmers. All is wonderfully scenic and the historic sites are secondary to the scenery.

Due west of the city of Sligo are the **Carrowmore Megalithic Tombs** and **Knocknarea (21)** – perhaps the largest area in Ireland containing megalithic tombs. They have not been restored as has Newgrange, Co. Meath, and are therefore not impressive in the same way. North of Sligo you can detour to **Lissadell House (22)**, the home of the descendants of the Gore-Booths and Constance Markieviez. William Butler Yeats was a frequent visitor. Although the Classical style of the exterior is severe, the interior does not share the austerity and contains family memorabilia. As you go farther north, **Creevykeel Court Tomb (23)**, a court cairn, is on your right with **Benbulben (28)** (see next page) in the distance.

Donegal's **Glenveagh Castle and Gardens (24)** are extraordinary: the luxurious gardens, a storybook castle in an idyllic setting on a rock promontory on Lough Veagh and the rugged

surround of the National Park. To the far north is **Doe Castle (25)** – a great medieval castle. As you proceed south, if you have decided not to go on to Londonderry, you will find the restoration of the ancient fort **Grianan of Aileagh (26)**, which played a part in the early history and mythology of Ireland.

As you pass through Sligo, take a more eastern route to see other interesting sites. You may go east into Fermanagh and visit Boa Island where the **Double Idol (27)** is found. As you go south, do not miss **Boyle Abbey (30)** which is an excellent example of the Cistercian foundation. **Clonmacnoise (30)** borders the River Shannon. There, the high cross, called the Cross of the Scriptures, is located in the Interpretive Center and, though not as well-preserved, is on a par with the high cross at Monasterboice. Don't miss the Irish-Romanesque **Nun's Chapel** across the road or the Irish-Romanesque doorway at **Clonfert (31).**

In southern Galway is a restored tower house called **Thoor Ballylee (32).** It was the residence of Yeats. It is worth a visit, both as an example of a 16th century tower house and as a memorial to the poet.

As you return to County Clare and Shannon Airport, I hope that you have participated in those activities that you enjoy, as there are wonderful opportunities for golf, horseback riding or horse racing, fishing, hiking, boating or whatever pleases your fancy. Ireland is truly a wonderful and interesting playground.

Cottage and Thoor Ballylee

Benbulben

4. *The Land*

Scenic Ireland

IRELAND WAS FORMED by the combination of mountain building upheavals, weathering, flooding, volcanic activity and glacial scouring. This all began as early as 600 million years ago and left Ireland with mountains, lakes, rivers, caves, cliffs and scenic beauty that are unequaled. Mankind, also, has had its impact over the past 9000 years in Ireland.

The climate is mild and moist, which accounts for the wonderful greenness of the land. The Gulf Stream prevents the frigid temperatures from the north gripping the country. The rivers and lakes are pure and not polluted. They are a haven for those who appreciate their natural beauty. There are beautiful scenic drives with pastoral views that are unequaled.

The rugged coastline with high cliffs, the rolling hills and mountain ranges as well as the verdant valleys offer enchanting meanders. Nearly every map will show green lines along those roads which are considered scenic. The secondary roads are the best.

The Golden Vale

There is the rugged west coast. The Burren is a limestone plateau with great fissures, caves and underground rivers. There is little vegetation and the Atlantic Ocean's winds and waves sweep and batter the coast. Just to the north is Connemara, another wild and splendid area. There are lakes and streams, mountains and fields of bog. There is a great feeling of isolation and natural beauty. Cities and suburbs will not invade this region.

The secondary roads are the best.

Hedgerow plantings

Canal boat rentals may be obtained through the Irish Tourist Board.

Another important ingredient of the splendor is the Irish and their talent for horticulture. Since they are excellent gardeners and the climatic conditions are ideal, the gardens are exquisite. There are unexpected varieties of plants – for who would expect palm trees at the same latitude as Goose Bay, Labrador, which is north of Newfoundland! The exposure to the ocean brings abundant rain. There are formal gardens and delightful hedgerow plantings.

There is also a network of **inland waterways** which are available for cruising. Different kinds of boats may be hired, with or without crew. Boat travel will be dependent upon the weather, to some degree, as the loughs can be quite rough. Travel by boat along the canals with a bicycle aboard is a relaxed and interesting way to explore the roads of Ireland. Information for rental may be obtained through the Irish Tourist Board.

Bogs

There is more that needs to be said about the bogs or peatlands. Much of the Irish heritage has been influenced by or recorded in the peat bogs that now cover only 17% of the country.

Peat bogs cover 17% of Ireland.

There is an excellent booklet, *Peatlands*, published by the Wildlife Service of Ireland and available at the Dúchas sites, which explains the formation of the fens and bogs as well as their specific composition.

The map at left shows the distribution of raised bogs in Ireland. This area is referred to as the

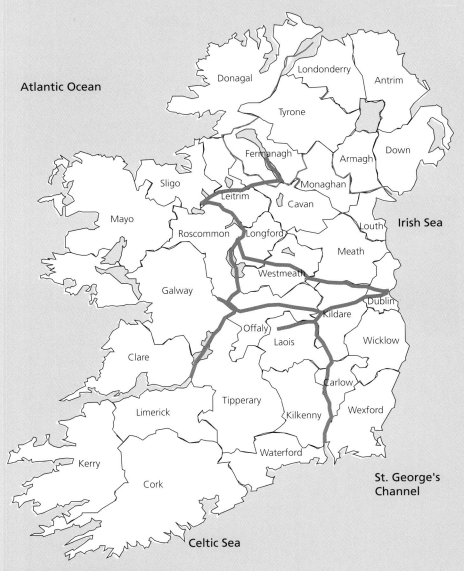

Ireland's network of inland waterways.

midlands. This map does not include the mountain bogs, which cover much of the Wicklow Mountains, the hills of Connemara or the coastal lowlands in the west. There are also many fens (similar to marshland) throughout the countryside.

Peat bogs, which have been developing for 8000 years, are common throughout the northern latitudes. As the glaciers retreated they left depressions without drainage. This standing water in a climate with abundant rainfall gave rise to the raised bogs. Generally it can be said that peat is 95% water while 5% is a combination of preserved dead plants (mostly sphagnum moss). Sphagnum moss, which is able to survive on rainwater, colonized the fen, made it more acidic, and prevented the process of its own decay; in this way, over hundreds of thousands of years, a peat bog was created. You cannot travel through these areas in Ireland without being aware of the bogs. The roads undulate, giving the sensation of driving over slight swells and dips of water – which indeed you are.

Bog cotton

Early man also contributed to the formation of blanket bogs. In prehistoric times Ireland was covered with forests of sessile oak. The Neolithic farmers felled trees to make pastureland for their cattle. Without the roots of these trees to absorb the heavy Irish rains, the soil became waterlogged. In the damp cool climate sphagnum moss was able to invade the swamped farmland, and bogs developed relatively quickly. There are wonderful plants in the bogs, with bog cotton the most prevalent and least seasonal.

For centuries, bog material, or peat, has been used as fuel for cooking and warmth. You may see the harvest of peat from these blanket bogs in the hilly areas. Many people have turbary rights, or the right to cut from a local bog.

The turf is cut with a slane, a narrow spade with a side blade set at a right angle, and laid on a spread ground to dry.

The sods are turned as each side dries and then loosely stacked into footings. When thoroughly dry the sods are stacked into clumps near the house.

The raised bogs found in the midlands are a rich source of fuel. After World War II the Republic of Ireland established Bord na Mona (Irish Turf Board) to centralize the peat industry. Farmers with small bogs were bought out by the government to make large-scale, mechanized peat production economical. Ireland currently meets one-fifth of its energy needs and generates 21% of its

Ireland currently meets one-fifth of its energy needs and generates 21% of its electric power with peat.

32

electric power with peat. More than 200,000 acres of peatland have been drained or cut away (mostly in low-lying central Ireland). There is a Peat Interpretive Center at Lullymore in Co. Kildare which traces the history of the midland bogs. At one time fens and bogs were common all over northwestern Europe. Through drainage and harvesting, Ireland is the last country in Europe to have significant bogs. They are valuable for study and wildlife preservation as well as being places of beauty and interest.

From Shannonbridge, Co. Offaly, a Bog Rail Tour, sponsored by the Bord na Mona, offers an excellent way of seeing and experiencing the world of the bog, particularly on the industrial level. Arrangements may also be made for a guided study tour of bog life.

During the pre-Christian times, executions and sacrifices took place in the bogs. There is also some thought that items were thrown into the bogs as offerings to the gods. During the harvesting of peat, many interesting finds or "hoards" were discovered. These artifacts are the only record which survives from the pre-Christian era. Now, many that demonstrate the wonderful workmanship of this period are on display at the National Museum of Ireland in Dublin.

With the coming of Christianity, these practices were abandoned although the fear of the bogs remained. Folklore is rich with tales of these forbidding lands. An Irish poet and winner of the Nobel Prize for Literature, Seamus Heaney, wrote "peat is the dark casket where we have found many of the clues to our past and to our cultural identity." Will-o'-the-wisp and jack-o'-lantern were the names the Irish gave to the strange lights that beckoned and led men astray on the bogs.

Cut turf drying on a spread ground

Gardens in Ireland

Gardening in Ireland is a way of life as Ireland has a friendly climate – not too cold with lots of rain – so plants are happy. This book mentions many of the gardens that are open to the public and you'll find booklets and brochures that list more.[1]

The early castles had domestic gardens which were designed within the confines of the available space. The walled enclosure of the castle became the safe haven from the marauding bands in the countryside and provided relaxation, exercise and food for the family. As times became more secure, the intimate formal gardens were expanded to include areas with more informal plantings and space for more energetic leisure, especially riding. These demesnes became a focal point of the culture and life of the aristocracy of Ireland. The outer space was usually designed to set off the surrounding landscape in harmony and beauty, whether it be a lake, river, mountain or ocean.

This development of the formal garden in Ireland occurred during the eighteenth century. Members of the aristocracy who had traveled abroad on the Grand Tour were enamored of the magnificent Italianate gardens of Europe. Their gardens became a statement of wealth and privilege with statuary, fountains, canals, topiary and formal flowerbeds to create perfect harmony. Hidden

The view from Powerscourt Gardens to the mountains

away were the kitchen garden, herb garden and orchard. The best example of this Italianate or formal garden is Powerscourt.

Gardening as a science also became popular in Ireland. The climate is conducive to a wide variety of species and there are those who have devoted their lives to collecting plants throughout the world and successfully introducing them to Ireland.

There are also many small intimate gardens which exhibit a knowledge and expertise in horticulture which is a pleasure to see and enjoy.

Gardens in Ireland by Type

These are gardens which have been created over the centuries and incorporate gardens of many types. The domain becomes a biome. The following features are often included: water, woods, trees, shrubs, formal plantings, bog plants, herb gardens, roses, shade and woodland shrubs and rolling lawns with appropriate statuary.

Altamont Gardens, Tullow, Co. Carlow are all-inclusive and offer residential gardening courses during the summer. A newer addition is the bog garden. There has been a great surge of interest in protecting the bogs, as they have been drained, cut away and used as fuel for electricity, and could near extinction.

Anne's Grove, Castletownroche, Co. Cork has many unusual specimens. Of particular interest is a water garden created in the early 20th century by soldiers from the nearby barracks, who diverted the Awbeg River so that it flowed closer to the house. They created an island, weirs, rapids and bridges.

Mount Usher, Ashford, Co. Wicklow was started in the mid-19th century as a small retreat for the Walpoles of Dublin. It now extends over 20 acres and is a horticultural wonderland including many species and environmental settings. The trees, shrubs and lawns interact with the water (river, weirs, cascades and bridges) to create a balanced and varied landscape.

These gardens have an international flavor, with trees, shrubs and flowers that are native to countries throughout the world. Ireland, with its mild wet climate, can host an extensive variety of species which are not native to either Ireland or northern environs. There is an emphasis on the science of horticulture, with a variety of species and texture which otherwise would not be available.

National Botanical Gardens, Glasnevin, Dublin 9, has collected 20,000 species. It was established by the Irish Parliament in 1795 to "promote a scientific knowledge in the various branches of agriculture." It encompasses 27 acres and has imported and distributed new species within Ireland. There are interesting greenhouses and pleasant grounds through which to wander, enjoy and learn.

John F. Kennedy Arboretum, New Ross, Co. Wexford which began in 1964, covers over 600 acres with 4,500 species of trees. One can walk through the various biomes for two miles or ten miles. There are two botanical circuits – conifers and broadleaf trees. From the summit of Slieve Coillte is a view of the whole arboretum and the countryside. Managed by the Irish Forestry Board, the arboretum can be enjoyed as one of scenic beauty at all times of year or as a research and learning center.

FORMAL
GARDENS

The formal garden usually includes the Italianate style terraced walks with boxwood hedges, statuary, topiary, fountains and rooms with different romantic themes. In Ireland it also includes a variety of naturally contrived spaces, such as a woodland path, bog gardens, Japanese themes and walled gardens with pool and colonnaded shelters.

Ilnacullin, Garinish Island, Co. Cork, was created in the early 20th century from a barren windswept island. There are several places along the coast near Glengariff where private boats will take you out to Garinish Island. To add to your pleasure, the boat passes by rocks which are often laden with sleeping seals. The island, topped with a Martello tower, is a myriad of gardens that include areas known as the Jungle, the Dell and Happy Valley. The Italian garden is spectacular; the Casita, or Tea House, with its columned portico looks down on a sunken garden with a reflecting pool beyond which is the Medici House or pavilion and a delightful view of the bay and nearby islands. The island was

The Casita, Ilnacullin, an Italianate garden

given to the state in 1953 and is now under the care of the Dúchas. Gardeners bustle about maintaining the grounds and the exquisite flower beds.

Powerscourt Gardens, Enniskerry, Co. Wicklow, are magnificent. Although the vast house was recently burned, the terraced gardens from which you view the Great Sugar Loaf peak represent the apex of 19th century landscape gardening. The present design was superimposed on the earlier style when the Viscount traveled extensively through Europe bringing home with him the impressive statuary and wrought ironwork. The setting, terraces and statuary are of great beauty and well maintained. The stark contrast with the burnt shell of the magnificent house inspires one to wish for restoration and continued access. Several miles away is the Powerscourt Waterfall in a woodland setting which is particularly spectacular after a spell of rain.

WOODLAND
GARDENS

The woodland garden features meandering paths with many shade-loving shrubs. Rhododendrons in Ireland are exquisite. There is usually an appropriate ruin with a suggestion of water creating a nice harmony of balance. These gardens are normally informal or natural and often adjoin the grounds of an estate.

Creagh Gardens, Creagh, Co. Cork, has an old mill and pond as well as many paths to wander through.

Kilfane Glen and Waterfall, Thomastown, Co. Kilkenny, was designed to display the rugged and untamed side of Mother Nature. According to the Irish Tourist Board, its "winding paths, cliff tops, cascading stream, a hermit's grotto, a waterfall and a tiny cottage orne work their magic on every visitor."

Demesnes were the landscaped confines of early castles which included the woods, fields and gardens. These could be quite varied and often included walled gardens for herbs and produce as well as formal social gardens. For the family to travel beyond these confines was dangerous so the demesnes provided an extension of living space for the residence. These areas have been cultivated and developed for many generations. Some are open to the public for viewing while others are in various states of restoration and preservation.

Johnstown Castle Demesne, Murrinstown, Co. Wexford, includes a castle that is now an agricultural research center. It is a delightful 19th century castle with towers, battlements, Gothic windows, color and texture in the facade, ornamental lakes and the ruins of a tower house that conjures up a wonderful setting for a medieval romance. This combination of the grounds as a setting for the castle defines a demesne.

Birr Castle Demesne, Birr, Co. Offaly, is an 18th century park and garden extending over 150 acres. Interest in horticulture and astronomy continued in the succeeding generations. The demesne has an interesting history, with the castle being added to and turned around to face the park in the early 19th century. During the potato famine, over 500 were employed to enlarge the lake and make other impressive additions to the demesne. It contains many exotic species and is particularly spectacular in the spring.

Heywood, Ballinakill, Co. Laois, is under restoration and in the care of the Dúchas, since the house was accidentally burned and demolished. It is an 18th century-style park that includes formal lawns, lake and pergola, an alley of lime trees and a pavilion, overlooking garden terraces and an ornamental pool.

Abbey Leix Gardens, Abbeyleix, Co. Laois was once the site of a Cistercian abbey located on the banks of the River Nore. The extensive pleasure grounds are charming.

Kilmokea,* Campile, Co. Wexford, is a privately owned garden that is a blend of creative horticulture and great care. It includes an Italian garden with loggia and pool and wide lawns. There is a lower garden with a lake, stream and woodland that suggests a different type of ambience.

*Indicates limited access or access by appointment

Japanese gardens create a separate world that unites one's soul to the earth. The elements and ideas are expressed symbolically. To enter a Japanese garden, one enters a different world.

Tully Japanese Gardens, National Irish Stud, Tully, Co. Kildare, is a garden created in the early 20th century that symbolizes the life of man. Plants, bonsai, stone ornaments and a geisha house were imported from Japan. It was designed and built by a Japanese landscape architect. While in this garden, you walk the paths of human life through which man passes.

These gardens are usually found in private homes, small hotels or country houses with accommodations. They are casual and natural and often are gems for those who wish to gain new ideas from what others have done. Visits to these gardens are limited to season and time. Contact the Irish Tourist Board to request their booklet, *Gardens of Ireland.*

Fairfield Lodge,* Monkstown Avenue, Monkstown, Co. Dublin, is a small and delightful city garden.

The Shackleton Garden,* Beechpark, Clonsilla, Co. Dublin, includes a natural walled garden with a perennial collection and some interesting trees and flowers in the surrounding grounds.

The Dillon Garden,* 45 Sandford Road, Ranelagh, Dublin 6

Primrose Hill Garden,* Lucan, Co. Dublin, is a traditional garden.

Wicklow Gardens Festival runs from approximately the 20th of May to the 26th of June with about 50 participating gardens. Information can be obtained through the Wicklow County Tourism Office at the County Building on the outskirts of Wicklow town.

The gardens in this category are of historical interest and open to the public. They reflect the genre of the period and are an integral part of the house complex.

Glenveagh Castle and Gardens, Churchill, Co. Donegal, were given to the nation of Ireland to form the focal point of the Glenveagh National Park. The garden encompasses 10 acres and includes both formal and informal plantings and landscaping. The breadth of the plantings include a formal walled garden, pleasure garden, Belgian walk, view walk, Swiss walk and an Italian garden. The castle and gardens are situated on Lough Veagh.

*Indicates limited access or access by appointment

Tully Japanese garden

Malahide Castle Gardens, Malahide, Co. Dublin, are also referred to as the Talbot Botanical Gardens. They were created in the 20th century and include shrubbery and walled gardens. The plants are particularly of the Southern Hemisphere. For the horticulturist the highlight of this garden is the 4-acre walled garden, which is best seen by appointment.

Muckross House and Gardens, Killarney National Park, Co. Kerry, is awash with pleasant lawns, shrubs and excellent vistas.

Emo Court and Gardens,* Emo, Co. Laois, has a classical house with dome, columned portico and Greek-style statuary that is impressive in its size and restoration. A house of this style and dimension would not be complete without the appropriate landscaping and gardens, which include woodlands, rhododendrons and azaleas in the spring, rare specimen trees and the required vista.

Lough Rynn Estate and Gardens, Mohill, Co. Leitrim

Castle Leslie and Pleasure Grounds, Glaslough, Co. Monaghan

Tullynally Castle and Gardens, Castlepollard, Co. Westmeath

Kilruddery House and Gardens, Bray, Co. Wicklow, is a 17th century garden in the French style. There are two parallel canals which extend from the house and lead across to the park along an avenue of lime trees.

Rose garden, Powerscourt

The gardens nurtured by hotels are unique and spectacular although not intimate or natural. These hotels are usually former castles which have been converted. The trees and shrubs on the grounds have been left intact and tended. The texture and colors of the flower beds are pleasant although not unusual. Some of these have excellent golf courses in superb settings. It is more comfortable to view these gardens as a hotel guest but one can also call ahead for an appointment specifically to see their gardens.

Hotel Dunlow Castle Gardens, Beaufort, Killarney, Co. Kerry, was created in the 20th century during ownership by an American who created a fine arboretum in the mountain landscape. The gardens have been expanded with this purchase by a hotel company. The hotel is a large modern complex through which one approaches the gardens. This includes a walled garden and the ruins of a 13th century castle.

Mount Juliet, Thomastown, Co. Kilkenny, is a great house with some wonderful stucco work and the gardens are a perfect setting for such a house. There is park land which extends to the River Nore as well as walled gardens, lawns, rose garden and water garden.

These gardens are often based on the foundation of an older garden but reflect the interest and cares of the new owner-designer.

Kinoith, Ballymaloe, Co. Cork, is among trees and hedges of an old garden but is directed toward culinary plantings by its owner, a renowned cook. There are vegetable gardens and a formal fruit garden with some of the trees trained to arch. The herb garden is contained within a Renaissance parterre with boxwood hedges protecting the herbs – both culinary and medicinal. It is also a country house and restaurant with accommodations.

Butterstream Garden, Trim, Co. Meath, is located in Trim and is a new creation by its owner. The garden is separated into 'salons' – each with its own temperament and ambience. The colors and textures of the separate gardens are planned as carefully as a landscape painting. Although not large, it is inclusive and selective.

Mount Congreve,* Co. Waterford, is a private garden created during the past 60 years to include every possible plant that will grow in this area. The species of magnolias are all-inclusive and there are over 500 species of camellias.

*Indicates limited
access or access
by appointment

5. *The Mythology*

THE ROOTS of the mythological stories in Ireland lie deep within the culture of the ancient Irish. Their social structure included the storytellers who recorded the customs and history of their people – not in writing, but orally. In this way the history, morals and standards were learned and embellished by new generations. Later, it was the druids, poets and bards who wrote them down at the druidic schools after the written word was brought to Ireland with Christianity. The early Christian scribes, who copied down the sacred texts in Latin, also wrote down the Irish legends and stories in the vernacular of Gaelic. The legends were copied again in the 11th and 12th centuries, and it is from those texts, now found in the National Library, that the rich literature of the Gaelic Irish survives.

The stories have been studied extensively and books have been written to evaluate the accuracy of these tales. Scholars have divided the sagas into cycles – each a somewhat separate unit in time and tale. On a less scholarly level these tales have been widely narrated and illustrated so we may also enjoy and know the rich literature of ancient Ireland. For example, *Over Nine Waves* by Marie Heaney is an enjoyable retelling of the Irish legends. And *A Guide to Irish Mythology* by Daragh Smyth is a good source for defining the theories of who and where. The question of when is more difficult. The above are just two of many available books that are well worth reading. Another extensive telling of these tales is *Lady Gregory's Complete Irish Mythology*. It includes a preface by W. B. Yeats.

The following streamlined summaries are included here not merely to whet your appetite but to stimulate your imagination when you see the ancient forts and the Treasury Room at the Museum in Dublin. Throughout these sagas, there is the universal theme of the banished rightful heir who is nurtured by lowly pastoral folk, learns the greatest of honorable skills and succeeds in claiming and holding his rightful place of authority.

Mythological Cycle

These tales tell of the coming of the ancient gods and how the Tuatha De Danaan seized the land from the Fir Bolgs. There was

Early Christian scribes who copied down the sacred texts in Latin also wrote down the Irish legends and stories in Gaelic.

Deirdre of the Sorrows O'Connell Street, Dublin

a fierce battle at Moytura (near Lough Arrow, Co. Sligo) after which the Fir Bolgs fled to the Aran Islands. "These newcomers were the People of the Goddess Danu and their men of learning possessed great powers and were revered as if they were gods. They were accomplished in the various arts of druidry, namely magic, prophecy and occult lore."[2] The stories of Balor of the Evil Eye, the birth of Lug, the Reign of Bres, and finally the second Battle of Moytura in which the Tuatha De Danaan were successful, arise from this period. Then there was peace. The following quotation from *Over Nine Waves* describes the beauty of Ireland:

"Ireland was a beautiful country, the coastline fringed with high mountains and below the wooded slopes lay deep valleys, fertile plains and marshy bogs. The rivers and lakes were full of fish, cattle grazed on the plains and herds of pigs rooted for acorns in the oak forests. Bees hummed among the heather in the bogs and the woods rang loud with bird song. The weather was not too hot in summer, nor too cold in winter, so crops grew abundantly and there was plenty of food. The island wasn't overcrowded and there was room enough for everyone."[3]

But nothing is forever. In northwestern Spain there lived a tribe, the Sons of Mil. They were skilled in magic and had been wanderers to lands as far away as Egypt and Greece. These Milesians came to visit Ireland under the leadership of Ith, who was ambushed there and left mortally wounded. The Milesians gathered a great army among the Gaels and returned to Ireland to avenge his death. There was a great battle which the Milesians won, with witchcraft playing an important role on both sides. The dates of the Milesians' arrival differ greatly. Some say they arrived as early as 1498 BC and others as late as 500 BC. Mil is considered the ancestor of the Gaels in Ireland.

Although the Tuatha De Danaan had been defeated, they did not leave Ireland, but went underground to live in the mounds, or sidhes. Throughout the ages it was believed that the Tuatha De Danaan could and did return from the Otherworld, at will. Their presence was accepted by all and they played an important role in the sagas and the heroic exploits of the kings and warriors. For these pagan people, the De Danaans were the gods who gave them strength, knowledge and wisdom.

The wonderful tale of the Wooing of Etain is a delight and the following is only one crisis in a great love story which I include to increase your interest in reading more of the Irish legends.

King Eochaid Airem (c. 135–110BC) was in search of a wife. He sought and won Etain, of whom it was said, "Never a maid fairer than she, nor more worthy of love, was till then seen by the eyes of men." They returned to Tara and were most happy.

However, she was also the wife of Midir, the handsome and immortal son of the Dagda of the Tuatha De Danaan who lived in the Otherworld. When Midir came to Tara to claim her, Etain declared that she would not leave Eochaid unless he gave his permission. Midir planned a campaign to gain that permission. He arrived at Tara in the form of a young warrior with a silver chessboard and challenged Eochaid to chess. The stakes were greatly in favor of Eochaid, who won 50 horses after the first night of play and 50 boars, 50 cattle and 50 sheep after the second night of play. The third night the ever-confident Eochaid made the stakes very high: the first "to clear the land of stones and with them to lay a causeway over the Bog of Tethbae; the second to make fertile the rushy ground around his fort; and the third to clothe the bare hills of the district with trees."[4]

Midir agreed to the stake on the condition that no one in the household look out from the ramparts while he honored the conditions. Eochaid agreed and won the game of chess. But during the night, he became so curious that he sent his steward forth to see what was happening. In the morning Midir knew he had been betrayed, accused Eochaid and was very angry at the dishonor of the King. They agreed to one more game, at which Midir would set the stake. Eochaid could only agree. The stake was "to take your wife, Etain, in my arms and to give her a kiss." Naturally Midir won, took his reward and no great number of warriors could prevent Midir from taking Etain. The couple rose into the air, became two swans, circled Tara and flew away. This was not the end of Eochaid's search for Etain, nor the end of the challenging confrontations between her two husbands. It was through them that the great high king, Conaire Mor, was descended.[5]

Ulster Cycle

Navan Fort, known as Emain Macha, is situated west of Armagh, Co. Down, in Northern Ireland. It was the ritual and political center of Ulster and the scene for the tales of the Ulster Cycle or the Red Branch Knights. There are many tales of which some very special ones are Deirdre of the Sorrows and all the aspects of the great hero Cuchulainn. The beginning of Navan Fort as a royal seat starts with Macha whose story follows.

Macha was the daughter of Aed Ruad who became King of Ireland in 728 BC, a kingship which he shared with his cousins, Cimbaeth and Dithorba. Their fathers had imposed a geis upon the three cousins to maintain harmony. A geis is either an obligation to perform or a taboo against performing a certain act. The kingship rotated on a seven-year cycle from one cousin to the next with the poets, magicians and chiefs ensuring compliance with the geis. This worked well for 45 years until Aed Ruad drowned.

Macha decided to assume the sovereignty on behalf of her father. Her uncles refused to allow the position to be held by a woman. A war followed, in which Macha was the victor. The defeated Dithorba was expelled to Connacht and Macha married Cimbaeth. She gave him the kingship. She had the ring fort at Navan built, which became the royal center of the Uliad or Ulster warriors. Macha succeeded Cimbaeth upon his death in 658 BC and reigned for seven years until she was slain. The palaces of the kings of Ulster remained at Emain Macha for 855 years.

Conchobar mac Nessa was king at Emain Macha, or Navan Fort, in the 1st century BC. His son was Cuchulainn whose adventures and exploits are told in numerous tales filled with imagination. You can visit Navan Fort where, according to J. P. Mallory in *Navan Fort, the Ancient Capital of Ulster:*

"You can stand on the mound where King Conchobor played fidchill, an early Irish board game. This is also the mound on which Sualtaim, the father of Cuchullain, raised the alarm that Ulster had been invaded by the armies of Queen Medb in the greatest Irish epics, the Tain (Cattle-raid of Cooley). You can also stand on the ramparts where Deirdre first met her lover Noisi, and shamed him into breaking the king's commandment and running off with her, thus setting in motion Ireland's most famous and tragic love story. It was also from these same ramparts that Emer, wife of Cuchullain, watched her husband go off to his final battle.

"A walk around the area outside Navan takes you to the playing fields where Cuchullain first came as a small boy to defeat single-handed the macrad, the 'boys brigade' who played and practiced warrior skills on the green of Emain. After play, we are told, they would swim in the Callan to the east of Emain Macha. To the northeast of the fort the druid Cathbad instructed his students and it was on the green of Emain that..."

The sites of his adventures have been identified. Cuchulainn's death occurred in 12 BC. Wishing to die standing up, he tied himself to a pillar stone that can be seen at Knockbridge near Dundalk, Co. Louth.

Fenian or Ossianic Cycle

The tales of the Fianna are about the military guard of the king in the 3rd century AD. This army was a group of highly skilled warriors who defended the state, supported the king and protected the safety and property of the people. It was a militia of the most honorable and most skilled of men. Cumhall was the leader of the Fianna. He was killed by Goll mac Morna, who then became their leader.

Many of the tales of this saga concern Cumhall's son, Finn mac Cumaill. After his father died, he was forced to go into hiding for the mac Morna clansmen were often in pursuit of him. He learned many skills and became a great warrior. When he had reached maturity, he went to Tara where Conn of the Hundred Battles reigned and welcomed him. It was the time of the feast, when there was a geis against war, battles, quarrels and feuds. Finn reclaimed his rightful position in the following way:

Every year the Tuatha De Danaan came forth on Samhain (Halloween) and Aillen, one of the Ever Young, would lull them to sleep with his enchanted music and burn down Tara. Finn received a pledge from Conn that his heritage would be restored, should he prevent the burning of Tara. An old trusted friend of Finn's father gave him the means of resisting the spell of the enchanted music. With the help of a magic cloak and spear he accomplished this deed and killed Aillen.

Under Finn, the Fianna became famous for their adventures. This elite force accepted only the most able, and their training was rigorous. Finn lived at the hill fort on the Hill of Allen. Among the best known of these tales are The Birth of Finn's Hounds, The Enchanted Deer: the Birth of Oisin, and The Pursuit of Diarmuid and Grainne.[6] Throughout his life, Finn sought the love of a woman who had spurned him, which led eventually to his death. His tales are, not surprisingly, linked to the Tuatha De Danaan.

The years of Finn ended in 283 AD. He had served bravely and well under Conn of the Hundred Battles and Cormac mac Airt, both High Kings at Tara.

Cycle of the Kings

This cycle features Conaire Mor (105–27BC) and is the tale of Leinster. It has been credited with being a mixture of history and fiction. The genealogy of Conaire returns to the mythological cycle and the tale of the Wooing of Etain. Eochaid and Etain gave birth to one daughter named Etain. She married Cormac, the king of Ulster, and produced only one daughter. Although her husband ordered this daughter to be killed, she was spared and taken to the cowherds of King Eterscel, where she was known as Mes Buachalla (the cowherds' fosterling). A bird informed her that she would be with child by him and the child's name was to be Conaire. King Eterscel, a king of Tara, married Mes Buachalla, and thus Conaire became the son of a King.[7]

Conaire was also the son of a bird. When King Eterscel died there was, according to custom, a bull feast. "One man would eat his fill and drink his broth. He would then fall asleep, an incantation chanted over him. In his sleep the person he should see would be king, and were the sleeper to tell a lie about this he would be killed."[8] Accordingly, the sleeper saw "a naked man carrying a stone in a sling coming after nightfall along the road to Tara."[9]

Conaire had been told to do just that, and at the right moment he arrived in Tara appropriately unclad. He became High King and received his geis. One of these forbade him from hunting or harming birds – not surprisingly.

This was a time of great strife and warring in Ireland. Although Conaire was able to expel to Britain the many marauders in Ireland, they returned with hired soldiers from foreign lands. Conaire was killed at Da Derga's hostel, however, not from the superiority of the marauders with their hired soldiers, but because he was not faithful to the many obligations and geis conferred upon him when he became High King. The Plunder of Dinn Rig and The Destruction of Da Derga's Hostel are tales and stories of war and vengeance from this cycle.

These tales in the Cycle of the Kings, or the Historical Cycle, are grim, reflecting the times. As the tales of the mythology end, the era of Christianity, with the arrival of the early monks, changed the society of Ireland. Perhaps this climate during the Cycle of the Kings opened the way for the very peaceful conversion of the people of Ireland.

6. Stone Age

7000—2000 BC

T HE STONE AGE in Ireland is uniquely apparent. Since Ireland has never had extensive industrialization or development, the Stone Age monuments still exist. Archeologists continue to make new and worthwhile discoveries. Knowledge of the **Mesolithic Era** of the Stone Age developed from the excavation of settlements at Mount Sandel, Co. Antrim, which dated from as early as 7500 BC. Formerly believed to be merely a temporary shelter for hunters and gatherers, the discovery of microliths (tiny shaped pieces of flint) made of chert, a mineral native to central Ireland, changed the evaluation of the evidence. Chert microliths have also been found at Carrowmore, Co. Sligo, and Lough Boora, Co. Offaly, where excavations have revealed well-established communities. This indicates a developed industry of making stone tools within Ireland during the Mesolithic period.[10] Individual interest in these excavations should be directed to the Dúchas or the National Museum of Ireland.

Settlements at Mount Sandel, Co. Antrim date from as early as 7500 BC.

The **Neolithic Era** of the Stone Age is even more easily seen as Ireland is rich in the stone field monuments of these early farmers, of around 3000 BC. There are artifacts and indications of their domestic and community life in the excavations at Lough Gur, the Ceide Fields, and the scattered stone field monuments which are numerous and impressive. Since Ireland was never subjected to massive industrialization, these monuments were relatively undisturbed and are now being protected and restored. If you want to see more than an artist's rendition of the Stone Age, Ireland is the place to explore.

The stone field monuments, mostly funerary in purpose, are located throughout the countryside in pastures, fields and reserved areas, which are under the aegis of the Dúchas. For these ancient people there was a strong emphasis on the afterlife. They believed that after death, their god/kings passed into the World of the Ever Young and must, therefore, be provided with adequate facilities. These facilities were cleverly conceived and well constructed. Since they were built of huge stones, which supported and defined the actual burial chamber, they are referred to as megalithic tombs. These include **passage tombs, court cairns, portal tombs** and **gallery graves,** as described below. After putting the megaliths in place, the chamber was covered with more stones, clay and sod, which gave it the appearance of a mound.

It is probable that many tombs have been destroyed when the stones were quarried by later generations for other purposes. The significance, if any, of every mound of stones is not known. "An archeological survey of the country is in progress and Sites and Monuments Records have been produced on a county basis....The ultimate aim is to produce a detailed published survey on every county but this will take many years."[11]

In the meanwhile, if you see a mound in a field, it could possibly hide a burial chamber, an early crannog, or a fort. Or it could simply be a mound of dirt covering an outcrop of rock. Exploration of possible sites is restricted to archeological teams with the approval of the Irish government.

Megalithic Tombs

A passage tomb "is an artificial cave built of large stones and usually covered by a mound. The normal practice was to erect the cave using massive slabs or dry stone walling covered by lintels or corbelling. Over this skeletal structure was thrown a massive mound of clay or stones."[12] It usually consists of an internal passage leading to inner chambers — one on each side and one in the rear. Found in these chambers were cremated remains as well as beads and carved objects. The mound is usually round and has a retaining wall of kerbstones. It was utilized in ceremonial functions. Not only is the construction of these mounds remarkable but these stone slabs give us our only examples of megalithic art in Ireland. Beside the Boyne River, just west of Drogheda, is a series of passage tombs which are well preserved. Since access to these is only by bus from the Interpretive Center, I would recommend driving through the small tertiary roads of the area first to have a feel for the location and to come upon the site of Newgrange somewhat unexpectedly.

The passage tomb at **Newgrange** (restored) is particularly significant as it has been carbon-dated to about 3000 BC and shows great knowledge of astronomy.

Newgrange has been carbon-dated to about 3000 BC

The mound stands 36 feet high and is 280 feet in diameter. The outside of the mound is faced with white quartz and is topped with sod and thick green grass as it was originally. The actual tomb is composed of a roof box, passage and chamber. Around the outside of the mound is a large circle of standing stones which may

have preceded the building of the mound to determine the exact position of the sun at the winter solstice.

This is an impressive site. With or without the tourists and the 20th century, this would be a place of grandeur and mystery. Can you imagine the countryside five thousand years ago? It's raining and very misty and you have debarked on the shore of the Boyne River not far from the Irish Sea. As you step out to explore, perhaps in search of food, this site looms out of the mist. I would be sore afraid.

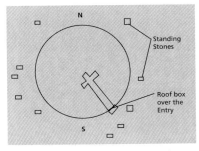

This layout of Newgrange shows the remaining stones of the Great Circle as well as the relation and position of the chambers and the passageway.

The roof box rests on the front of the passage roof and it is through here that the rays of the sun reach the inner chamber on the morning of the winter solstice (December 21). Although you cannot actually see the entrance from the inner chamber, your guide will shine a light through this roof box from the outside and the inner chamber will be lit.

How were these Stone Age farmers able to move these megaliths and calculate their proper placement? They were certainly not as primitive as our image of Stone Age man.

The passage into the chamber is nearly 60 feet long and about 5 feet tall and is faced with standing stones, of which many are decorated. The central chamber is the focal point of the tomb with three small side chambers. There are basin stones in the chambers which held ashes, bones and offerings. Mythology tells us that Dagda, the chief of the Gaelic gods, and his three sons, Aengus, Aed and Cermad, are buried at Newgrange. Dagda was also one of the five chieftains of the Tuatha De Danaan and when they were defeated by the Milesians, they went *into* the mounds rather than leave Ireland.

The roof is a corbelled arch, which consists of angled overlapping flat stones, that allows for the runoff of water away from the chamber. In the east of Ireland there is an average annual rainfall of 30 inches. Without this arch, a great deal of unwanted water would have drained into the chamber. However, the chamber has remained dry. These people were not only knowledgeable in astronomy but also in adapting to the environment.

Decorated stone at the Newgrange passageway entrance.

This decorated stone (above) at the entrance of the passageway at Newgrange is divided by a straight groove which is deliberately in a direct line with the entrance of the tomb. Before restoration the entrance was sealed with a large flat stone. On one side are three spirals carved out of the stone and on the other is a series of double spirals. These patterns are repeated on the carefully placed stones within the passage.

Many designs appear haphazard with overlap as though each generation supplied its own creation. The most significant advance

Passage tombs at Knowth

was the development of three-dimensional designs which conform to the shape of the stone. On the right side of the entrance stone (previous page) the end spiral follows the snub shape at the upper edge of the stone, while on the left side the diamond or chevron shape tapers and also follows the contour of the stone. This represents a more sophisticated composition in the application of designs to rigid objects.

Simple designs are found on the kerb stones at the back of the Newgrange mound as well as on the orthostats, or roof stones. The designs were chipped or picked into the stone using another sharp stone. These processes are called picking, ribbon picking, blanket picking and incision, depending on the breadth and subtlety of the design. Since no tools or areas with waste chippings have been discovered, it is not known where the designs on the stones were created – at the site or at a separate quarry. We do not have any solid evidence to explain the meanings of the designs or clues as to their symbolism and significance, although these same designs continued in use into the Bronze Age upon axe heads and pottery.

At **Knowth** the kerb or supporting upright stones along the edge of the mound are visible and are often decorated with lines and geometric shapes. The artwork on these stones is over 7000 years old. This community of passage tombs has no accessible entrances.

This area contains as many as twenty tombs. Restoration and excavation are ongoing and the team in September 1996 reported that they "represent the finest examples of megalithic art across Europe…" and were used in Neolithic, Iron Age, Early Christian and Anglo-Norman cultures.

The passage tombs at Knowth were used by four cultures: Neolithic, Iron Age, Early Christian and Anglo-Norman.

55

After the Neolithic farmers, Knowth became a center for the druid priests of the Iron Age; during the early Christian era it was used as a religious center or perhaps an early monastery; and the Normans used these mounds to build their defenses to repel attack by the local clans. But as time passed, these structures were deserted, decayed and became landfill – an unnoticed and unrecognized part of the natural landscape. Excavation has revealed that these mounds were not natural after all.

Fourknocks, Co. Meath, does not have a kerb although the interior of the chamber has some spectacularly decorated stones in which the designs are plastic and incorporate the shapes of the stones. The mound is restored and the key is available nearby.

Loughcrew, Co. Meath, is a superb, though strenuous, site with many outstanding features, and now has guided tours.

COURT
TOMBS

[The] "court-cairn or court-tomb...has the form of a rectangular burial chamber, often divided up by jambs and sills, and entered from a court or forecourt which is roughly semi-circular in shape and in which some form of funerary ritual probably took place."[13]

These tombs appear now as foundation stones and are in various states of preservation. They exist primarily in the northern half of the country and on lower ground. Cohaw, Co. Cavan, **Creevykeel,** Co. Sligo (with a lovely view of Benbulben), and Maghaghanrush (Deer Park), Co. Sligo, are examples.

The tomb known as **Creevykeel** is a very elaborate example. The photo below shows part of the layout with the entrance and the open courtyard beyond, which is an entrance to the stone covered tomb. The area is surrounded by a dry stone wall and there

Creevykeel

are entrances and evidence of other tombs. Creevykeel was taller and covered with many stones which followed the pattern of those that remain.

The portal tomb, or dolmen, has two large upright stones forming the entrance or portal of the chamber with a third upright in the rear. On this tripod is balanced a huge capstone. These are also called giant's graves.

Proleek Dolmen

It was within this shelter that the cremated remains were placed. The structure was covered by stones and/or earth. How did these men in 2000 BC place these immense capstones on the uprights? The accomplishment of this feat is most impressive when one considers the lack of machinery in 2000 BC. The **Proleek Dolmen,** Co. Louth, and **Poulnabrone,** Co. Clare, are excellent examples.

The **Burren** is an area in the northwest of County Clare with many portal tombs on the limestone karst. The stones are not as massive as Proleek and are of limestone. The road from Corofin to Ballyvaughn has a great abundance of these portal tombs. The flora which survive in the cracks of this near-wasteland is delicate and beautiful. The most famous and most photographed of these sites is **Poulnabrone.**

Knocknearea, Co. Sligo, the dolmen of Queen Maeve's Grave, is the largest unopened megalithic tomb in Ireland. It is well worth a hike to the hilltop for the view. Another significant portal tomb is that at Drumanone, Co. Roscommon.

Poulnabrone

Gallery tombs are smaller rectangular-roofed chambers which are enclosed by a U-shaped series of stone slabs. These occur more in the south and later (after 2000 BC). They were used and reused during the Bronze Age. Although the wedge-shaped tomb is more widespread than the other types, it blends into the landscape

Gallery tomb

and is not as noticeable. The chamber narrows in width and lowers in height toward the back. It is roofed with slabs of stones.

Stone Circles

It is believed that these circles represented a strong religious culture with a high degree of social organization. The **Great Stone Circle** at Grange, near Lough Gur, consists of a ring of 117 accurately placed orthostats, or standing stones, set in sockets with a diameter of nearly 50 yards. It was elevated by manually scraping the soil from the surrounding pastures. Although fragments of human bones have been found, there is no evidence of actual burial sites. The flints, scrapers, pottery shards and other tools present were not sufficient to indicate the presence of dwellings. It seems to have been religious and ceremonial in intent whose construction would have required zeal as well as an organized plan and work force. With carbon-dating the likely date is 2000 BC.[14]

Other circles include **Dromberg Circle**, Co. Cork, which consists of 14 evenly spaced stones which form a circle 30 feet in diameter. This is on a much smaller scale than the Great Stone Circle near Lough Gur.

There is also **Beltany Circle**, Co. Donegal, where there are 60 stones in a circle with a single upright stone on the outside. It is thought that this ring was used by the Celtic pagans to celebrate a May Day festival as early as 2000 BC.

Dromberg Circle

Artifacts and Excavation

At these sites some artifacts have been discovered which consist of shards of pottery, ornaments, offerings and tools made of stone, flint or bone. Although these are not exciting to everyone, they have been valuable for the understanding and dating of the sites in Ireland. These are on display at local interpretive centers and at the **National Museum of Ireland** in Dublin.

Evidence of domestic and community life is mostly limited to these artifacts, post holes and stone circles.

At **Lough Gur,** Co. Limerick, several house sites have been excavated and identified to this period by the pottery shards found there. Foundation stones and post holes have been unearthed. It is thought that the thick walls at the base of the structures were topped with mud and posts which supported the thatch roofs of bog reeds. The Interpretive Center here is an "imaginative reconstruction of two of the Neolithic house types of the area."[15] Further south there are other artifacts: Cush earthworks, Duntry league megalithic tomb and a motte at Kilfinnane. There are also artifacts from later periods.

The motte is a large mound with a flat top.

A somewhat recent discovery under the blanket bog at Ballycastle, Co. Mayo, is the **Ceide Fields.** This excavation represents only a small section of an extensive farming community dating from 5000 BC. The ongoing project includes a walled field system, dwelling site and tombs. The Interpretive Center gives an excellent presentation of the early history and geology of the area. This is an excellent example of man's creating the conditions for the formation of a blanket bog – the underlying bedrock prevented good drainage, the sessile oak forest, which once maintained the balance of moisture and earth, was cleared for pasture and the heavy rainfall saturated the pastures. All that was needed was time and some special plants. The Neolithic farmers left this inhospitable bog land they had created. Beneath the bog-covered hills are extensive stone-age monuments such as stone walled fields, dwellings and megalithic tombs.

The Ceide Fields excavation represents only a small section of an extensive farming community dating from 5000 BC.

For hundreds of years this bog land has provided peat for the surrounding area homes. While visiting here, another member of our guided group, who had emigrated years before told us, "As a child I was required to come here to help cut peat, now I have paid for entry to see and learn."

The views from here are superb. Not only is there a sense of the sea and cliffs, but the vast acreage of inhospitable bog land is overwhelming – particularly on a rainy windy day.

NOTE: For those whose interest in the Stone Age has been aroused, there are many sources including *Guide to National Monuments*, by Peter Harbison, the periodical *Archeology Ireland* and booklets by Eamonn Kelly and Muiris O'Sullivan.

Atlantic Ocean

Donagal

Grianan of
Ailough

Londonderry

Antrim

ULSTER

Tyrone

Down

Fermanagh

Navan
Fort

Armagh

Monaghan

Sligo

Leitrim

Cavan

CONNACHT

Rathcroghan

Mayo

Roscommon

Longford

Louth

Irish Sea

Hill of Tara

Meath

Westmeath

Galway

Kildare

Dublin

Offaly

LEINSTER

Dun Aengus

Clare

Laois

Wicklow

Carlow

Rathgall

Tipperary

Kilkenny

Wexford

Limerick

MUNSTER

Kerry

Waterford

Staigue Fort

Cork

St. George's
Channel

Celtic Sea

7. *Ancient Ireland*

2000 BC – 500 AD

Crucifixion plaque from Rinnegon, Co. Roscommon. National Museum of Ireland

THE PERIOD I call Ancient Ireland starts around 2000 BC and goes through the Bronze Age and the Iron Age up to the time of the conversion to Christianity around 500 AD. It is a period which extends for 2500 years and includes the arrival of the Milesians and the Celts. The Milesians, or Gaels, came from the area which is now Spain and probably introduced the technology and skills of the Bronze Age. They were great seafarers and had traveled all through the Mediterranean. The Celts came from the area which is now southern France and Germany and introduced La Tène art (see p. 72) and the Iron Age. These were an artistic, educated and fiercely independent people who brought their skills and knowledge to Ireland. It is believed that they arrived in small groups over a long period of time, and the culture of Ireland modified and advanced gradually while assimilating the knowledge and cultures of the new settlers. Trade flourished and the social structure of Ireland was developed.

Although tin, the essential component of bronze, is not native to Ireland, there was gold in the Wicklow Mountains (the parent vein has never been discovered!). Gold has forever been a precious and important material for trade and the craftsmen of Ireland were highly skilled. The export of gold and the import of copper and tin for the manufacture of bronze opened the trade routes and brought further exchanges of ideas and materials. To support this scenario, many gold ornaments with Irish provenance have been found on the continent of Europe. With the introduction of tin and copper – and the technology of melting, molding and combining metal ores – the Bronze Age begins.

Penannular brooch found with Armagh chalice. National Museum of Ireland

Trade and manufacture require organization, which in turn influences the life of the people. From the **Stone Age** there was a strong social organization, as witnessed by the construction of the passage tombs, the stone circles and the extensive walled fields at Ceide Fields. The Milesians and the Celts utilized this organization which evolved into a society based on **Kingship** and the Brehon laws (see p. 112). The country was divided into royal provinces and it is around their centers that the society and community life revolved and from which the mythology evolved.

There are three areas which give us clues about the people of ancient Ireland: mythology, field monuments and artistic design. It is from the rich tales of **mythology** that we perceive the life and culture of the people. Without these tales to stimulate our imaginations, the Hill of Tara and Navan Fort are merely hills with incredible vistas.

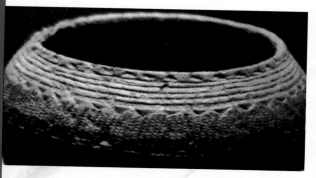

The Treasury at the **National Museum of Ireland** in Dublin is full of artifacts – the tools, bronze weapons, golden ornaments and decorated pottery shards. There are objects of bronze and gold which have been found preserved in bogs – some truly great finds, or hoards. They support the tales of mythology which describe the richness of Irish life in earlier times. From them you can more easily envision the setting fit for a king at Tara, such as the handsome Cormac mac Airt, who was described as wearing a fine purple garment, a golden brooch, a finely wrought collar of gold, a belt ornamented with precious stones and shoes of gold.

It is most rewarding to see the gradual progress and paths of transition in the designs and skill from the Stone Age forward.

Field Monuments

Many **field monuments** such as the royal seats or palaces of the kings, forts, crannogs and souterrains, earthworks and roadways are scattered throughout Ireland. Some forts were very elaborate, like Tara and Navan Fort. Others were great stone bastions like those on the Aran Islands, others were extensive with walls and passageways like Staigue Fort, Co. Kerry, and Grianan of Aileagh, Co. Donegal, while still others were small defensive family units.

Royal Seats

TARA WAS THE CENTER of Ancient Ireland and the royal seat of the high kings until the 6th century AD. It was the center of rich grazing land where cattle were the symbol of wealth. It was also a center of ritual activity where the burning of Tara occurred every Samain (Halloween). It is difficult to imagine the grandeur of the area when today there are only mounds, banks and ditches. These represent the Royal Enclosure, the Banquet Hall and other forts. Looking at an aerial view before you explore helps you to visualize the size of the enclosure. At the top of the hill is the Stone of Destiny which is thought to be the inauguration stone of the Kings of Tara. Although a visit to Tara requires much imagination, *it should* be visited as it **was** Ireland.

The Feis of Tara was a very important event in the social structure of the country. All the kings and chieftains met at Tara on the first of November with the high king to settle all matters of national importance. Each pledged to do no violence to another or his life would be forfeit. These assemblies settled matters of histories, genealogies, tribute, territory and precedence.

For those readers interested in the history and mythology, the high kings at Tara who were involved in the cycles were Conn of a Hundred Battles, Conaire Mor (105–27BC), Conn Cet Chathach (122–157AD), Cormac of the Exiles, Cormac mac Airt (226–266AD), Niall of the Nine Hostages, Niall Noigiallach (379–405AD) and Leogaire (428–458AD), who was the king during the arrival of Saint Patrick.

NAVAN FORT, also known as Emain Macha, is west of Armagh, Co. Down, in Northern Ireland. It was the ritual and political center of Ulster as well as being the focus of the Ulster Cycles and is a site worthy of a visit. During extensive excavation the earth on this mound was peeled back, the site was examined and then the earth was replaced so it appeared again as a mere mound. Although this site was not restored or rebuilt, the archeological exploration was excellent and revealed the following:

"Prior to 100 BC the site was a great center of importance. Many houses existed in the area and even a skull of a barbary ape was found in the excavation – probably a gift from a personage from Spain or North Africa to the king of Ulster.

"What is most interesting is that the 'destruction' of the site was not from quarrying but from a deliberate act of sacrifice.

"In 100 BC all the buildings in the area were removed. A huge round structure, supported with wooden posts, with a diameter of 125 feet was built. In the center, a huge totem or oak post was placed. This structure was temporary. After ten years and without disturbing the structural posts, the floor of the interior was covered with three feet of limestone cobbles to form a cairn. Then, the upper part of the wooden structure was burned and ten feet of earth and sod were deposited upon the cairn. During the excavation the holes made by the posts were found within the cairn."[16]

Why did they build this great structure and then destroy it? It is thought that perhaps they were creating a mound in which the Tuatha De Danaan would dwell in the Otherworld.

The landscape surrounding Emain Macha also contains sites of archeological interest. To the northeast is Loughnashade where a three-foot trumpet was unearthed – perhaps used in Celtic rituals. Human skulls and animal bones were also discovered – probably from sacrifices. To the west is an area known as the King's Stables and an artificial lake around which were found clay molds for making bronze swords. This also was probably a ritual lake.

A quarrying industry developed in this region during the 19th and 20th centuries. It is assumed that many artifacts and foundations from the Iron Age settlements were destroyed. In 1986 this area was declared a prime archeological site where quarrying is no longer permitted.

Bronze trumpet, National Museum of Ireland

Forts

THE WORDS *Dun* and *Rath* are the Gaelic words for Fort. There are several types of forts which are found throughout Ireland. One of these, the ring fort, is "a space surrounded by an earthen bank formed of material thrown up from a fosse or ditch immediately outside the bank...in the west of Ireland, a massive stone wall enclosed the site in place of a bank and ditch. This type of ring fort is called a caher, cashel or stone fort and well preserved examples may have terraces and steps in the inner face of the wall."[17]

Stone/Hill Forts

THESE ISLANDS are accessible for a day trip by boat or plane from Galway City Docks, Co. Galway, or Doolin, Co. Clare. The three islands of Inishmore, Inishmaan and Inisheer offer not only six or seven stone forts but also many early Christian monuments. When the weather is good, they also offer a wonderful opportunity for exploration and relaxation. It is thought in mythology that it was to the Aran Islands that the Fir Bolgs fled after their defeat by the Tuatha De Danaan.

The forts built on these islands (perhaps built by the Fir Bolgs) are impressive, while the locations and structures attest to their serious purpose of defense. An outstanding site is **Dun Aengus** on Inishmore Island. It is a large dry stone fort situated atop a high ocean cliff and surrounded with three walls of defense.

Interior of Dun Aengus...   *and the outside wall*

It also features a defensive structure called "cheveux de frise." Sharp stones are angled into the ground to injure and hinder the approach of enemy forces.

Entry into the fort is prevented by the combination of the inner and outer walls, the cheveux de frise and the almost insur-

Dun Aengus backs up to this cliff which is about 60 meters above sea level.

mountable cliffs on the Atlantic. This is indeed a safe haven although the storms from the sea and the stony, inhospitable earth continue to make life very difficult

On the other side of the fort is a sweeping hill with little vegetation, many rocks and little chance of a surprise attack.

Another fort, Dun Conor on Inishmaan Island, has been restored and gives an excellent example of a prehistoric fort. **Rathgall Stone Fort,** Co. Wicklow, has been restored and is another example of a defensive stone fort.

Throughout the countryside and away from the royal forts, there are smaller defensive communities which reflect the independent and warlike nature of the Irish/Celtic culture. They come in many sizes. The economy and topography of each area determined the site of the fort. In cattle country, the forts were atop the hills, while on the coast they abutted the water and were usually protected by a cliff. Others were beside a river when transport was important for trade. The larger ones were normally built on high ground, walled, often circular and had many passageways. They would often enclose a whole community.

Some of these have been restored and there are two good examples: **Grianan of Aileagh,** Co. Donegal, is a reconstruction of a 1700 BC stone fort which crowns the hilltop. The original was the royal seat of the O'Neill sept which was destroyed in 1101 by Brian Boru, King of Munster, in his push to rule all of Ireland.

Staigue Fort, Co. Kerry, is a stone fort on the Ring of Kerry. The sloped stone wall, built without the use of mortar, rises up to 5.49 meters and in places is 4 meters thick. It encloses a round area which is nearly 29 meters in diameter. On the interior there are '×'-shaped stairways for easy access to the top with two small chambers within the wall. Outside are a large bank and ditch. It is thought that, although the inside is now empty, at one time it might have contained houses made of wood.[18]

Smaller ring and hill forts found throughout the countryside were more for domestic homesteading of a somewhat extended family unit, with the outer walls keeping the animals in and the predators out.

Staigue Fort

A CRANNOG is an artificial island on which people built houses and kept their livestock. It was made by placing layers of stones on the bottom of the lake. When the waters of Lake Gara (on the borders of Sligo and Roscommon) were lowered, many small artificial islands emerged. The Crannóg Research Programme is working here. These islets were covered with brushwood, tree trunks and sod and secured with wooden pilings. An island was often surrounded with a wooden fence for protection and accessed by dugout canoe. The houses were thatched and made of mud and wattles. There is a reconstruction of a crannog at the **Craggaunowen Bronze Age Project,** Co. Clare, which also has examples of a souterrain, megalithic tomb and cooking area.

CRANNOGS
AND
SOUTER-
RAINS

The souterrain (right) was an underground passage in which the temperature remained constant for use in food storage or refuge in time of attack. Occasionally there would be access to the outside of the compound by a tunnel.

THE STANDING STONES in the stone circles during the Stone Age were used either to delineate a circle or were positioned to aid in astronomic calculations. Other huge stones standing singly have been associated with mythology, for example, the stone at Knockbridge. The single standing stones of this era are thought to mark a grave. Some have alphabetical markings and are called Ogham stones. Others are decorated and their function is not known.

The **Ogham stones** seem to have had several purposes and are primarily found in counties Cork, Kerry and Waterford. The Beara Peninsula and the Dingle Peninsula have excellent examples as well as a good sampling of sites from the Bronze and Iron Ages.

They are inscribed with an ancient alphabet of dots and strokes cut along the edge or edges of the stone. This is not to say that it can be translated easily as they were often written in ancient Gaelic.

Other Field Monuments

Earthworks and roadways have been discovered and more are being found. Aerial views of the terrain have brought to light many formations which were heretofore unrecognized. **Rathcroghan,** Co. Roscommon, is full of legend and field monuments. While hard facts are few, it was here that Queen Maeve discovered that her husband Ailill's herd of cattle had a better bull than hers. It was from here that she gathered her army to go forth to fight Cuchulainn and the Ulster warriors. The site includes the King's Cemetery (Relignaree), the pillar stone of Dathi's mound, and a large ring fort as well as round earthworks, flat-topped mounds, linear earthworks and a souterrain with Ogham stones. All this indicates it

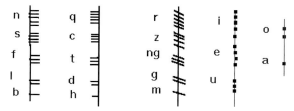

Ogham Stone Alphabet

Ogham Stone,
Ring of Kerry

was the center of an ancient kingdom. Some ancient Irish thought this was the place for entrance into the Underworld.[19]

There is another type of earthwork which consists of large banks of earth with ditches. It ran long distances and was the territorial boundary of the clans as well as a barrier to prevent cattle rustling. Although most of these earthworks have been destroyed by the laying of new roads, the Black Pig's Dyke, Co. Leitrim, is still evident and marked on some maps. There were also toghers, timber roadways running across bogs; one has been constructed at the Craggaunowen Bronze Age Project. The **Motte** was the forerunner of the towerhouse and bawn. It was a high mound of earth with a flat top on which was built a wooden tower that served as a lookout and a place of defense during an attack. Knockgraffon Motte, Co. Tipperary, and Granard Motte, Co. Longford. are good examples.

Another ancient monument which is often not recognized and survives only as a small horse-shaped mound is a **Fulachta Fiadh,** or cooking place. A rectangular pit was lined with stone slabs or wooden planks to form a trough. Water was heated by rolling hot stones from a nearby fire into the trough water. It has been proven that water can be boiled in this way. There is one at the Dromberg Stone Circle, Co. Cork.

Artistic Design

The Bronze Age signified the introduction of weapons, implements and ornaments of bronze and gold. According to Peter Harbison in *Irish Art and Architecture,* Ireland **"was probably Western Europe's greatest producer of gold in prehistoric times... The manufacture of magnificent gold finery continued throughout the Bronze Age."** The designs were geometric using parallel and crossed lines, triangles, zigzags and diamond shapes, and circles.

Perhaps the most accurate way of tracing and identifying the stylistic similarities in the development of art in Ancient Ireland is to follow a time line. It begins with the spirals, triangles and chevrons chipped into the megalithic tombstones during the Neolithic era. Although

Gold plated lead pendant, National Museum of Ireland

Ireland was rich in copper, the tin necessary for making bronze was not a native element. On the other hand, gold was abundant, did not require smelting and was soft and malleable. These materials characterized the implements created during the Bronze Age, which prevailed from 2000 to 300 BC, the beginning of the Iron Age.

In the 7th and 8th centuries BC, there was a large goldsmith industry in the lower Shannon River area. The Bog of Allen yielded a typical **gold-plated lead pendant** (photo, previous page). It is less than 3 inches in height with the design composed of concentric circles, punched holes and furrowed triangles. The designs became more intricate and refined in gold, which is a more supple and elegant material. It is apparent that the tools for working the designs also became more sophisticated.

Gold gorget Gleninsheen, Co. Clare, National Museum of Ireland

The gold gorget from Gleninsheen, Co. Clare, (photo left), is finely wrought and of an intricate design using repoussé, where the metal was hammered from the underside. Of particular interest in developing continuity of style are the furrows between the rows and the spirals on the discs (below left).

Not to be forgotten is the bronze work. These pieces include axe heads, scabbards, sword handles, crowns, discs, box covers and vessels as well as figurines. Although not as showy as the gold, they represent the more practical aspects of this ancient culture and include the same geometric designs.

Bronze disc. National Museum of Ireland

Bronze axe-head. National Museum of Ireland

Three-faced head.
National Museum
of Ireland

The Celtic Traditions

It is probable that the Iron Age began with the arrival of the Celts, who brought the necessary expertise and skill. They came in small groups over a long period of time. They, as the Milesians had, merged with and adapted the culture of the native Irish, whose seers and sorcerers became as one with the Druids. Not only were the Druids learned, but their schools trained future advisers and helped to maintain order and perpetuate knowledge. The Celts were very independent and it was they who divided the country into five territorial units: Ulster, North Leinster, South Leinster, Munster and Connacht. They established the division of classes and defined the role of the high king. It is probably through them that the Brehon laws were established and enforced.

Their contribution to the artistic designs was significant, not only in stone sculpture but in La Tène design.

Stone sculptures are not prevalent from this era for several reasons. First, they would not have withstood the weather and, second, they were pagan images which were usually destroyed by the early Christians.

Double Idol
front. Boa Island

There are two exceptional examples of stylistic human representations in Northern Ireland. One is in the Anglican Cathedral in Armagh, the **Tanderagee Idol,** and the other on Boa Island in Co. Fermanagh, the **Double Idol,** or Janus figure, where the upper parts of two figures stand back to back and the figures are belted together. It is thought that they represent Celtic deities.

There is also a three-faced head of a Celtic god found in Corleck, Co. Cavan, in the National Museum of Ireland.

Double Idol back.
Boa Island

THE CELTS introduced La Tène style of art. It came from what is known as the Hallstadt material culture in the Alps and southern France. It is a graceful biomorphic adaptation of the ancient spiral and is a complete departure from the geometric designs. There are two standing stones decorated with La Tène design: the **Turoe Stone** at Turoe, Co. Galway, and the **Castlerange Stone** at Castlerange, Co. Roscommon.

The Turoe Stone is located in a park area and fairly well signposted.

Castlerange Stone, the more difficult to find, is in a cow pasture. It is also smaller. Both are under the protection of the Dúchas.

La Tène design, prevalent on much of the gold jewelry in the National Museum, marked the beginning of the late Bronze Age. The designs are exquisite in style and workmanship. The objects, of both gold and bronze, include jewelry, ornaments, tools and weapons. They may be seen at the **National Museum of Ireland** in Dublin.

The designs became more intricate as the level of craftsmanship increased. Not only did they appear in gold and other metals, but also in enamel, amber and glass. The more ornate designs which include these materials are considered the high points of La Tène design. The gold Torc, or collar, found in Boighter, Co. Kerry, is an outstanding example of the repoussé technique and is of Irish manufacture.

Gold Torc with model boat in the background. National Museum of Ireland (photo, right)

An excellent book for more in-depth information is *Early Celtic Art in Ireland* by Eamonn P. Kelly.

The Celtic designs also include step and key patterns although the spiral patterns and their many variations were the most prevalent. There is a series of books on Celtic design by Aidan Meehan which gives instruction in the making of all the patterns. The key and step patterns were made with the use of a grid and the designs were created by connecting the grid points. Establishing the grid by pin pricks, the designs were done freehand in a great variety of patterns simply by varying the connecting lines. This is called the tile method. Repeats were attached to form a larger design.

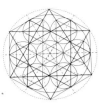

The step and key patterns and the spiral designs continued to be used by Celtic artisans after they converted to Christianity. These designs adorn the high crosses, the Irish-Romanesque doorways, early gold ornaments and Christian shrines and are seen in all their glory in the **Book of Kells,** on display at the Library at Trinity College in Dublin. The Irish preferred elaborate spiral designs.

Illuminated manuscripts in Ireland were created in the early monasteries. The inspiration came from Italy with much Coptic influence. (Note: The Copts were Egyptian Christians who founded Christian monasticism. St. Anthony was the first and is often depicted meeting with other saints on the high crosses of Ireland.)

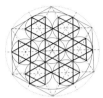

The earliest manuscript to survive is a copy of the Psalms, the **Cathach,** which is located at the Royal Irish Academy. The decoration is limited to the first letter of each paragraph. The **Book of Durrow** is also a significant manuscript of the gospels and is a great deal more elaborate. This may be seen at the Library at Trinity College along with the Book of Kells. These books represent the zenith of artistic design in illuminated manuscripts. They include the animal decoration and interlacing bands from the Mediterranean style, but it is the spirals with all their variations and intricacies which were Celtic in origin.

These spirals, a natural and intricate part of La Tène design, were created and expanded with a ruler, grid and compass. With the help of Aidan Meehan's *Celtic Design: A Beginner's Manual,* I was able to make the designs in a reasonable fashion although erasures and smudging were a problem. Then I turned to the computer and Adobe Illustrator®. Hours and hours later I created the diagrams to the right, which show the mechanical process by which the elaborate designs in the Book of Kells were created.

If you follow the spiral of the Stone Age to the spirals of La Tène art of the early Celts, and then to the variations of these designs on the weapons, you can see a definite developmental trend. This is a reasonable assumption because the wise ones of the Tuatha De Danaan became as one with the Milesian seers and magicians of the Bronze Age, who in turn became as one with the Celtic Druids. The Druids then became the historians or bards of the kingships, converted to Christianity and continued their role of recording and teaching, perhaps even as monks.

Sculpture at the entrance of Clonmacnoise

8. *Early Christianity Through 1100*

T HE CHRISTIAN PERIOD in Ireland begins in 432 AD with the arrival of St. Patrick, although he was preceded by other missionaries. These early missionaries, like the Celts before them, converted, merged and adapted the Irish culture. Many of the seers and prophets of the kingships became the teachers and historians of the monasteries. Some of these early priests went into the wilderness for a solitary life of prayer and study while others founded monasteries which became great seats of learning. The monasteries usually included clusters of small churches, an oratory, high crosses, and round towers and were probably surrounded by embankments. The monks probably lived in small wooden huts. These early sites were quite different from the large Cistercian and Franciscan abbeys which followed the internal restructuring of the Irish Church in the 12th century. Old Melifont Abbey was the first Cistercian monastery in Ireland.

The Saints

SAINT PATRICK was a Roman Briton who was captured during an Irish raid, brought to Ireland and sold off as a slave. After six years he was "led by miraculous prompting" to escape, which he did successfully. He traveled by sea to Gaul and Italy, studying at many monasteries. He was carefully trained for fourteen years and decided to return to Ireland in 432. He helped to organize the already converted Christians, converted kingdoms which were still pagan and formally made Ireland part of Christendom. He is said to have also banished snakes and reptiles of all kinds from Ireland.

There are many tales and legends which give an understanding of this man and how he was able to achieve the conversion of Ireland without any bloodshed. One tale concerns his journey to Tara to seek the conversion of King Laoghaire. It is from a "Life of St. Patrick" written in the 12th century, is retold in *The Legend of Tara* by Elizabeth Hickey, and here is my summary: "Reaching the nearby Hill of Slane, he decided to abide there for Easter eve as it would be more fitting to reach the Royal City on Easter Day to spread the Gospel. It was the custom that no fire be lit within the sight of the Hill of Tara on the eve of the festival of Spring and then only by the chief druid. King Laoghaire's followers and attendants were indeed dismayed when they looked across the plain and saw the fire on the Hill of Slane. Emissaries of the king were sent forth to extinguish the fires. The fires of St. Patrick were not quenched. He arrived at Tara the next day. Patrick was challenged by the magician and a trial by fire was arranged. The magician, wearing the robe of St. Patrick, was placed in a new building made of green wood while the boy Benignus, wearing the robe of the magician, was placed in an old worm-eaten building. Both structures were set ablaze. The magician was burned to an ash although the robe of St. Patrick was untouched. The boy, Benignus, was untouched by the fire although the robe of the magician which he wore was totally burned. St. Patrick was unable to convert King Laoghaire but he permitted his followers to become Christians."

Another legend, repeated by H. V. Morton in *In Search of Ireland*, explains the Irish belief in the inflexible determination of their saint as "a steady and imperturbable man" with their best interests at the center of his beliefs and care. It goes as follows:

When Lent came in the year AD 449 St. Patrick retired to a great mountain in Connaught to commune with God. He fasted for forty days and forty nights, weeping, so it is said, until his chasuble was wet with tears.

The medieval monks possessed detailed accounts of St. Patrick's fast. They said that to the angel, who returned to him every night with promises from God, the saint said:

"Is there aught else that will be granted to me?"

"Is there aught else thou wouldst demand?" asked the angel.

"There is," replied St. Patrick, "that the Saxons shall not abide in Ireland by consent or perforce so long as I abide in heaven."

"Now get thee gone," commanded the angel.

"I will not get me gone," said St. Patrick, "since I have been tormented until I am blessed."

"Is there aught else thou wouldst demand?" asked the angel once more.

St. Patrick requested that on the Day of Judgment he should be judge over the men of Ireland.

"Assuredly," said the angel, "that is not got from the Lord."

"Unless it is got from Him," replied the determined saint, "departure from this Rick shall not be got from me from today until Doom; and, what is more, I shall leave a guardian there."

The angel returned with a message from heaven:

"The Lord said, 'There hath not come, and there will not come from the Apostles, a man more admirable, were it not for thy hardness. What thou hast prayed for thou shalt have…and there will be a consecration of the men of the folk of Ireland, both living and dead.'"

St. Patrick said:

"A blessing on the bountiful King who hath given; and the Rick shall now be departed therefrom."

As he rose and prepared to descend from the mountain mighty birds flew about him so that the air was dark and full of the beating of wings. So St. Patrick stood, like Moses on Sinai, and round him all the Saints of Ireland, past, present, and to come.

This mountain, Crough Patrick, rises 2,510 feet above Clew Bay. It is Ireland's Holy Mountain. Once a year in July (the last Sunday) a pilgrimage is made to the little chapel at the crest. As many as 40,000 pilgrims have climbed the mountain in one day – and many of the more devout remove their shoes and socks and take the hard path barefoot.

It is on this height, as told by the medieval monks, that St. Patrick flung his bell from him only to have it returned to his hand; and at each sound of the bell the toads and the adders fled from Ireland.

It is at the top of another hill in Downpatrick, Co. Down, where it is said the bones of St. Patrick lie in the shadow of the cathedral. There is a big slab of rough granite with a Celtic cross on it and the word "Patric." There is a legend that Saint Columcille (St. Columba in English) and Saint Brigid are buried with St. Patrick in this little graveyard.

SAINT COLUMCILLE was born in Gartan in Donegal in 521. The royal blood of Ireland ran in his veins. He belonged to the northern Ui Neill, the descendant of Niall of the Nine Hostages. Over the green mountains of Donegal, beside a little lake, tradition has preserved the stone on which he lay. It is said that anyone who sleeps on this stone will be saved the agonies of homesickness.

The education of a child like Columcille in the Ireland of the sixth century illustrates the culture of Ireland and how it was preserved at that time. In contrast, in Europe, western civilization and Christianity were being destroyed by the invasions of the Islamic Moors to the south and the barbaric Huns to the east.

First, the child was sent to the school of St. Finnen at Moville on Lough Foyle. This saint was of royal blood and had spent seven years as a student in Rome. Columcille then went to the Leinster School of Bards, which was ruled by an ancient poet, Gemman, who must have taught the boy the ancient druid lore of Ireland. His next school was that of Aranmore, founded by St. Enna. He passed on into the great college of Clonard on the Boyne, where St. Finnen taught three thousand pupils from every part of Europe. His last school was that of the Mobhi at Fin-glas near Dublin. This school was broken up by the plague that swept Ireland in the year 544.

In order to avoid the plague, Columcille went to Ulster, where his cousin gave him the grove of Derry where he started his first monastery. During the next fifteen years of his life he founded monasteries at Kells, Swords, Tory Island, Lambay (near Dublin) and Durrow.

His new monastery at Durrow was the cause of his exile and the cause of the coming of Christianity to Scotland and the north of England. It happened in this way. His old master, St. Finnen of Moville, had returned from a second journey to Rome with a rare manuscript. Finnen valued this manuscript highly and did not want anyone to copy it. He wanted to be the sole owner of this precious document. Columcille would not wait for Finnen to change his mind, as he wanted a copy of St. Jerome for his new foundation. He borrowed the book to read, but secretly copied it, sitting up by night and working by the light of a lamp. When Finnen was told of this, he was furious. He appealed to the high king of Tara and brought forward the first action for violation of copyright. The king decided in favor of Finnen on the theory that, as every cow owns her calf so every book owns its copy.

Another event complicated matters and hastened Columcille's departure from Ireland. During the Festival of Tara the son of the King of Connaught lost his temper and killed another youth, thus violating the annual truce (or feis) proclaimed at this time. The murderer fled to Ulster and was placed under Columcille's protection. The high king had the boy seized and, in spite of Columcille's protests, put to death. The saint raised his clan against the high king. A furious battle was fought in which 3,000 lives were lost.

The legend is that, in order to make penance for the battle, Columcille decided to leave Ireland and seek some desolate place from which he could not see his native land. He landed at Iona (an island off the coast of Scotland). There he was most beloved until he died.

SAINT BRIGID was the daughter of a chief and the slave woman Broicseach. The chief's wife was very jealous of Broicseach, when she was with child. To keep peace with his wife, he sold the slave woman to a druid, but having heard that the child would be marvelous and famous he granted the child to be freeborn. This child was Brigid, who grew up to be beautiful, wise and kind. One day she heard a monk preaching and became a Christian. Brigid longed to see her father and received permission from the druid to return to her father's house.

There, she was put in charge of running the house; this was not a great success because she gave to the poor anything available. Her father was most unhappy with this and decided to sell her as a slave to the King of Leinster to curb her pride. While he was arranging the deal, Brigid gave away her father's sword. Upon hearing this, the King of Leinster decided that she was most unique in God's sight, presented her father with a new sword and sent her home a free woman.

Brigid was very beautiful and many men wanted to marry her, but she would not accept any. The first convent that she founded was in Kildare beside an oak. Her community grew and, in need of more land, she went to the king. He had said that he would give her some of his land but never seemed to get around to it. Brigid finally asked him if he would give her the land that her cloak could cover. That sounded quite acceptable. Each of her nuns took a corner of the cloak, but instead of laying it down they ran as fast as they could in a circle and as they ran the cloak proceeded to grow longer and broader. The king then agreed to give her what was covered as long as they stopped running. It was agreed, and Brigid had the site for her church.

Saint Brigid lived to be eighty-eight years old. She died in Armagh and is buried at Downpatrick next to St. Patrick and St. Columcille.

The Gallerus Oratory

Early Churches and Monasteries

The earliest churches, made of wood, have not survived. Some early monasteries were ascetic retreats for the monks in search of peace, solitude and meditation. They encompassed a defined area which contained a collection of small stone churches having little ornamentation. The monks lived in wooden huts or stone beehive huts.

Beehive Hut

Within the confines of these early monasteries were stone oratories which had the appearance of upside-down arks. The walls were very thick, while the roofs were corbelled. This is the same construction as the early passage tombs. The overlapping and slant of the stones allowed for the rain to run off the roof without leaking into the interior of the structure. A stone lintel or beam spanned the simple opening.

The **Gallerus Oratory** on the Dingle Peninsula, Co. Kerry, is an excellent example. The rocky mountain landscape, the pounding surf of the Atlantic Ocean and the dark gray atmosphere of the peninsula create a sense of isolation and otherworldliness fitting for the reclusive monastic life.

Beehive huts, located on the south shore of the Dingle Peninsula, were used either as cells for the monks of a monastery there, or may have been used as a hostel for the pilgrims en route to the Gallerus Oratory or perhaps to the monastery at Reask also on the Dingle Peninsula.

80

There are many **island sites of monastic ruins.** Some are for the adventurer, as travel to them is usually made by special arrangement and is dependent upon the weather. These islands were suitable for the early hermit monks, as they could easily provide the isolation the hermits sought. **Holy Island,** Lough Derg, Co. Clare, is easily reached by boat. Inishglora Island, Co. Mayo, and Inishmurray Island, Co. Sligo, are doable, while the Skellig Islands are restricted. Other accessible monasteries grew to be very large as they attracted disciples. New churches were built as the need increased. Some of these became great seats of learning such as Armagh, Bangor, Kells, **Monasterboice, Clonmacnoise,** Lismore, Cork and **Glendalough.**

Christian activity in Ireland was abundant. When St. Patrick chose Armagh as his headquarters, it became an important center of religion and learning. The Book of Armagh, written in the 8th and 9th centuries, consists of pen and ink sketches of the evangelistic symbols. It is now in the library at Trinity College, Dublin. Bangor Abbey was founded by St. Comgall in 558, becoming most famous in Europe, where its monks founded monasteries. It was the work of these monks who converted the Carolingians to Christianity and thus 'saved Christianity in Europe.' Kells is the site where the Book of Kells was produced and it is here that the monks from Iona fled during the Viking raids. The monastery on Iona, an island off the coast of Scotland, was founded by St. Columba (St. Columcille in Irish).

Monasterboice, founded by St. Buithe in 521 for both men and women, became an important center of learning connected with Armagh. Clonmacnoice, founded by St. Kieran, was also the burial place of the kings of Connacht and Tara. The monastery at Lismore, founded by St. Carthach in the 7th century, became a distinguished European university. At its peak in the 8th century, there were twenty seats of learning within its walls. St. Finbarre founded the monastery in Cork in 650. Since this seaport was an easy prey to Viking raiders, its development was often interrupted. Glendalough was founded in 498 by St. Kevin. It was first an ascetic monastery but developed into one which attracted many disciples from Europe. These great institutions are no more, but they were an important part of Ireland. The support of the kings for ecclesiastical life and learning was an integral part of their lives. Their sons were educated at these monasteries.

Early Cross at Reask

81

Other monuments from these monastic sites were the high crosses and round towers. Some of the stone high crosses are in good condition and many are topped with stone likenesses of the early churches. They were dedicated to the benefactors of the local monasteries and probably carved by the abbots. They were often divided into panels with scenes from the scriptures. The designs reflect the combined culture of Celt and Christian. They may be found throughout the countryside on former monastic sites and at the more accessible sites like Clonmacnoise and Monasterboice.

Many round towers have survived, although some are in better repair than others. They are found within the boundaries of former monastic sites. Their function was as a bell tower, although often the doorway was well above the surrounding terrain, which indicates a defensive use, as well.

High Crosses

The high crosses were not funerary monuments. The inscriptions (normally at the base), where they have survived weathering, only ask for a prayer for the men who erected them. The designs on the crosses of this period are divided into three groups: Celtic, decorative (geometric designs or hunting scenes) and scriptural.

It is thought that one type of high cross was a copy of an early wooden processional cross. In the North Cross at Ahenny (right) the large studs represented bosses that were originally used to

cover the nails of a wooden processional cross. The shaft and arms are decorated with interlacing. The spiral designs and the fretwork patterns are visible on the shaft. Although it is not clear, the base of this cross has an unusual scene: a man chasing animals under a palm tree. On the other side is carved a procession of men. Be sure to look for the unusual, as Irish stonemasons were highly individual.

Celtic design includes spirals and intertwining. The section on the left (from the North Cross at Ahenny) shows the use of the familiar spiral designs in the center as well as the step and key at the lower edge and the braid or figure-eight designs at the top.

North Cross, at Ahenny, Co. Tipperary

The scriptural crosses were dedicated to scenes from the Old and New Testaments as well as Celtic designs and representations of their benefactors. The same scenes were carved on many crosses and, if you know your Bible, the iconography can be easier to identify. Since these crosses have withstood the weather for over a thousand years, the figures are not always clearly defined. The crosses were not shrines. Since they are located on the grounds of former monasteries and the bases usually make reference to the lay benefactors, it is thought that they were commemorative and instructive, as they depict the power of God and demonstrate his care and protection of the faithful. They probably served the same purpose as other descriptive art in the great cathedrals – to instruct the uneducated. The scenes from the Bible were recognizable for those who could not read the texts in Latin.

An appropriate place to start is the beginning and most every cross has a panel representing Adam and Eve having eaten from the Tree of Knowledge as well as Cain slaying Abel.

Moone Cross

The **Moone Cross,** Co. Kildare (left), demonstrates the simple earlier design, which is quite stylized.

At Monasterboice on **Muiredach's Cross,** Co. Louth (lower left), Adam and Eve are coupled in the same panel with Cain and Abel. The ax-like weapon behind Abel's head is the identifier. This panel shows more skill in carving than the earlier Moone Cross and the figures are more realistic. This cross is made of a more durable stone so the figures are more clearly defined.

Muiredach's Cross

In the west at **Drumcliff,** Co. Sligo (right), the spiral is elaborately used in the stylish tree with evidence of more Celtic design. The animal above the panel is a surprise and a delight.

The **Moone Cross** marked the site of an early monastery founded by St. Columcille (St. Columba). This 8th century cross is an absolute gem. The primitive designs are charming and easy to identify. It is, however, very difficult to locate (on an unmarked road, through a stile and a field). There has been extensive restoration and the cross has been moved within the frame of a roofless chapel to protect it from the weather. These panels tell the stories without embellishment – the sincerity and honesty are apparent. They are useful in identifying the iconography, or clues to biblical tales. These scriptural scenes are located around the base of the cross with the rather narrower shaft containing images of animals.

On the Moone Cross other examples from the Old Testament are Daniel in the Lion's Den, a lone figure surrounded by vicious animals, and the Sacrifice of Isaac, showing Abraham ready to take his son's life with the Golden Calf floating above.

From the New Testament are the Flight into Egypt by the Holy Family and the Miracle of the Loaves and Fishes. Here two fishes and five round loaves of bread illustrate the scene with an eel on either side of the loaves. Of all the famous high crosses, this scene is special because it is not normally included and because of its simplicity.

This scene on the Moone Cross shows some of the fantastic figures and imagination of the Irish stonemasons. This treatment of elongated animals becomes popular in Romanesque art.

Muiredach's Cross at Monasterboice (right) is in excellent condition and is a masterpiece of Irish art. The most spectacular scene is the center of the east side depicting Christ in Judgment. The top of the cross is capped with a structure which resembles early churches.

The detail is exquisite and the iconography complete. Christ is holding a cross and a scepter. To his right is David playing the harp and all the good souls are facing him. On his left is a man playing the pipes of Pan with the devil and triton behind and all the bad souls are facing away from Christ.

St. Michael is below the scene with a two-pan scale weighing a soul. Underneath him is the devil lying on his back trying to weight the balance in his favor with a long pole. St. Michael has forced his staff down the devil's throat to neutralize his effect.

For those purists who like to be able to identify everything, there is a chart at the site.

Arrest of Christ

Three Children in the Fiery Furnace

On the other side, the center of the cross presents the crucifixion of Christ. The figures on this side are quite different in style from the east side as well as being from the New Testament.

On the West Cross, also at Monasterboice, the lowest panel (left) is of great interest as it not only shows the Arrest of Christ, but his cloak is fastened by a brooch bearing the Tara design. This was more recognizable before weathering.

Another easy find is the panel of the Three Children in the Fiery Furnace.

It shows three small figures protected by the wings of an angel. In essence, Shadrach, Meshach and Abednego refused to worship the golden hind as commanded by King Nebuchadnezzar. They were thrown into the furnace, but, no matter how hot, they walked away unscathed. This convinced the King of the power of their God.

This theme demonstrates specifically the protecting power of God. This is also the basis of the legend of St. Patrick when he first arrived at the Hill of Tara.

Muiredach's Cross

Although those who are familiar with the Bible will be more adept at recognizing the panels, some panels are quite worn and the references are not well known.

King Flann's Cross, or the Cross of the Scriptures at **Clonmacnoise,** Co. Offaly, is also noteworthy. The original high cross has

been moved into the Information Center to protect it from further damage from weathering. A reproduction exists within the grounds of the monastery from which the expanse and measure of the monastic grounds can be appreciated. Since this cross is early 10th century it is simpler in design and style, perhaps a transition between the Moone Cross and Muiredach's Cross.

The Crucifixion scene is in the center of the west side in which the figure of Christ dominates, while the

King Flann's Cross

Last Judgment (above) is on the east side.

The scenes on the shaft include two interesting panels, Christ in the Tomb and the founding of Clonmacnoise.

Christ is shown in the tomb (right) with two soldiers sitting atop asleep, leaning on their spears. Martha and Mary are in the background. Below the slab is the body of Christ wrapped in a shroud with a bird in his mouth to indicate that the moment of Resurrection is near.[20]

Christ in the Tomb

The panel (left) represents the founding of the monastery with the

Irish king and the abbot. The king is identified by his sword and the abbot by his apparel. They are erecting the cross for the new cathedral at Clonmacnoise. Chiefs, kings and soldiers are identified by their swords.

These examples of panels and other significant high crosses are located at Monasterboice, Co. Louth; Clonmacnoise, Co. Offaly; Castledermot and Moone Cross, Co. Kildare; Kells, Co. Meath; and Kilkieran, Co. Kilkenny. When you try to decipher the scenes, remember that as some have been badly weathered a bit of imagination is required. It also helps to be familiar with the Bible, symbols and iconography.

The decorative crosses show geometric designs and hunting scenes. There is an excellent one from Banagher, Co. Offaly, which is now at the National Museum.

Round Towers

Beginning in the 10th century, monasteries in Ireland usually had a round tower. The structure was tall, slender and tapering with a cone-shaped cap. "They possess the feature of entasis, an invention of classical architecture whereby the line of the side of a column is slightly convex to counter the optical illusion of concavity which an observer would get if the sides were straight." [21]

The towers were usually in excess of one hundred feet tall, and served as a bell tower, a lookout and a defensible place in which to store valuables during an attack by Vikings or neighboring clans. There are many round towers about the countryside and some have very interesting features. This tower, right, is at **Glendalough**, Co. Wicklow.

Some have been partially restored while others are missing their caps. Generally the earlier ones were more slender, four storied with four windows on the top story and only one on the others. The levels were reached by wooden ladders and the entries were often more than a few feet above ground level. The entry ladders were drawn up into the tower during attacks.

Although many monastic sites still have round towers, there are exceptional examples at **Ardmore**, Co. Waterford, **Timahoe**, Co. Laois, and **Kilmacduagh**, Co. Galway.

Glendalough, Co. Wicklow

Monasteries

THE NAME Glendalough means the glen of two lakes. It is a charming spot in the Wicklow Mountains which is completely picturesque – a valley and lakes surrounded by mountains. On a beautiful day it is an ideal picnic spot with fields for games, and trails to hike and the Dúchas visitor center is helpful. The guides will take you on the tour which is a wonderful blend of history, legend and humor. There are also significant architectural sites: a round tower, Romanesque door, Celtic cross and an oratory, or a church, with a corbelled roof.

St. Kevin came here about 520 in search of solitude. According to H.V. Morton:

"There is an ancient tradition, the source of a thousand songs and poems, that he was driven into solitude by the passion of a beautiful girl named Kathleen, who favored him with relentless ardour. The old chronicle states that 'the holy youth rejected all these allurements.' One day finding the young monk alone in the fields, she approached him and clasped him in her arms. But the soldier of Christ, arming himself with the sacred sign and full of the Holy Ghost, made strong resistance against her, and rushed out of her arms into the wood, and finding nettles, took secretly a bunch of them and struck her with them many times in the face, hands and feet. And when she was blistered with the nettles, the pleasure of her love became extinct."[22]

Another legend says that he pushed her into the lake! In the 1930's, when Morton visited Glendalough, he wanted to climb up to St. Kevin's Bed, the cell in which the saint lived before the monastery was built. It sits high up in the cliff overlooking the Upper Lake and was accessible only by boat. His boatman and guide was skilled in the art of "putting over a bit of blarney." Morton asked him if these stories were true and he replied: "On that stone Kathleen appears every night at ten. I've seen her with me own eyes, that I have, and the loveliest creature that ever stepped she is."

To corroborate his honesty, when asked how deep the lake was, the boatman replied: "It's that deep, sir, that when my sister went bathing there awhile back and sank...we heard not a word from her until we got a letter from Manchester, England, asking us to post her some dry clothes."[23]

It is also purported that the monastery from which St. Kevin came started these stories in order to discredit him in the spirit of rivalry and jealousy. The facts do support his coming here as a hermit. Many disciples were attracted to Glendalough by his holiness. He set up the monastery and became its first abbot. During his rule, over a thousand students came here from Ireland, Britain and all over Europe, and it became a school for saints.

The guides of today have not lost the art of the blarney nor the Irish love of story telling. They tell of the time that Kevin healed the son of the local Irish king and, in return, asked for the land within the circle of the flight of a swan. The bird set off and swept around the entire valley and the king was true to his word.

In the 9th and 10th centuries, Vikings and local kings ravaged the wealth of the site. In the 12th century Saint Lawrence O'Toole revived the site when he became abbot at the age of 25 years. The site again fell into ruin and disrepair and was finally destroyed by the English in 1398. In 1875 major restoration work was carried out.

In the 18th century and 19th century the monastery site was used for "riotous assembly" or games on the feast day of St. Kevin, June 3rd. During this festival the women were included in the games. They were allowed to attack the men, but the men were not allowed to retaliate. The ladies then took off one stocking, filled it with a large stone, swirled it above their head and let go. It was, needless to say, an effective and safe form of attack for the women. This dangerous festival was eventually banned.

At the Upper Lake is an information office. They have maps of all the nature trails through the reserve. In this area, there are sessile oak trees, a remnant of the primeval forest that covered Ireland. Do not stint on time at this wonderful spot, particularly if it is a sunny day.

...Kevin healed the son of the local Irish king and, in return, he asked for the land within the circle of the flight of a swan. The bird set off and swept around the entire valley and the king was true to his word.

ONE OF THE most famous monastic sites in Ireland, Clonmacnoise was founded in 545 by St. Kieran and was the burial place of
the Kings of Connaught and Tara. Kieran went there with seven
companions and settled on the field, by the River Shannon. He
died seven months later of the plague.

The settlement grew from an original wooden oratory to a
cluster of stone churches, many monks' dwellings and a round
tower within an earth or stone enclosure. There was no single
large church or abbey with a cloister. The ruins today are no earlier than the 9th century. The monastery was plundered many times
by the Irish, Vikings, and Anglo-Normans until it was finally
reduced to a ruin in 1552. Within the Visitor's Center is a model
of how this early monastery would have appeared.

The most important feature of this monastery is the site,
which is located on a natural gravel ridge overlooking a marsh
and the River Shannon. There is a wonderful painting of the
ruins, George Petrie's *Pilgrims at Clonmacnoise*, c. 1840, at the
National Gallery of Ireland, Dublin. Within the Visitor's Center
are the original high crosses and grave slabs, which were placed
inside to protect them from
more damage from the ele-
ments. Replicas were created
and are in situ on the grounds.

*Model of early
Clonmacnoise*

The ruins on the site are
predominantly 12th century with
additions through the 15th century. According to the Visitor's
Guide, the grounds include a
"group of fairly late ruined stone
churches in a large graveyard together with a round tower or a
detached stone belfry."

Among these ruined stone churches are numerous high
crosses. There is an excellent map in the visitor center of the
grounds, and a guided tour is also available and highly recommended.

The South Cross dates from the 9th century. It is a free-
standing Celtic cross similar to the Ahenny High Cross. The
shaft is all that remains of the North Cross which dates from
around 800. There are tail-biting lions and a curious figure with
crossed legs which is perhaps a Celtic god. These are well worth
a look.

There are also the 10th century O'Rourke tower without a cap and a small round tower attached to the Temple Finghin which is much newer. It is important to note that the early round towers were taller, more slender and very graceful.

Early Irish gravestones were usually flat rectangular slabs of stone with an incised cross of some kind as decoration and a simple prayer for the person the stone commemorates. There are excellent ones in the Visitor's Center.

There are some interesting ones next to the Durrow High Cross, Co. Offaly, as well.

A wonderful site which should not be missed is this restored Romanesque doorway of the Nun's Chapel (right). It is beyond the entrance to Clonmacnoise and across the road. This is pure

Nun's Chapel Romanesque doorways

Irish Romanesque with dragon heads on the drip moldings. There is also the step-key pattern. The detail (below) shows only a small sample of some interesting designs. The benefactress was Derbhforgaill, daughter of the king of Meath, who, while she was married to the king of Breifne, eloped with the king of Leinster in 1152. This is the same king of Leinster who sought the help of Henry II of England and brought about the Anglo-Norman invasion. She completed the church in 1167 and died in religious retirement in 1193 at the age of 83 years.

Two bronze artifacts originally from Clonmacnoise are displayed in the National Museum of Ireland. They are the Crucifixion plaque of the mid-11th century and the crosier

Nun's Chapel detail

of the abbots of Clonmacnoise of about 1100. The plaque is a blend of the Celt and the Romanesque. The angels on Christ's outstretched arms have the Celtic spiral design but the body is not decorated with the Celtic spirals. There is a beast's head on the crook and animals on the shrine of the crosier of the abbots.

THERE ARE three high crosses to mark the site of the Monasterboice monastery founded by St. Buithe, who died in 521. It
was a foundation with both men and women in holy orders and
an important center of learning connected with Armagh. This
site is worthy for its high crosses. As well as Muiredach's Cross
and the West Cross mentioned ealier, a third or North Cross
shows the crucifixion on its west side. The original shaft is in the
same enclosure as well as a monastic sundial indicating hours of
the Divine Office. The round tower and its treasures were burned
in 1097.

Romanesque Influence 10th to 11th Centuries

The Romanesque influence on the stonemasons of Ireland took
on its own flavor. These churches were normally small rectangular buildings with decoration limited to the arches and the doorways. These decorations became known as the Irish-
Romanesque style and included many of the earlier Celtic geometric designs as well as heads of animals and dragons. The
stonemasons of Ireland used their imagination and creativity to a
delightful extent. The prototype for this style is **Cormac's Chapel**
on the Rock of Cashel, Co. Tipperary. This was the first and the
most elaborate – those which followed incorporated some of its
ideas and decoration, but none the entirety. The decoration
includes chevrons and various styles of heads. These styles are
reminiscent of the Carolingian style of the 9th century in
Europe, but also of the Celtic designs. When the Judgment Day
of the Apocalypse (from the Revelations of St. John) did not
occur in the year 1000 AD, the church in Europe encouraged the
use of reminders that all was not secure. The depiction of monsters, devils and the weighing of souls was a reminder to Christians
that the Church was their only salvation from damnation and
these monsters.

The Rock of Cashel rises above the vast plain of the Golden Vale
in Tipperary.

It is said that this rock formation was dropped there by the devil.
St. Patrick baptised King Aengus here on the ancient coronation stone of
the high kings of Cashel. Legend says that St. Patrick accidentally drove the
spiked point of his crosier firmly into the foot of King Aengus. When the cer-

The Rock of Cashel

emony was over, St. Patrick saw the blood on the grass and in perplexity asked Aengus why he had remained silent. The King responed that he had considered it a part of the ritual.

This was once an ancient stronghold of ancient Ireland. The views of the surrounding countryside are wonderful. Within the walls are the ruins of the Bishop's palace, a round tower and a roofless 13th century cathedral with wonderful windows, but the real gem of the site is Cormac's Chapel.

Muirchertach O'Brien, King of Munster, granted the fortress of Cashel to the church in 1101 AD as a seat for the archbishop. Cormac MacCarthy, king of Munster from 1127 to 1134, was the patron of the chapel. This chapel is the prototype for Irish-Romanesque architecture of which the round arch was an integral part.

According to the brochure, *St. Patrick's Rock, Cashel*, issued by the Office of Public Works, Cormac's Chapel was the earliest Romanesque church in Ireland. It was begun in 1127 and completed in 1134. It reflects a high degree of sophistication, knowledge of architiecture and the advantages of the round arch. Monks from Ireland had traveled, studied, and lived in Europe. Those who built this chapel were in touch with and influenced by what was going on in Europe.

Round Arch at Glendalough

The photograph at left, taken at Glendalough, shows an excellent example of a round arch, which forms a simple barrel vault, or passageway. At the top of the arch is a wedge-shaped stone. When any structural weight is placed on this center stone, the stress is transferred to the abutting stones and travels to the ground. This architectural wonder, the round arch, made possible multilevel buildings with large interior spaces. Before the development of the arch, columns supported stones placed horizontally, called lintels, and the lengths of these stones defined the frequency of the columns.

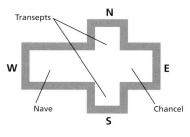

The typical Christian chapel followed a cruciform (cross) pattern. The altar is in the area of the chancel. The transepts are side arms of the cross.

In Cormac's Chapel, the transepts have been replaced by two square towers. The southern tower has a circular stair to the upper floor which once housed a library. The chancel is off center to the south from the nave and has a ribbed vault ceiling. Here the walls are nearly two feet thick.

The chapel ceiling is little more than half the height of the outside wall. A barrel vault supports the nave, while a ribbed vault supports the chancel ceiling.

The building is made of stone and stands tall. But the thick walls and arched stone croft (unique to Ireland, see diagram at right) resting on the barrel vault of the chapel were not sufficient to prevent buckling of the thick heavy wall topped with a heavy high-pitched stone roof.

The round arches, which appear as blockaded windows, form a blind arcade that supports the roof. The arcade is the same concept as the round arch in windows, doorways and vaulted

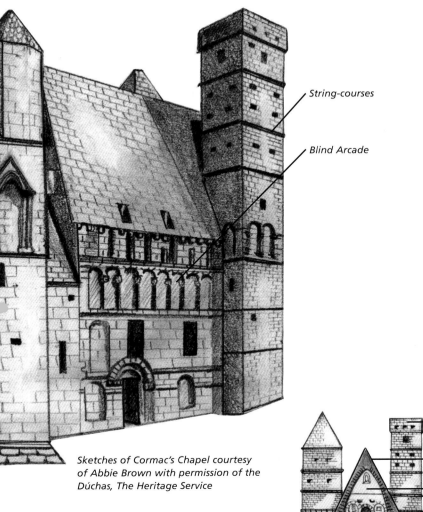

String-courses

Blind Arcade

Sketches of Cormac's Chapel courtesy of Abbie Brown with permission of the Dúchas, The Heritage Service

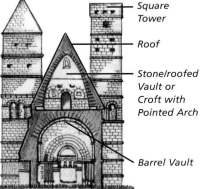

Square Tower

Roof

Stone/roofed Vault or Croft with Pointed Arch

Barrel Vault

ceilings. In this instance the arches rest on columns which are attached to the wall. The weight from the heavy stone wall is directed along the curve of the arch to the columns to relieve the downward pressure. This structure prevents the wall from buckling or collapsing. These blind arcades were also used within the chapel for additional support.

These features are also seen in other Romanesque architecture, but Cormac's Chapel was probably the first use in Ireland.

The string-courses on the tower were prevalent during this period. They often marked the floor levels.

This stone sarcophagus demonstrates the **Urnes** *style of design.*

In Cormac's Chapel the sarcophagus shown at left has large and small intertwining, elongated, footed animals, of a kind often found in Celtic decoration. This is the Urnes style which was introduced into Ireland by one of the many migrations of the Celts.

Cormac's Chapel also exhibits the influence of Europe in its design. Of particular interest is the tympanum (or semicircular area within the arch) decorated with a centaur shooting a lion with a bow and arrow. This is not typically Irish. It is located above the north door and opposite the entrance. It is important, particularly in the religious houses, to look for detail. There are many hidden treasures that you will miss if you concentrate too much on the whole.

Since this site is undergoing restoration, the south side of Cormac's Chapel is covered with scaffolding which is not likely to come down in the near future.

Art in Romanesque Churches and Doorways

Stonemasons throughout Ireland borrowed ideas from Cormac's Chapel. The churches which still exist that are variations of that style are: Kilmalkedar Church, Dingle Peninsula, Co. Kerry; and Clonkeen Church, Co. Limerick. Remains of Romanesque doors are found in Kilmore Cathedral, Co. Cavan; **Clonfert Cathedral,** Co. Galway; Dysert O'Dea, Co. Clare; Ardfert Cathedral, Co. Kerry; Killeshin Church, Co. Laois and **Nun's Chapel,** Clonmacnoise, Co. Offaly.

The feature most popular with Irish stonemasons was the ornamentation. They used the basic designs from Cormac's Chapel and elaborated on the geometric and biomorphic Celtic designs. A delight of imagination and style, their designs include triangles with a variety of leaf designs, weird dragon heads and elaborate chevrons, as well as interlacing and spirals.

The Nun's Chapel at Clonmacnoise, now preserved, is an excellent example of Irish Romanesque design.

Tower, cathedral and bishop's palace on the Rock of Cashel (north face).

This doorway sketch is from Dysert O'Dea. A reconstruction of the original, it is an excellent example. Dysert O'Dea, Co. Clare, is worth a visit if you are in the area. A reproduction of this doorway is also at the National Museum in Dublin.

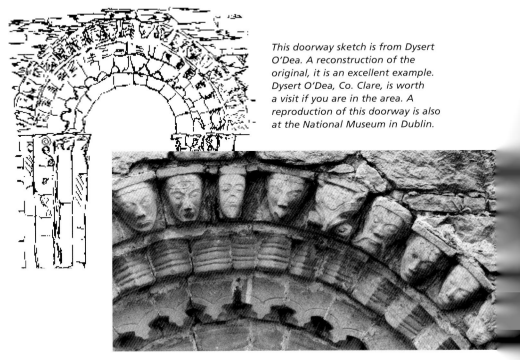

The most remarkable Romanesque door may be that of **Clonfert Cathedral,** Co. Galway (below). The church was built in the 13th century and its west doorway is the thing to see.

Above the arch is a pointed gable which is rich in early geometric design as well as foliage and animals biting the molding. It is unusual that the figureheads on this gable, like those in Cormac's Chapel, are not dragons and gargoyles but the heads of people, perhaps identifiable patrons or priests.

Romanesque door at Clonfert Cathedral

In every Romanesque-style church or ruin in Ireland, the stone-masons left many hidden treasures, strange animals, unique designs and wonderful gargoyles and dragons. Be sure to look, as they are delightful. I particularly like the flowers that take hold between the stones and are charming.

9. *The Monasteries of Ireland*

1100 TO THE DISSOLUTION, 1539

Art and Architecture

During the first millennium AD, the kings and the church structured Irish life. It was an advanced culture where arts, literature and learning flourished, and the reputation of the Irish scholars was famous throughout the continent of Europe.

Kingship was an important and powerful institution. The sagas of Old and Middle Irish literature preserved the ideals of kingship which identified the required qualities for a king as an individual and a ruler. Heroism and courage were paramount. In the literature his coronation was the holy marriage of the king to the goddess of the land for the benefit of the people and the land. The vernacular law tracts describe three grades of kings: king of the local petty kingdom; great king, who was overlord of a number of petty kings; and king of great kings, who was king of a province and a ruler of considerable power and significance.

The five or six kings of the provinces were the big players who exercised the power. The churches backed their pretensions and expected to benefit from their protection. Canon law laid down that if an offense was committed against the church, the final appeal was to the king of the province. The churchmen drew from the Old Testament to develop the idea of the ordained and consecrated king. They were interested in promoting effective kingship and stressing the coercive powers of the king. They also believed that the church should not be taxed and the kings must not overtax their subjects or plunder them. It was during this time that the great monasteries grew and flourished and became seats of religion, royalty and learning.

The world of the Irish kings changed in the 11th and 12th centuries which led to a period of new growth in religion, literature and the arts. There was a movement for religious reform which opposed the power and influence of the royalty in the church in Ireland. Many of the monks traveled to Rome and were not only enthused by the higher position of the church, but more particularly by the Cistercian monasteries whose beliefs and practices were serious and dedicated. In the 12th century the Cistercians were invited to establish new monasteries in Ireland. This was an attempt to reinforce religious fervor.

Cistercian Monasteries

The Cistercians were an order of the Benedictines called the "white monks" who chose remote pastoral land, normally at a river's edge, where they built self-sufficient communities. Their monasteries were located far from activity and temptation and their numbers included monks and lay brothers. Since they were efficient and industrious, making good use of the land, the monasteries became wealthy.

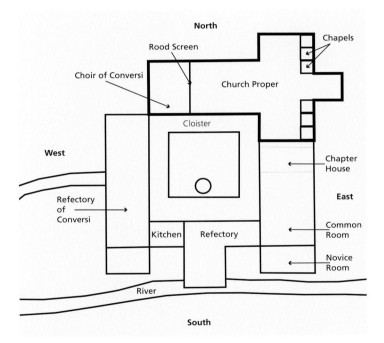

There was a standard pattern to their monastery design which was created at the mother house in Citeaux, France (see above). Their churches were in the shape of a cross and made of white hand-hewn stone on a single continuous stone base which supported the columns, pillars and windows. Stone vaults spanned these to support the roof structures. The design conformed to a strict rectangularity and was based on a ratio with the total length of the church twice the width of the transept. The chancel was square. The rood screen separated the conversi (lay brothers) from

103

the monks. The altar was in the east while the church was directly north of the cloister. There was no adornment with plaster or decoration. There were no statues, pictures or towers, but the placement of the clear paneled glass windows gave light and a beautiful ethereal quality to the churches. The Cistercians scorned scholarly and artistic creativity as well as knowledge and literature. They came to Ireland at the request of St. Malachy and established many monasteries.

Old Mellifont Abbey, Co. Louth, was the first Cistercian House in Ireland. It was founded by a group of French and Irish monks. The original simplicity was continually modified until it became a huge, high Gothic structure. The remains are fragmentary although there is a unique wash house or **lavabo** (left) within the cloister in the Romanesque (or round arch) design.

Lavabo at Old Mellifont

This abbey is under the care of the Dúchas and the guides are interesting and informative.

The French and Irish monks soon began to disagree, with the result that the French monks returned to France. The Cistercians received support from the lay and clerical rulers before the Normans landed. It was to Old Mellifont that Dervorgilla (wife of O'Rourke of Brefni who went off with Dermot MacMurrough, King of Leinster) gave a gold chalice and to here that she retired and died.

This abbey also became the center of a great rebellion known as the Conspiracy of Mellifont during the 13th century. Although it lost prestige and popularity, it remained one of the wealthiest monasteries until the Dissolution of the Monasteries in 1539. It then became a fortified residence, and during the Battle of the Boyne was William 1's headquarters.

These lancet windows, and all windows in the Cistercian style, were placed to create excellent lighting. They are often seen in Romanesque ruins although only the first Cistercian monasteries followed the strict standards set in France by using clear glass.

Jerpoint Abbey, Thomaston, Co. Kilkenny, exhibits many of the classic Cistercian features: the nave, cloister and ruined walls of the complex define the structure of the whole abbey, and the rood screen is visible.

The early monasteries established by the Cistercians during the 12th and 13th centuries underwent changes. The strict adherence to the principles of severe simplicity was modified by the Irish artisans and benefactors of the Church. The plans became more elaborate with taller arches, with towers and with decoration on the capitals. The architectural decoration of these Cistercian monasteries, particularly in the west, was in the Romanesque style. This version of the Romanesque – between the simple Cistercian and the ornate Gothic – is referred to as the Transitional Style.

In these structures, there are both round Romanesque arches and pointed Gothic arches. The more elaborate the style, the later the period of construction. This is a good way of determining the sequence of building in regard to additions and modifications.

Round arch

Pointed arch

Boyle Abbey

Boyle Abbey, Co. Roscommon, (left), started as a Cistercian abbey. During the years of construction, the design was altered, making this an excellent example of transitional style. In this photograph the floor space is the nave, which shows a wonderful and typical blend of round and pointed arches. The round arches and the layout are from the earlier Cistercian period while the pointed Gothic arches and rather bulky square tower are of the later period. At the end is the triple lancet Gothic window of the choir.

In wandering around religious structures there is always a tendency to look up. The taller the structure, the greater its need for stability. In order to achieve the height with stability, the ceilings were vaulted. This approach carried the weight to the sides where other arches and columns could help to bear the weight and thus prevent collapse. Two types of vaults that are typical from this period are the groin vault and the ribbed vault (below).

You are able to identify these by the number of ribs on the ceiling. The groin vault is created by the juncture of two barrel vaults with the formation of a stone "×" in the ceiling. The ribbed vault is created from the meeting of two ribbed vaults. This gives you a design in the ceiling of a "+" superimposed on an "×" as illustrated below right.

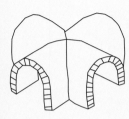

Groin Vault

Ribbed Vault

In the later Gothic-style cathedrals, the vaults became very ornate and intricate, showing a great deal of grace and design. Throughout this period the influences of the Gothic from Europe did not prevent the Irish stonemasons from continuing with their own designs. This is seen in column capitals, window and arch adornment and sculptures on the columns in the cloisters. Some have been restored, others are there to find. You need a sharp eye.

Other Cistercian monasteries include Bective Abbey, Co. Meath, Tintern Abbey, Co. Wexford, and Baltinglas Abbey, Co. Wicklow. They are all good examples although there is little left of the original simplicity in the structures.

A typical decoration by the Irish stonemasons of the 12th and 13th centuries from Boyle Abbey.

These panels are from the columns of the cloister at Jerpoint Abbey. The 'Knight' to the far left is reminiscent of the high crosses and probably represents the patron of the Abbey. Immediately to the left is a typical Celtic design showing a long body and tail with short legs.

Other Monastic Orders

Other orders came to Ireland from Europe: the **Franciscan, Dominican** and **Augustinian** were the most popular. The Franciscans were founded in the early 13th century by St. Francis Assisi, who believed in following in the footsteps of Christ. His magnetism attracted many followers, who entered the theological schools in Paris and Oxford to became theologians and confessors, who went forth from their friaries to preach. Throughout the centuries there was, within the order, a conflict concerning the vow of poverty. In the early 16th century this caused a permanent split which gave rise to the Observants, who followed the belief of total poverty. They became very influential in the western part of Ireland. Unlike the Cistercians, they went among the people and preached. Their

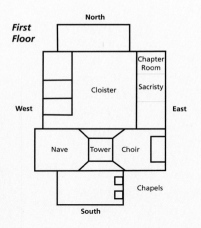

First Floor

North

West · East

South

Chapter Room
Sacristy
Cloister
Nave · Tower · Choir
Chapels

Franciscan style friary floor plans

The tower is in the middle of the long narrow church between the nave and the choir. Here at left is an approximate floor plan of a Franciscan friary.

Although there are many ruins of old monasteries, few have the **second floor** intact. An exception to this is Ross Abbey, Co. Galway.

The castellated battlements on the **tower** of a typical Franciscan friary or Dominican priory are illustrated at lower left. The string-courses usually mark levels. A battlement is a low guarding wall or parapet. The openings are called crenels and the solid part is called a merlon.

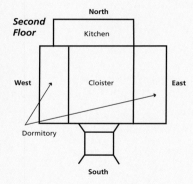

Second Floor

North

West · East

South

Kitchen
Cloister
Dormitory

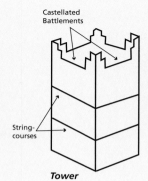

Castellated Battlements

String-courses

Tower

Moyne Abbey

monasteries were large and often well fortified. Moyne Abbey, Co. Mayo, **Ross Abbey**, Co. Galway, and **Rosserk Friary**, Co. Mayo, are good examples of the Franciscan style, which is identified by the tall slender rectangular tower with battlements and string-courses to divide the tower into stories.

Ross Abbey is in the process of conservation work. After the Dissolution of Monasteries in 1539, Franciscan brothers continued to live there under the protection of the local earl. You can easily see the huge oven of the bakery, fireplaces and other parts of the monastery which follows the general Franciscan floor plan. The view from the tower is excellent.

Ecclesiastic architecture has its own emphasis. In this period, the Roman arch and the Gothic arch played an important role in the design of the religious houses. Another important contribution was the windows. Architecture is an art form. Although most of the buildings from this era have been destroyed, there are sufficient ruins to give us a clue to the elegance of these buildings which were thought to be the passageway to the afterlife or Paradise.

As the monasteries were modified and enlarged, the trend moved toward the Gothic, which came to be very elaborate. The style of window is an important feature, the development of which is easy to trace. These windows are usually in an end wall with a gable roof.

The following definitions are based on information from Spiro Kostof's *History of Architecture:*

Mullion – An upright within a window which divides a series of openings or window panes.

Lancet – a narrow window with a pointed arch at the top; a three-light lancet window has a pointed arch with three sections of window pane divided by uprights or mullions.

Tracery – A pattern of curves and lines (usually geometric) which form the support and frame for window panes within the pointed area of the arch.

These windows show the transition in the development of the Gothic window which became far more elaborate in the 18th century. These are all from Kilmallock Abbey, Co. Limerick. The "five light" above is 13th century, while the one on the left (below) is 15th century with tracery within the gable that was in the chapel on the south side.

Some of the ruins of the Franciscan monasteries have evidence of the symbols of St. Francis in the form of pictures or statues with the stigmata. Askeaton Friary, Co. Limerick, is one of these. There are also wonderful carvings to look for, such as the one at Ross Abbey.

This carving in stone is located in an obscure corner of Ross Abbey.

The Irish stone-masons were influenced by Europe but were not controlled by it. They developed their own style.

During the 14th century and the period of the Black Death there was little activity with respect to church building. However, activity resumed in the 15th century on new sites as well as established sites. All the monastic ruins exhibit a succession of styles. Until the Dissolution of the Monasteries in 1539 by Henry VIII, these were active, living institutions which reflected the fiber of the community. It is natural that modification and embellishment occured as new styles were introduced.

The choice of what to see depends on where you are traveling. Those under the auspices of the Dúchas are accessible and often have guided tours. Others, like Moyne Abbey, Co. Mayo are deserted, in an isolated setting (a cow field) and entry is not always available without inquiry. These are not often frequented by tourists and offer a special charm. Ennis Friary, Co. Clare, Muckross Abbey, Co. Kerry, and Rosserk Friary, Co. Mayo are further examples of the Franciscan style.

The **Dominican Priories** founded by St. Dominic were similar in structure to the Franciscan, as at Kilmallock Abbey, Co. Limerick, Portumna Priory, Co. Galway, Roscommon Friary, Co. Roscommon, and Sligo Abbey, Sligo, Co. Sligo.

The Augustinian houses worth a visit include Kells Priory, Co. Kilkenny, Ballintubber (Ballintober) Abbey, Co. Mayo, and Ferns, Co. Wexford. St. Canice's Cathedral, Co. Kilkenny, is in a 13th century early Gothic style with an interesting effigy from the 16th century.

Kilmallock Abbey, Co. Limerick

In the 15th century the power of the local lords was reestablished and they again became the dominant political influence in Ireland. Lay interference in the ecclesiastical world was again prevalent. This led to another great reformation of the church. Within the Franciscans were several splinter groups. The strictest

Kells Priory

of these were the Observant Friars, who, as the first to state their concerns, became a dominant influence. This emphasized and assured that religion in Ireland would play a major role in politics. The focus increased when Henry VIII and Parliament declared the churches of England and Ireland to be independent of Rome. The Observant Friars became the leaders of the Counter-Reformation in Ireland. This became a political battle, not an architectural one.

In 1539, when Henry VIII announced the Dissolution of the Monasteries, all the monastic lands were confiscated. They lost their wealth and power. Elizabeth I supported these policies and quickly squelched any form of rebellion against the power of England and the Anglican church. The separation of the Catholics and Protestants continued. The Protestants were those who were "planted" on monastic lands or land confiscated from unsuccessful rebels. The Catholics were those, who were the native Gaelic Irish, mostly under the leadership of the Observant Friars. Another group of Catholics were the descendants of the Anglo-Normans who had married the daughters of the Irish kings.

They had a rather bumpy road to ride until total disaster and mayhem reigned with the onslaught on Catholicism by Oliver Cromwell in 1649. His troops destroyed churches, homes, monuments and virtually everything Catholic. As you visit the ruins of all of these monasteries, you realize the breadth of the destruction – even to the small monastic islands and the Aran Islands.

10. *Anglo-Norman Invasion Through William* I
1170–1700

Residential Architecture

The development of art and architecture is usually dependent upon the economic and political climate of a country. The interests and needs of the powerful determine the type and nature of this development. During the period from the 12th century through the Dissolution of the Monasteries in 1539, there was generally a great expansion in the growth and embellishment of the monasteries. They were great centers of learning and wealth. The building of cathedrals and abbeys surged. These were founded under the auspices and protection of the Irish chieftains and the Anglo-Normans.

The development of residential architecture was based on necessity during this period, not grandiosity. The homes or castles were functional and defensive. Each spurt of growth was not indigenous but a response to new settlements or plantings from England. These plantings usually came in response to a rebellion or uprising after which land would be confiscated and redistributed to planters.

Ireland was divided into many small kingdoms which were constantly changing and getting smaller. According to the Brehon Laws of succession, when a chief died, the new chief was elected on the spot. The bulk of his estate (results of conquest and allegiance) went to the new chief – not the natural progeny. For this reason, great palaces were not the means of showing wealth or prestige. The chiefs preferred to grant their largess to the monasteries to pave the way for their journey to the after life.

The clans were constantly at war and sacking of property was normal. The early chiefs had used the circular forts as dwellings and security. This style of living persisted for many centuries and was utilized by the Anglo-Normans as well as the later English colonists. It continued up to the time when defense was no longer a necessity for domestic safety, which was as late as the 18th century. The early architecture of the Irish was for domestic use and defense.

The Anglo-Norman invasion began in 1170 and ended in 1175, when Henry II received the allegiance of the chiefs and was held as overlord of Ireland. The chiefs had hoped that he would restrain his Anglo-Norman knights, but, on the contrary, this was the beginning of the colonization of Ireland by the British.

After conquering, the Anglo-Normans needed to occupy and secure the territory against the Irish. The early burial mounds had been used by the Celts, then by the early Christians. Now the Anglo-Norman invaders built wooden towers on these mounds. There is evidence of this at Knowth. From the rocky heights, hills or mottes one could see and prepare for the attack of an approaching enemy. The typical early castle perched atop the motte was protected by a stockade fence with a watchtower. The area within the fence was the bawn, wherein lay the necessary wooden structures for livestock, shelter and food. An excellent example of this is the **Granard motte,** Co. Longford. It was erected by the Normans and looks like an upside-down bowl. Attached was a half-moon-shaped area defended by an embankment and a ditch. **The Rock of Dunamase,** Co. Laois (under restoration), was an ideal site for a defensive fortress.

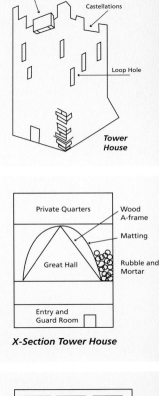

Tower House

As the Normans became more established, stone was used for building. These early stone castles, usually square and multistoried with the living quarters at the top level, consisted of a keep and walled bawn to provide security. Although there were no windows, there were narrow loopholes for firing weapons and murder holes over the entrances for throwing stones and hot liquids on those trying to enter the building. Those tower houses, or keeps, which survived have been the basis for restorations and additions into grander castles.

There are many ruins that were burned or destroyed during the turbulent 17th century. Some remain as ruins while others have been restored and are open to visitors.

One of the most interesting aspects of the tower house was the use of an arch on the third level, the Hall. An A-frame of wood was erected and then covered with a woven matting of twigs in the shape of a

X-Section Tower House

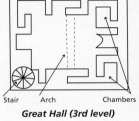

Great Hall (3rd level)

barrel or a ribbed arch. Then, stone or rubble was placed over the matting upon which mortar was poured. After it hardened, the A-frame was removed. The twigs usually decayed, although the imprint of them can often be seen on the ceilings. This was the same system that was used in the early oratories. **Ross Castle,** Co. Kerry, has been restored using the same materials and techniques.

The floor plans of the tower houses varied although the basics were the same. As time passed, towers were placed at the corners of the rectangle, which offered more private sleeping quarters, a chapel and a garderobe. The accessibility correlated to the rank of the user. When more peaceful conditions prevailed, the Great Hall was a separate structure although still within the bawn.

Newcastle West left, Enniscorthy Castle, right.

"The tower house is the late medieval Irish castle par excellence. From the 1300s to the 1600s the great majority of Irish castles included, or were comprised solely of, tower houses. What is perhaps most remarkable about the tower house tradition is that by the end of the 15th century, all three populations in medieval Ireland – the Gaelic Irish, the English and the gaelicized English – had embraced it."[24] Examples of the 13th century stone castle include Athenry Castle, Co. Galway,

Mannan Castle, Co. Monaghan, Roscommon Castle, Co. Roscommon, and **Newcastle West,** Co. Limerick. An excellent reconstruction of an Irish stone castle is **Enniscorthy Castle,** Co. Wexford. Lesser lords also made use of this single fortified tower house style while the peasantry lived in mud cabins.

The great Norman lords lived in large fortified castle grounds with their relatives. These stone fortresses usually contained a keep and stone tower house within a bawn surrounded by a curtain wall with round towers at the corners. They were usually at the edge of a river. This style was evident in England as well. Examples of these fortresses are King John's Castle in Dungarvan and Limerick, **Trim Castle,** Co. Meath, and Dublin Castle, Dublin.

Some of these were built by King John to prepare for a royal visit. The keep had very thick walls (11 feet) and was within the bawn, which was extensive.

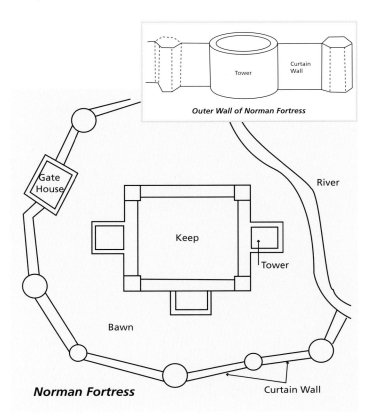

Outer Wall of Norman Fortress

Norman Fortress

Trim Castle

By the mid 13th century the Normans controlled three-quarters of Ireland. They introduced feudalism, founded walled towns, and began to divide the land into counties. Dublin became an administrative center with an independent Irish Parliament.

During the great famine and the Black Death of the 14th century, which plagued all of Europe, many settlers returned to England to become absentee landlords in Ireland. This allowed the Gaelic Irish and Anglo-Normans who had married the daughters of the Irish chiefs and adopted the Irish ways to regain some of their lands. These two groups became the Irish aristocracy who would refuse to accept the Protestant Reformation and thus remained Catholic.

Excellent examples of the 14th century castle are Malahide Castle, Co. Dublin, which has many later additions, **Castleroche** (left), Co. Louth and Ballintubber Castle, Co. Roscommon.

In the 14th and 15th centuries, various architectural features were added to embellish the basic tower house. A few of these are: a crenellated parapet, machicolations, turrets, garderobes and hooded mullioned windows.

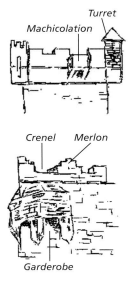

Parapet — The wall that rises above the roof level of a building and is made up of crenels and merlons.

The **merlons** became quite ornate and were later used for decorative features rather than for defensive purposes as at Waterford Castle.

Machicolation is an opening in the floor of a projecting stone gallery through which missiles, stones or hot water were dropped: also called a murder hole.

Turret is a small tower which is usually projecting from a larger structure.

Garderobe is a latrine or lavatory which may be at a low level over a river or on an upper story of a tower castle.

The 15th century saw the establishment of the Pale, an area about the size and location of present Dublin County. There, English was spoken and English law enforced. The remainder of the country became known as "beyond the Pale" or colloquially not the English and therefore uncivilized. These were the Irish or those who spoke the Gaelic language. More castles and defensible towers were built within the port towns and along the borders of the Pale. These towns included Trim, Naas, Dundalk and Kells. The economy was based on warfare, not agriculture. Productivity and life outside the fertile valleys were very primitive. Life within the Pale was grand. This was the time of the Geraldine Supremacy, when the Geralds of Kildare and Desmond were the appointed Lord Deputy and representative of Henry VII and Henry VIII and built many castles. The polarization of the Irish and the English continued to intensify.

The rectangular keep continued to be popular, but often was surrounded by a moat beyond the high walls, which were still fortified with round turrets at the corners. Some boasted their station in life by the addition of a banqueting hall and the title of the Lord of the Manor. Examples which have been restored (or are under restoration) include Bunratty Castle, Co. Clare, Dysert

O'Dea Castle, Co. Clare, **Blarney Castle** (right), Co. Cork, and Cahir Castle, Co. Tipperary.

It was Elizabeth who also gave Blarney Castle its fame. In 1931 H.V. Morton described it:

"In the middle of a pretty wood rise the ruins of Blarney Castle, with rooks cawing round it, moss growing over it, and damp green slime in its dungeons. It is the third castle built on that site. The first was a wooden fortress erected in remote times by Dermot McCarthy, king of South Munster; the second was built about AD 1200, and the present tattered shell was constructed in the reign of Queen Elizabeth. It was the strongest castle in that part of Ireland.... The word 'blarney' entered the language, so they say, when Dermot McCarthy was required to surrender the fortress to Queen Elizabeth as a proof of his loyalty. He said that he would be delighted to do so, but – something always happened at the last moment to prevent the surrender! His excuses became so frequent and were so plausible that the Lord President, Sir George Carew, who was demanding the castle in the name of the Queen, became a joke at court.

Kissing the Blarney Stone

Queen Elizabeth (probably) said, when these excuses were presented to her: "Odds, ikins, more Blarney talk!"

If you visit Blarney Castle to kiss the Blarney Stone, you will have satisfied a whim or a burning desire. Today it is much safer than in years past, as there are not only an iron grating over the opening and steel bars to hold onto, but a guide to hold you. You lie on your back with your head lowered. The purpose of this physical endeavor according to H.V. Morton:

"There is a stone there,
That whoever kisses,
Oh! he never misses
To grow eloquent.

Tis he may clamber
To a lady's chamber,
Or become a member
Of Parliament."

Cahir Castle is of the Norman castle style with huge bastions along the banks of the River Suir. Morton in 1930 wrote:

"Cahir Castle is one of the finest buildings of its kind I have seen in Ireland. It lifts its towers above the river Suir beside a pretty bridge.... If I owned this castle and had the money to indulge a fancy I would restore it and furnish the finer rooms in it with armour and furniture of the period. It is in remarkable condition for a castle that knew the cannon of Cromwell. I believe that if a very little money and thought were spent on it, Cahir Castle would become one of the sights of Ireland."

Cahir Castle. Courtesy of Dúchas: The Heritage Service

The 16th century in Ireland was chaotic for the aristocracy as well as the church. During the reign of Henry VIII, there occurred the Kildare Revolt in 1534 in which Lord Offaly made a symbolic gesture to show Henry that he would not be able to rule Ireland without the support of the Kildares. He went too far in denouncing Henry as a heretic and declared himself champion of pope and emperor. His supporters in the Anglicized community deserted him as his actions were seen as a threat to the English crown rather than a mere symbolic gesture. All the males of the FitzGerald family except for an infant half-brother were put to death and all the vast lands were confiscated by the crown. Henry then forced legislation in the Irish Parliament which declared that the state catholicism of England was the sole legal religion for Ireland. More colonization followed on the confiscated lands of the FitzGeralds.

Those who accepted the Anglicized state church became the rulers and power brokers of Ireland. They became the Protestant Ascendancy and would be in the financial and social position to develop the styles of architecture.

In 1579 the Desmonds revolted, to which Elizabeth I responded with firmness. All the leaders of the revolt were slain in battle or executed. Their lands were confiscated and a new plantation scheme was initiated. Over 4000 English settled in Munster. The test of loyalty was no longer obedience to the crown

Desmond Castle unrestored.

but acceptance of the Protestant faith. She responded with equal firmness to the intrusion of Spain in support of Hugh O'Neil, earl of Tyrone, who had ambitions for the whole of Ulster. He advanced himself as the champion of the Counter-Reformation. England was victorious at the Siege of Kinsale, 1601, and the earl of Tyrone fled into exile.

The 16th century brought forth some interesting square tower castles in the west of Ireland along the same lines as the earlier ones. There are notably Doe Castle, Co. Donegal, Aughnanure Castle, Co. Galway, **Barryscourt Castle,** Co. Cork, **Dunguire Castle,** Co. Clare, and **Thoor Ballylee,** Co. Galway, which is where Yeats lived. It has been restored and as you ascend the circular stairs to the upper levels, you hear a recording of his poem the "Tower Stairs."

Dunguire Castle

The 16th century also saw the building of great houses. On the foundation of an earlier castle (the tower can be seen rising above it) the Tudor style Ormond Castle (below) was built. The Tudor style used brick and stone, gables, and mullioned windows which were often hooded – all the elements that gentrified the old Norman castle. Now it was possible to have windows (although there are loopholes by the entry) and decorations and soften the austerity of the medieval style castles. This castle was designed to please Elizabeth I in a style that was the rage in England. Much of the decoration used not only her coat of arms, but her profile in the tiles of the banqueting hall in anticipation of a visit she never made there.

Ormond Castle

Rothe House in Kilkenny was built by a wealthy Irish merchant. Also there is Shee's Almshouse, which is now an information center but was a typical plain stone structure of this period. Merchants, artisans and their employees and families lived within the town walls for protection.

The 17th century was not a happy time for Ireland. Oliver Cromwell arrived in 1649 and left a wide path of destruction of monasteries, cathedrals and all things belonging to the Catholics. With the Dissolution of the Monasteries in 1539, the monasteries had lost much of their land and wealth, but with the arrival of Cromwell they lost all. All Catholic proprietors who survived were bundled to the northwest across the Shannon River. Their land was confiscated.

In 1661 the restoration of the Stuarts, Charles II and James II, brought little relief or significant return of property to the

Catholics. It did bring fear to the planters, and the Protestant community imposed more restrictions and introduced the Penal Laws, which effectively restricted property ownership by Catholics.

The architectural growth of Ireland continued to be in the Protestant community while the Irish were still limited and controlled by their landlords. The plantation of Ireland increased as these planters from England and Scotland were offered the best of the land upon which to settle. They were pleased with their status and built elegant houses. A new wave of Englishness spread through Ireland. Irish proprietors who had adopted the Anglican religion also adopted English ways to exhibit their loyalty to the crown. Dublin developed as a metropolitan center of importance. There are many houses to see from this period. Some were built on former foundations, others were additions to earlier buildings and others were additions upon additions. The best way to have a feeling for the development of architecture and the confusion of ownership in these periods is to follow this abridged history of Monkstown Castle, Co. Cork taken from *Houses of Ireland* by Brian de Breffny and Rosemary ffolliott.

The house was built in 1636 by John Archdeacon under his wife's supervision while he served in the King of Spain's Army. He did not like the house even though his wife had contrived that it cost, according to legend, either two-pence or fourpence. She had charged the stonemasons room and board while they worked! The Archdeacons were removed in 1647 when it was given to Captain Thomas Plunkett of the Parliamentary Navy. They were soon out and Cromwell gave it to Colonel Huncks who was also soon out and the Reverend Michael Boyle received a full grant to the property in 1685. It remained in the hands of his descendants who let it out to tenants. The Shaws (as in the family of George Bernard) held it in tenancy during the 19th century until 1869. Private residents resided there until 1908 at which time it became the property of the Monkstown Golf Club. It was used as the Club House for many years when a fire occurred that damaged much of the building. The shell still stands although unsafe to enter and the surrounding land has been divided for development. The intentions of the owner with regards to this ruin are unknown. It is sad that such an interesting historical landmark was destroyed so recently and no effort has been made at this date for restoration.

Derryhivenny Castle, Co. Galway, Burncourt Castle, Co. Tipperary, Portumna Castle, Co. Galway and Jigginstown House, Co. Kildare are examples from this era.

The 17th century was devastating for the Gaelic/Irish and the Catholic church. The reigns of James I and Charles I were filled with corruption and poor judgment. The people of Ireland were

Leamaneh Castle, co. Clare

divided into two separate societies. The division not only became more pronounced but it was no longer based on language and culture but religion. The people did not live in elaborate castle/houses. Theirs were the vernacular structures which were made of stone or clay and roofed with thatch. Although these dwellings normally consisted of only one room with one window, perhaps the more successful farmers would have an attached stable for the animals. These were often in the country, clustered in groups and were inhabited by the poor Irish. The very poor lived in mud huts.

II. *18th Century Through Independence, 1937*

U NTIL INDEPENDENCE, it is really necessary to view the culture of Ireland as two separate entities: the Protestants and the Catholics. The Protestants were the social elite, the politically significant and the landowners. This ruling group was first-generation English settlers, descendants of Englishmen who arrived during the 16th century, landowners of Scottish descent (primarily in Ulster) or descendants of Anglo-Norman and Gaelic landowners who had accommodated themselves to English ways. All were Protestant in religion. The wealth of these Irish landowners was dependent upon the agricultural economy, and the collection of rents was their source of income. The Catholics encompassed two major groups: the old Irish aristocracy who had refused to convert and the peasantry (75% of the total population). These peasants were the payers of the rents and the workers in the mills.

This is the beginning of the Georgian era, which is not represented by a specific style but by variations of style which evolved during the reigns of King George I through King George VI (1714 to 1837). The reign of Victoria added a new dimension in architectural style.

Although this seemed a period of peace and general economic prosperity, beneath the surface there was insecurity and discontent. Much of this was the direct result, on the one hand, of the determined efforts of the Protestant Whigs in England to maintain control and, on the other hand, the persistence of the Jacobites to restore the Catholic Stuarts. If the latters' efforts had been successful, which they were not, the Protestants feared a great redistribution of assets in Ireland. This insecurity within the Protestant Ascendency is reflected in the penal laws. A Catholic was forbidden to own a horse worth more than five pounds, or to bear arms, or to own land or to vote. However, Catholic religious communities continued to exist and grow and the laws were gradually ameliorated, if not corrected. In the northwest, Catholics were able to retain their land – often with the aid and complicity of their Protestant neighbors.

Careers in the British Army on the Continent and the "Grand Tour" introduced the Protestant aristocracy to the architectural styles and grandeur of Europe. They built houses in these styles and furnished them with the spoils of war. The Irish Palladian style was introduced by William Conolly, the Speaker of the Irish House of Commons. He was a lawyer from Ballyshannon, Co. Donegal, and although of humble origin, he was later acknowledged as the wealthiest man in Ireland in 1720. He made his fortune with land transactions following the Williamite Wars. His house, **Castletown House,** which is now under the care of the Dúchas, is the grandest of the grand.

Palladian Style Houses

Andrea Palladio was one of the major architects in Italy during the sixteenth century. He studied the simplicity and harmony of ancient Greek structures and emulated them using the temple front as a roofed porch with columns. He also wrote *The Four Books of Architecture* which contained the classic designs and drawings that have been used by architects throughout the western world. The following diagrams are simple representations of the Palladio style.

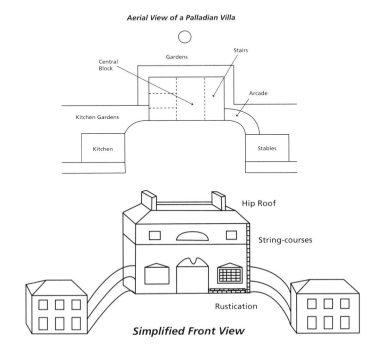

Aerial View of a Palladian Villa

Simplified Front View

The covered curved arcade joined the pavilions to the central block to facilitate dry travel during the rains in Ireland. One pavilion housed the stable while the other, the kitchen. They were often built on a high hill which afforded views in all directions. Beyond the area immediately surrounding the house were the pleasure gardens, fields and forests.

This layout was an ideal way for the landowner to have his office, dairy or stable all within a unified structure. This was not only for defense but a dry access in inclement weather. It was practical and therefore appealed to those who could afford it. Many of these were not designed by architects but by the local builder with instructions from the owner as to his desires.

The drawings, photographs and definitions below are descriptions of those features which are used throughout Ireland on many Georgian houses.

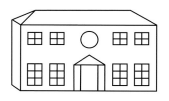

Bay is a regularly repeated spatial unit which may be defined by a window or door. The diagram (left) is of a five-bay facade with a hip roof. A seven-bay facade would have three windows on each side of the door bay and a three-bay facade has one window on each side of the door bay.

The influence of the Greek style of architecture has been prevalent throughout the centuries. In this period in Ireland it was most prominent for governmental and domestic buildings. Although some of the features were modified or enhanced, their origin is clearly recognizable. The following photographs are from objects in Greece.

Ionic Capital *from Delphi, Greece, showing spirals and designs.*

Corinthian Capital *(from the Agora in Athens). This is a good example showing acanthus leaves.*

In the photograph below you can see some of the significant features which are typical of the Palladian style and rely upon the classical worlds of Greece and Rome. Although the photograph does not include both pavilions, the simplicity of the lines and gracefulness of the proportions are evident. This is a thirteen-bay house with the hip roof hidden by a balustrade. The pediments above the windows of the second story alternate between the Greek triangle and the Roman round arch. Demarcating lines of stone which show the locations of the stories are called string-courses. Other classical features

Castletown House

include Ionic capitals on the arcade and the Grecian vase sculpture on the balustrade of the arcade. There is an excellent tour of the interior and a visit is recommended.

There are many elegant houses available for view from this period. Among these is **Russborough House** in Blessington, Co. Wicklow, which also houses the Beit Art Collection and contains fine examples of Francini plaster work. Another excellent example is Strokestown Park House, Strokestown, Co. Roscommon. Other examples of the Irish country house of the Palladian style are Mount Ievers Court, Sixmilebridge, Co. Clare, Derrynane House, Caherdaniel, Co. Kerry and Belvedere, near Mulligar, Co. Westmeath.

The Greek temple style entry was used in Ireland as well as all Renaissance architecture for porticos and window design or merely for embellishment.

Balustrade is a railing supported by small ornamental columns. This is a photograph of the balustrade on the top of Leinster House, Dublin.

Neoclassicism or Classical Style

The Neoclassic theme looked to Rome for its inspiration for domes, arches and porticos. The antique motifs were copied from ancient etchings and drawings based on the Palladian style while the stucco work was in the Greek tradition of wreaths and amphorae.

Marino Casino, Clontarf, Co. Dublin.

This style is best shown by the **Marino Casino,** Clontarf, Co. Dublin. The Earl of Charlemont had spent a great deal of time in Italy and was enchanted with its culture. With the need to return to Ireland to secure his inheritance by producing an heir, he married a local girl and participated in the affairs of Dublin. He was a scholar and a patron of the arts. His town house is now the Hugh Lane Municipal Gallery of Modern Art. The Marino Casino was designed as a pleasure house to entertain his friends and was connected to his principal house (no longer standing) by an underground passage. It is the ultimate of classical architecture. It looks, from the outside, like a one-room mausoleum. In fact, it contains a total of sixteen rooms on three floors: a basement, ground floor and first floor. The cleverness of its construction is worth a visit.

The lion sculptures are delightful. Certainly a study should be made of the poses and expressions of lions in architecture. Much of the statuary in Ireland is enigmatic.

Lion from the front of the Marino Casino.

Other examples of the classical style include Newbridge House, Donabate, Co. Dublin, the **Custom House** and the **Four Courts,** Dublin, Emo Court and Gardens, Emo, Co. Laois, Westport House, Westport, Co. Mayo and Lissadell House, Drumcliffe, Co. Sligo.

ANOTHER IMPORTANT aspect of the Palladian style is the plaster work. The artists who did this were called stuccodores with the most famous being the Francini brothers from Italy. Some decoration was in the flamboyant Rococo style with life-size human figures while others were more classical, ordered and in lower relief. Robert West was the great native Irish stuccodore whose work was made more delicate by employing flowers, fruit, leaves and musical instruments in its design. Others were Michael Stapleton, Robert Adam and James Wyatt.

The stucco work on the ceiling of the **Rotunda Hospital Chapel** in Dublin is marvelous and reflects the theme of this maternity hospital. The entrance to this ornate and secluded chapel is through the main Lobby of the Maternity Hospital, a building without redeeming artistic features. Inquire at the Matron's office, as this gem is well worth the visit. The area has changed significantly since the Rotunda is now a cinema; the Assembly Rooms are now the Gate Theatre; and the pleasure garden is now Parnell Square.

Two other outstanding examples of plaster work include Riverstown House, Riverstown, Co. Cork and Slane Castle, Slane, Co. Meath.

Rotunda Hospital Chapel – section of the ceiling and detail of cherubs.

Victorian Style

The Victorian style and the Gothic Victorian style were employed in public buildings and castle houses.

The early Victorians found the classical style too severe, turning instead to the Renaissance style of the Italian villa and

palace. They sought richness and grandeur. Victorian splendor is not very evident in Ireland since the industrial revolution did not gain great dominance and a large *nouveau riche* middle class was not created. Ireland remained primarily an agricultural economy with some industry in linen and beer. The influ-

Royal City of Dublin Hospital

ence of this style is evident with the creation of a few large houses and some public buildings. In Dublin there are several buildings of brick which exhibit the texture and business of the Victorian era. One of these is the Royal City of Dublin Hospital, which is a wonderful conglomeration of all kinds of features.

The architecture of this period was also influenced by the Venetian style. This style has rounded arches with varieties of marble and mosaic as well as domed ceilings. A wonderful example of this is the **Museum** (now the Engineering School) **at Trinity College, Dublin**.

This was a return to the romantic notions of the middle ages – the setting for "Sleeping Beauty" and other fairy tale classics as well as King Arthur and his brave knights. The buildings were "sculptural, with heavy cornices and string-courses giving a strong horizontal accent, sometimes balanced by arcaded towers, called belvederes. It exploits the rich effect of rustication for quoins, basements and other wall areas."[25] They are frequently faced with brick and the battlements and turrets have no symmetry, a decided break with the Classical style of Greece.

The style was also used by those who restored and added to older tower houses or early castles. They feature architectural battlements and turrets with no symmetry – an artistic exercise. They are usually located on a large estate with wonderful gardens, including a pleasure garden, and rolling fields filled with horses and cattle, and create the ideal of a romantic landscape.

Malahide Castle is particularly significant as it also contains the original 14th century castle. This family played a significant and futile role in support of James II. Other examples are **Glenveagh Castle,** Churchill, Co. Donegal, Ardigillan Castle, Balbriggan, Co. Dublin, Castle Leslie, Glaslough, Co. Monaghan and **Clonalis House,** Castlerea, Co. Roscommon.

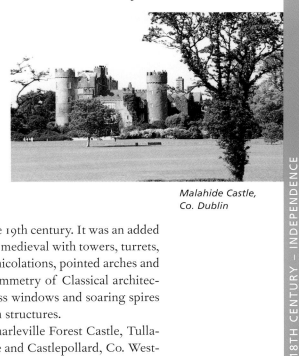

*Malahide Castle,
Co. Dublin*

Gothic Style

The Gothic style was popular in the 19th century. It was an added embellishment of the romantic and medieval with towers, turrets, battlements, crenellations and machicolations, pointed arches and a complete divergence from the symmetry of Classical architecture. The pointed arch, stained glass windows and soaring spires were particularly popular in church structures.

Glin Castle, Co. Limerick, Charleville Forest Castle, Tullamore, Co. Offaly, Tullynally Castle and Castlepollard, Co. Westmeath and **Kylemore Abbey,** Co. Galway represent this style.

Kylemore Abbey

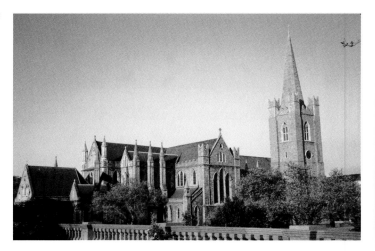

St. Patrick's Dublin in the warm glow of sunrise

SCOTTISH BARONIAL OR GOTHIC VICTORIAN STYLE

THIS STYLE seems to favor the medieval – more compact than the Gothic sprawl but with stepped gables, turrets, string-courses and rustication or texture in the facade. Blarney House, Blarney, Co. Cork is an example of this style.

The High Gothic of the late Victorian Age, also called Gothick, derived much of its style from the French. This is represented in the many churches and cathedrals which have been built or rebuilt. **Christchurch Cathedral** and **St. Patrick's Cathedral** in Dublin are both Anglican (Reformation of Henry VIII, 1530's).

The interiors with their arched ceilings give an excellent idea of the detail and extent of ornamentation of this period. The Archbishop of Dublin did not like living next door to Christchurch Cathedral, which was under the jurisdiction of the City Provosts. In 1181, he moved to where it is reputed that St. Patrick performed many baptisms. This new church, St. Patrick's, was then promoted to a cathedral. They have been rivals in restoration which has assured the continuation and preservation of these ancient cathedrals. As in all architecture in Ireland, these also reflect the many modifications (from Romanesque to Transitional to Gothic) of the different styles.

Christchurch Cathedral

Tudor Revival Style

This style reverts back to Elizabeth I with mullioned windows, gables and texture in the facade (like Ormond Castle). **Muckross House** and Gardens, Co. Kerry, Carrigglas Manor, Co. Longford and Kilruddery House and Gardens, Bray, Co. Wicklow.

Muckross House

Residential Castle Style

These castles were built in the 19th century to emulate the wealth of the aristocracy during this period. They often have incorporated an early ruin and are in the style of an "old castle." **Kilkenny Castle,** Kilkenny, Co. Kilkenny and Lismore Castle, Lismore, Co. Waterford, are excellent examples of this style and period.

Throughout the 18th and 19th centuries building occurred sporadically while imitating individual features of the different styles gleaned from travels throughout the world. This included creative and interesting divergences inspired by the Crystal Palace at Brighton. The **Hindu-Gothic Gateway,** Dromana, Co. Waterford was a surprise for a bridal couple off on their honeymoon to India. They liked the temporary creation so much that it was then built as a permanent structure. It is now under the care of the Irish Georgian Society.

Another wonderful spoof is **Ballysaggartmore,** the Towers. Just outside of Lismore, Co. Waterford, two sisters vied to own the most elegant home. In trying to outdo the other, one planned a grand house with great Gothic gateways. At the completion of the gateways, her husband suffered financial reversals, a modest house was built which was razed several decades ago. The two gateways are still there and offer a pleasant excursion.

Another is the **Swiss Cottage**, Cahir, Co. Tipperary. This was built for the dashing Duke of Ormond by the architect John Nash. It was anything but a cottage, since it sported Persian wallpaper and elegance in great

Lismore Castle

Hindu-Gothic Gateway

One of the two gates of Ballysaggartmore

Swiss Cottage

measure in a delightful setting on the River Suir. It is under the protection and care of the Dúchas.

Ecclesiastical building continued and showed a growth in style. The Gothic style became more popular after the building of the Parliament building in London. There were also variations in the Perpendicular style which was designed with greater simplicity with a vertical stress. St. Fin Barre at Cork, Co. Cork, is decorated in the ornate French Gothic.

Several excellent books offer photographs and details of the houses in Ireland. They are available for sale and easily found. Many houses are on exhibit or are open for house stays. The list continues to grow as this is a practical way to meet the cost of maintenance on these elaborate and costly houses. Not only the Dúchas is involved with the restoration and preservation – there are the Irish Georgian Society, Heritage Island and others.

The landscape of Ireland was gradually modified. Port cities developed, road, bridges, mills and canals were built, cattle raising encouraged the growth of market towns and small industries were developed. The growth of the cities marked a new era.

While the ports and farms in the south were flourishing, Ireland was devastated by the Potato Blight. The toll of lives lost from starvation and disease was extensive. The Famine Museum at **Strokestown Heritage Center,** Co. Roscommon, shows the story of these years with photographs. At Cobh, the Queenstown Story graphically shows the horrors of emigration in crowded vessels and stormy seas. These exhibitions are in sharp contrast to the scenic landscape and elegant houses, but both are an integral part of Ireland.

At right is a thatched cottage which was standard housing for many of the peasantry. This one is located in Donegal on St. John's Head and is maintained and enjoyed as a summer getaway. It is far more idyllic than those which served as the principal dwelling for a large family in earlier times. Thatch is expensive but the picturesque setting and wonderful garden make it seem a romantic landscape and life. These were small and usually of one or two rooms with the fireplace, which burned peat, the center of family life.

Map courtesy of Dúchas:
The Heritage Service

12. *Dublin City*

DUBLIN CITY straddles the River Liffey which forms a bay opening into the Irish Sea. The water from the bogs is dark in hue and called Black Pool, which in Irish is Dubh Linn, or Dublin. Although there are impressive Stone Age monuments north of the city, the earliest remains which have been discovered in Dublin date from the 9th century and the Norse Vikings. They built the first structure on the site of present Dublin Castle. On the south bank of the Liffey there is a dig in progress and many artifacts have been removed and preserved. The Vikings ruled here and used their strength to neutralize the power of the Irish. In 1014 they were defeated by Brian Boru in the Battle of Clontarf on the north shore of Dublin Bay. Since Brian was slain in this battle, they lost the battle but not their influence or power. The Vikings, or Ostmen, were then instrumental in defeating Dermot Mac Murrough, king of Leinster. He then went to England to seek the aid of Henry II. The Anglo-Normans arrived at the end of the 12th century.

Dublin remained a small medieval walled town within the Pale. This narrow strip along the shore of the Irish Sea became primarily an English settlement.

At the time of the Reformation and the Dissolution of the Monasteries in 1539 by Henry VIII, Dublin became Protestant or Anglican. In 1649 its residents did not join the Irish Catholic confederacy but yielded the city to the Parliamentarian, Oliver Cromwell. At the end of this era Dublin was in shambles: the city walls and gates, the two cathedrals and the castle were all in a sorry state.

With the repeal of the Edict of Nantes in 1685 in France, there was a large influx of Huguenots to Ireland. These were weavers and traders in cloth and the city of Dublin flourished. In the 18th century Dublin became a Georgian city dominated by the Protestant Ascendency. The Irish Parliament met in Dublin and it became a prosperous and cultured city. The growth and building within the city were planned with a sense of proportion and beauty.

In 1801, the Act of Union dissolved the Irish Parliament and many members of the Protestant Ascendency returned to England.

Dublin lost its prestige and elegant bearing. As the Penal Laws were gradually repealed, railways were built and a measure of prosperity returned, although some of the worst slum areas in Europe were in Dublin.

The city's development in the 20th century has progressed slowly and surely. There is now a balance between development and conservation. In touring the city, one can seek out the oldest remains of the Viking presence, which are seen in parts of the Dublin Castle and along the River Liffey at Wood Quay where archeological excavation has taken place. There is also an audio-visual presentation of the Viking presence, Dublinia, which is located near Christchurch Cathedral.

A signposted walking tour of Dublin, the 'Heritage Trail,' with guide books is available at the Writer's Museum near Parnell Square. However, in this book, these sites are sorted according to the era and architecture. The River Liffey which flows west to east and O'Connell Street are the main arteries for important sightseeing.

Dublin is the headquarters of the Dúchas: the Heritage Service, the Genealogical Office, and many other useful services for pursuing study, investigation or exploring. There is an excellent publication, *Archeology, Ireland*, which provides news of ongoing and recent discoveries from all eras as well as notification of conferences. There is much research in progress and many early monuments are being discovered.

Monuments of Dublin City

Dublin is not an easy city in which to find one's way – even with a map. The streets are higgledy-piggledy, change their names frequently and are often not signposted. Using a good street map with the general landmarks of the area does work. Although reference to north, south, east and west is not preferred, it is a valuable tool for Dublin. The River Liffey flows from west to east through Dublin. O'Connell Bridge connects the two parts of the city. Located to the south are such sites as Dublin Castle, Trinity College, St. Patrick's Cathedral, and Christchurch Cathedral, as well as the National Museum of Ireland, and the National Gallery of Ireland, and Leinster House where the Parliament sits. North of the Liffey are the Fourcourts, Custom House, General Post Office as well as the Rotunda Hospital, Garden of Remembrance and Phoenix Park.

The monuments in Dublin, which are generally of the Classical and/or Palladian style, are large and impressive and bespeak an era of style. Although rigid in design and faithful to the classical tradition, they are significant in their monumental size. But as in the early centuries, the Irish craftsman continued to embellish. The Age of Victoria introduced ornate designs with carvings, texture and color. Brick work became popular for the warmth of the earth tones. And the wonderful work of the stuccoteers is found in Dublin to perfection.

Crown, Urnes design. National Museum of Ireland

THE **National Museum of Ireland** is located in Dublin on Kildare Street. The heritage of Ireland viewed here should not be missed. As you enter through the impressive entryway into the Treasury, be patient – turn to the left and follow the progress of this ancient culture through the centuries. There are models of the curraghs (boats) and many other artifacts up through the Bronze Age. Then, into the center to see the Treasury – the golden artifacts of Ancient Ireland which have been found in the many bogs. The workmanship and design of these golden hoards are outstanding and illustrate a sophisticated and refined culture. Another gallery

NATIONAL MUSEUM OF IRELAND

displays the voluptuous religious objects which are decorated with jewels, gold and silver in intricate design. It is said that the lack of opulence in their domestic residences as opposed to that of the religious houses shows a greater interest in their salvation or afterlife than in their physical comfort. There is also a gallery devoted to the movement toward Independence.

Within the museum there is an audiovisual display which highlights the most important items. Like the many students who

Gold Ionula. National Museum of Ireland

Gold beads

Etruscan figure

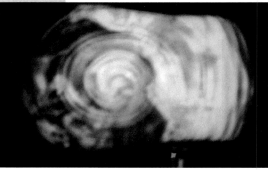

Mace head

come here, there are many things that one should seek and find. Ask a guard if you are having trouble finding them. Within the Treasury, notice particularly the shaped **gold beads** with intricate scrollwork. A **mace head** found at Knowth Passage Tomb is quite different from other finds as it uses the natural coloring of the stone to enhance the design. The **Etruscan figure** must have traveled to Ireland during the first millennium BC. During this same period there was much work in gold, including the model boat with oars and mast, the **Tara brooch** (and many other brooches) and ornaments including the **petrie crown**. The artifacts of the Christian era are many, elaborately adorned and bespeak the church's wealth.

The **Armagh Chalice (left)**, **Cross of Cong** and many other Christian relics should be viewed.

IN 1854, at Westminster, an Act of Parliament established the National Gallery of Ireland. The **National Gallery of Ireland** is located within a square that includes the National Museum of Ireland, the National Library, Leinster House and the History Museum. Leinster House is the seat of the government and is not open to the public. It is in the Palladian style and was the former town residence of the Earl of Kildare.

The new gallery was a technological treasure in the mid-19th century with top-lit galleries, special construction to avoid the dangers of fire and acoustic considerations. The collection was not great and consisted of only 125 paintings. Several large purchases were made from the Italian School. The collection continued to grow with an annual budget for purchasing works of art.

In 1903 a new wing was opened and they received the Milltown gift, which included the art and antiques at Russborough House. Many of these paintings had been obtained on the Grand Tour. Other endowments continued as did purchases which increased the size and quality of the collection. Sir Hugh Lane, as director, endowed the gallery with many generous gifts. This included some great masterpieces as well as funds for future purchases. He hoped to establish a Dublin Municipal Gallery of Modern Art. When he failed to gather support for this project, he lent his collection of French Impressionist paintings to the National Gallery in London. Upon his unexpected death in 1915 (he was aboard the Lusitania), both art galleries claimed the paintings. The paintings now travel between the two galleries – London and Dublin.

Another great benefactor of the gallery was George Bernard Shaw. He bequeathed a third of the royalties from his estate to the gallery to make possible the purchase of many excellent paintings.

In 1968 another new wing was opened. This provided exhibition space not only for a fine collection of French artists but for the rehanging of the older Baroque pieces. Included in the addition was space for support facilities for the gallery.

The National Gallery of Ireland is a vibrant and growing institution always worthy of a visit. One example of this is the permanent loan of a recently discovered Caravaggio. The discovery of this painting, the search for its provenance and the skill with which it was restored were exciting.

My recommendation for a visit to the art gallery is to first purchase a catalog showing their major works of art. From there, go to see your favorite artists and styles. The best of the best will be included in the catalog. The Irish artists are most impressive.

The musts are: Caravaggio's *The Taking of Christ*, Vermeer's *Lady Writing a Letter with her Maid*, Canaletto's *A View of the Piazza San Marco*, and Master of St. Augustine's *Scenes from the Life of St. Augustine*. If you plan to visit Clonmacnoise, Co. Offaly, be sure to look at the gallery's painting by George Petrie, *The Last Circuit of Pilgrims*. The famous *James Joyce* portrait by Jacques Blanche as well as two paintings by William Leech, *A Convent Garden, Brittany* and *The Sunshade*, are not to be missed. An amazing Irish artist is Jack Yeats, brother of the poet. *For the Road*, for me, captures the essence of Irish culture.

CHRISTIAN
HERITAGE

The Book of Kells is located in the Old Library at Trinity College. The book contains, in Latin, the text of the four gospels: Matthew, Mark, Luke and John. The pages are made of vellum or calf skin which had been treated to create a fine surface. The ink is made from the juices of plants, leaves and fruits and is applied with a quill, probably of a goose. The vellum is marked with pricks to set up a grid for the lettering. The pigments of the colors have been studied but it is not known how they were prepared. Since the colors are still rich after twelve hundred years, the loss of the formula for preparing the colors is indeed our loss. The books were inscribed by monks at a monastery founded by St. Columba at Iona, an island off the coast of Scotland. After the raids of Vikings, the monks fled to the monastery at Kells and continued their work there. Of particular interest is the detail and drawings in the text. Many designs of the Celtic type are apparent as well as both wonderfully fantastic and real animals.

St. Audoen's Church of Ireland was dedicated to St. Ouen. It was built by the Normans on the foundation of a church honoring St. Columcille. There is a 12th century doorway. The churchyard is now a park which leads to St. Audoen's Arch, a surviving gateway of the old city. It is located on Cook Street, which is south of the River Liffey.

St. Mary's Abbey was founded in the 12th century and was one of the most important Cistercian Abbeys in Ireland until the dissolution of the monasteries in 1539. The church buildings were used as a stone quarry for the Essex Bridge. What survives today are the Chapter House and a passageway, known as the slype, which connected the cloister to the outside world. The Chapter House includes lancet windows and four bays of ribbed vaulting as well as an exhibition on the abbey. This abbey is located north of the River Liffey and east of the Four Courts.

St. Patrick's Cathedral* (Church of Ireland) is built on the oldest Christian site in Dublin as it is said that St. Patrick baptized converts here. The present structure is 13th century early Gothic or Early English and was restored in the 19th century. The massive west tower is easily identified by the large public clock, 'that has the loudest peal of bells in all of Ireland.' The cathedral has some interesting historical monuments and history. It was built outside the city walls by John Cromyn, an archbishop appointed by Henry II, who did not wish to be under the jurisdiction of the City Provosts. Jonathan Swift was dean here during the early 18th century and his memorial is here. There is also the huge Boyle Monument which was erected by the Earl of Cork in memory of his second wife, Catherine. There is another such monument which he constructed in the St. Mary's Collegiate Church in Youghal, Co. Cork. These effigies represent an interesting aspect of this culture and comprise much of the art of the period.

Christchurch Cathedral* (Church of Ireland) is also an early Gothic or English style cathedral although there are remains of an earlier Romanesque structure on this site. These include a doorway and the foundation of a chapter house. The additions were built in the latter half of the 12th century by the Archbishop Lawrence O'Toole and the Norman Richard de Clare or "Strongbow." This cathedral was obedient to Henry VIII and became an Anglican church. It is located south of the River Liffey on Castle Street.

St. Michan's Church* is famous for the mummified bodies in its crypt which is still an active burial site. A guided tour is available. It is located north of the River Liffey and west of the Four Courts.

Dublin Castle is thought to be located on the site where there was first an ancient rath or earthwork, after which there was a Viking fortress (841); Strongbow, who led the Anglo-Norman invasion, erected a motte which officially became a castle under King John and included a central keep with a surrounding curtain wall with massive towers. Some features of this 13th century building can be found. In 1684 a fire destroyed the medieval castle and the present structure gradually evolved. It represented British rule for many centuries. The state apartments are now used when Ireland is President of the European Community and for Presidential inaugurations and state functions. Guided tours are available.

CASTLES

* Information about each of these is available at the entrance.

Ashtown Castle, Phoenix Park, Dublin, is a restoration of a 17th century tower house. It houses a visitor center for the park.

PUBLIC
BUILDINGS

Rotunda Hospital Chapel is within an active working maternity hospital. The stucco work is superb and should not be missed. Permission to visit the chapel is cordially granted by the matron of the hospital. Inquire at their information desk. The hospital is located north of the River Liffey on Parnell Street.

Leinster House was built in the 18th century as the town house for the Earls of Kildare. It was purchased by the Irish government in 1925 to seat the national parliament. It is located south of the River Liffey and west of Merrion Square. It is not normally open to the public. This large block also includes the National Museum, National Gallery, and the National Library, as well as other significant buildings.

Custom House was built at the beginning of the 19th century with much travail. In 1921 this wonderfully classical building was severely damaged by a fire which continued for many days. In 1926, the damage was repaired although it was learned that there had been more serious structural damage. In 1986 a large restoration project was started which is now complete. It is located on the north shore of the River Liffey and east of O'Connell Street. Although it is closed to the public, a wander about the grounds to view the architecture is worth a few moments of time.

Four Courts is a wonderful structure which played an important role in the Civil War. Located on the north shore of the River Liffey and west of O'Connell Street.

Trinity College was founded by Elizabeth 1 on the site of the Augustinian priory. There are many architectural treasures and a guided tour is a way to get one's bearings. The examination room contains some marvelous stucco but is not normally open to the public. The grounds include forty acres and a casual stroll is an excellent idea. The old museum building has a Venetian design.

Trinity Library or the Old Library is comprised of a wonderful 'Long Room.' The famous Book of Kells, located in this building, is the culmination of Celtic and Christian art of the 8th century. It is significant not only for its artistic excellence but also because it represents a major cultural contribution to the Christian world. A good text for appreciating this work is *Exploring the Book of Kells*, by George Otto Simms.

Leinster House

Custom House

Four Courts

National Botanical Gardens, Glasnevin, Dublin 9, is situated on the Tolka River which is one mile north of Dublin City center.

The Dillon Garden, 45 Sanford Road, Ranelagh, Dublin 6

Powerscourt Town House, South Williams Street, Dublin 2 – 18th century palazzo

Newman House, 85/86 St. Stephen's Green, Dublin 2 – 18th century townhouses – famous for the Irish-Georgian stucco work

Number Twenty Nine, Lower Fitzwilliam Street, Dublin 2 – 18th century middle-class merchant house – completely restored

Marino Casino is a small 18th century pleasure house which is exquisite. It is reached by Malahide Road and is northeast of the metropolitan center.

Kilmainham Gaol – 1796 – symbolizes Ireland's tradition of militant and constitutional nationalism with the leaders of all the rebellions being jailed here. It is located on Inchcore Road just south of the entrance to Phoenix Park.

Garden of Remembrance is a wonderful quiet space in the busy district of Dublin.

The Royal Hospital at Kilmainham was built in the 17th century as a home for retired soldiers. It is an outstanding classical building built around a courtyard. The building houses the Irish Museum of Modern Art. This classical building has a fine chapel whose baroque ceiling deserves particular attention.

Phoenix Park was created in the 17th century. It is a landscaped parkland with a deer herd, a People's Flower Gardens, Dublin Zoo, Wellington Monument, the Papal Cross, fields for cricket, polo and 'gentle exercise.' Here, also is located the house of the President of Ireland as well as the home of the U.S. ambassador to Ireland. During the first half of the 20th century, lions were raised here for export to other zoos throughout the world. They were unique and were nurtured by the Director of the Zoo, often playing with his children and dogs. Today the zoo is a member of the World Zoo Association and an active participant in their conservation strategy. All the animals here were bred at the Dublin Zoo or in other zoos throughout the world. They do not advocate taking animals from their natural habitat. It is run by the Royal Zoological Society of Ireland as a nonprofit organization which relies on the generous donations of its supporters, memberships and admission charges.

St. Stephen's Green was created in the 17th century before which time it was common land. It is a pleasant place to wander or sit, with water gardens, flowers, shrubbery and trees. The statuary is interesting. Many of the buildings abutting the green are architecturally interesting for their excellent Georgian doorways with fanlights and other features.

Merrion Square is an oasis within the busy City of Dublin. Since the gardens and lawns are well established, it is a pleasant place for strolling, reposing or eating a picnic lunch.

War Memorial Gardens at Islandbridge is across the River Liffey from Phoenix Park. This is a memorial for Irishmen killed in World War 1. The planting, rose gardens and lawns create a setting appropriate for this memory. There is a book room where an illuminated book lists the names of the 49,400 killed.

The **Hugh Lane Municipal Gallery of Modern Art** displays an excellent group of Irish artists.

The Irish Museum of Modern Art is located in Kilmainham Hospital with an emphasis on 20th century art as well as theater and music.

The **Writers Museum** includes memorabilia and information about the many Irish writers.

Sculpture in public places is an integral part of Dublin. In the Garden of Remembrance is a wonderful "Children of Lir," on the center strip of O'Connell Street is a fountain containing "Deirdre of the Sorrows" and close by is a statue of James Joyce (left).

Literature

It is said of William Butler Yeats that he "formed the idea of recreating a specifically Irish literature which would give dignity to Ireland's idea of itself, by making Irish readers aware of their heritage of a Gaelic civilization, by encouraging a new literature not dominated by political rhetoric but distinctively heroic in its return to past traditions." [26]

Story telling, the oldest form of literature, was an intrinsic part of the lives of the Celts. These narratives told of the gods, the warriors and their adventures and romances as well as describing the way of life. Their palaces were great, the clothing rich and elegant and their parties and feasts sumptuous. In the early monastic times, the scribes wrote down these tales and stories in Gaelic in the Book of Leinster. From this have come the wonderful mythological cycles.

In 1935 the Irish Folklore Commission began to collect many of the tales and poems recited through the ages by the Gaelic storytellers, seanachai. Peig Sayers of the Blasket Islands knew many of these ancient stories handed down from generation to generation.

This tradition of articulation with imagination has created literary giants in Ireland. Some became exiles as their work did not conform to the system. The Dublin Writer's Museum is located next to the Garden of Remembrance. It is a good starting place for a literary tour of Ireland.

JONATHAN
SWIFT

Jonathan Swift (1667–1745) was born in Dublin of English parents. Since his father died before he was born, he was dependent on the generosity of his uncles. He was not a great student at Trinity College, Dublin – perhaps, because he neglected his studies. He went to London as a young man to become a member of the household of Sir William Temple. He matured, wrote and formed a lasting friendship with the daughter of the housekeeper, Esther Johnson a.k.a. Stella. During this period he wrote *A Tale of A Tub* which ridiculed religious extremists. After the death of Sir William he became a well-known satirist, political journalist and churchman. In *Journal to Stella*, letters to Esther Johnson who was living in Dublin, he recorded his reactions to the political climate.

He retired to Ireland, became dean of St. Patrick's Cathedral in Dublin and became involved with the affairs of the nation. He wrote on many of the social and economic problems in Ireland with humor and extreme irony and tried to incite the Irish to do things to help themselves with his *Drapier's Letters*. He became greatly beloved in Dublin. He was pursued by Esther Vanhomrigh, a.k.a. Vanessa, who followed him to Ireland. There are many stories about Swift, Stella and Vanessa, but there is no proof of the actual situation. These relationships have given rise to much speculation.

His *Gulliver's Travels* achieved much acclaim. In a letter to Alexander Pope he said that it was written to "vex the world rather than divert it." He is entombed at St. Patrick's Cathedral where his epitaph (which he composed) reads:

"The body of Jonathan Swift, Doctor of Sacred Theology, dean of this cathedral church, is buried here, where fierce indignation can no more lacerate his heart. Go traveler, and imitate, if you can, one who strove with all his strength to champion liberty."

Oliver Goldsmith (1731–1774) was born and received his early education in Ireland near Athlone. His father was an Anglo-Irish clergyman. After an unhappy time at Trinity College, Dublin, where he received a BA degree and had several misadventures, he left Ireland in 1752 and never returned. Some of his poems recall sites from his childhood. He is considered to be an Irish-born English playwright, poet and novelist, who always retained his Irish brogue. His poem, "The Deserted Village," his novel, *The Vicar of Wakefield* and his comedy *She Stoops to Conquer* are the most well-known. Samuel Johnson said of him that no man was more wise when he had a pen in his hand, nor more foolish when he had not.

Oscar Wilde (Fingal O'Flahertie Wills) (1854–1900) was born in Dublin. His father was an ear and eye surgeon with interests in archeology, folklore and Jonathan Swift. His mother was a poet and authority on Celtic myth and folklore. Oscar was an outstanding student. He studied at the Protera Royal School in Enniskillin, Trinity College in Dublin and Magdalen College, Oxford. He traveled in Rome and Greece. By the 1880s he was a dilettante and brilliant conversationalist in London. An American tour was hugely successful. He married the wealthy daughter of an Irish barrister and was the father of two sons. At this time he wrote the "Canterville Ghost" and the "Happy Prince." His plays were great satirical comedies of which *The Importance of Being Ernest* was the most famous. Others were *Lady Windermere's Fan*, *A Woman of No Importance* and *An Ideal Husband*. His play *Salome* was written in French and the basis for the opera by

Richard Strauss. His great novel was *A Picture of Dorian Gray*. Oscar Wilde was accused of homosexuality, tried and imprisoned. He lived in France after his imprisonment and died a lonely and bitter man. His genius and abilities were outstanding and his literature is delightful.

JOHN
MILLINGTON
SYNGE

John Millington Synge (1871–1909) was born in Rathfarnham, Co. Dublin, of Anglo-Irish stock; his family was a part of the Protestant Ascendency. He became a leading figure in the renaissance of Irish literature. He was advised by Yeats to return to the west coast of Ireland to draw the material for his drama from life. He lived in the Aran Islands for three years and was able to master their language. His works were detached and not political – he understood and loved the harsh Irish landscape with its natural cruelty. He observed the peasants sorrowfully enduring the realities of their lives. These were the people in his plays: *In the Shadow of the Glen, Riders to the Sea, The Well of the Saints* and *Playboy of the Western World*.

He was associated with the Abbey Theatre where his plays gained gradual acceptance. He was a friend of the great dramatists of his time and often visited Coole Park, Co. Galway, the home of Lady Gregory, an early patroness of the Irish Theatre. He died at an early age.

WILLIAM
BUTLER YEATS

William Butler Yeats (1865–1939) was a poet, playwright and Irish nationalist. He was of the Anglo-Irish Protestant aristocracy but scorned their greed and commerce. He did not share the Catholic faith with the Irish, rather, he was drawn to the paganism and mysticism of ancient Irish mythology. As a poet, he bemoaned the ills and corruption of the world.

He loved Maud Gonne, who was an intense Irish nationalist. She admired and respected Yeats but did not love him. He proposed to her and she refused. He met Lady Gregory, a wealthy aristocrat and playwright. They became close friends and worked together on the Abbey Theatre. He spent many of his summers at her house, Coole Park, Co. Galway.

In 1917 he proposed to the daughter of Maud Gonne who refused him. Shortly thereafter he married Miss George Hyde-Lees and had two children. At this time he bought a 16th century tower house near Coole Park which he converted to a summer residence. When you visit this house and ascend the stairs to his study, his poetry is being read aloud. The following lines are embedded in my mind as I followed his words:

> ..."A winding stair,
>   A chamber arched with stone,
>   A grey stone fireplace with an open hearth,
>   A candle and a written page...."

His cares and concerns were communicated through his poetry. He identified with the peasants and felt that the aristocracy were neglecting their responsibilities to maintain courtesy and civility. He showed no sympathy with the middle class.

He served as a senator in the Irish Senate for six years. During that time he worked on the practical matters of censorship, health insurance, divorce, the Irish language, education and Ireland's membership in the League of Nations.

Yeats won the Nobel Prize for Literature in 1923. He died in Europe and was interred there because of the outbreak of World War II. In 1948 his body was returned to Ireland and he is buried in the churchyard at Drumcliffe, Co. Sligo, where his great grandfather had been the rector. This is his own epitaph: "Cast a cold eye on life, on death. Horseman, pass by!"

James Joyce (1882–1941) was born and educated in Ireland. Although the family fortunes were not constant and he knew poverty well, he received much of his schooling in Jesuit schools. At the University College, Dublin, he studied languages and read constantly. At one time he considered being a doctor to support himself while he continued writing, but found it distasteful. After a short stay in Paris, he returned to Ireland as his mother was dying. It was at this time he lived in the Martello Tower, Sandycove, Co. Dublin, which is now a Joyce Museum. Here, he wrote the tales of the *Dubliners*. He left Dublin in 1904 with Nora Barnacle, a chambermaid, whom he finally married in 1931.

He lived his life in exile in Paris, Trieste, Rome and Zurich in constant rebellion against his family, church and country although the setting of his books was always Dublin and his characters were its residents. *A Portrait of the Artist as a Young Man*, *Ulysses* and *Finnegan's Wake* were his masterpieces.

His daughter was beset with mental illness and was finally institutionalized near Paris. His eyesight continued to fail until he was nearly blind.

His style of writing is unique with the use of many innovative narrative techniques. His works found great difficulty in getting published and *Ulysses* was actually banned in the United States. The symbolism in his works was not accidental. Books have been written to help the reader or scholar read *Ulysses*. Joyce incorporates Greek mythology, Irish legend, history, astronomy, anatomy, Hebrew, Latin and Gaelic as well as the theology of the Roman Catholic church.

He is now considered one of the greatest writers of the 20th century with *Ulysses* placing first in the Modern Library list of the 100 best books of the 20th century. It has been said that his greatness in literature is attributed to the new styles he created which led the way for many other authors.

Twentieth Century Authors

SEAN
O'FAOLAIN

Sean O'Faolain (Sean Whelan) (1900–1991) was born in Cork. He fought in the Irish insurrection (1918–1921). He attended the National University, Ireland, and Harvard University. He taught Gaelic, Anglo-Irish literature and English in England and the United States. In 1933 he returned to Ireland to write. He wrote *A Life of Daniel O'Connell*, 1938, and *Vive Moi!*, an autobiography, in 1964. His novels include *A Nest of Simple Folk*, 1933; *Bird Alone*, 1936; and *Come Back to Erin*, 1940.

LIAM
O'FLAHERTY

Liam O'Flaherty (1896–1984) was born on Inishmore, Aran Islands and died in Dublin. He trained for the priesthood, served in WWI and then wandered throughout the Western Hemisphere and the Middle East. He labored as a lumberjack, miner, factory worker, etc., returning to Ireland in the mid-twenties. He was imbued with a respect for the Irish people – for their endurance, persistence and courage and he always wrote about the poor and the people from the Aran Islands. His writing is brutal, analytical and satiric. His best known work is *The Informer*, 1925. His works include *The Neighbor's Wife*, 1923; *The Black Soul*, 1924; *Skerrat*, 1932; *Famine*, 1937; and an autobiography, *Shame The Devil*, 1934.

FRANK
O'CONNOR

Frank O'Connor was born in Cork in 1903 and died in Dublin in 1966. He received little formal education although he worked as a librarian in Cork and Dublin. In the 1930's he was a director of the Abbey Theatre but is best known for his short stories which were characterized by humor and sensitivity. He was very popular in the United States. Among his stories are "Guests of the Nation," 1931, which narrates the Irish-English troubles; "Crab Apple Jelly," 1944; "Dutch Interior," 1940; and two comedies,

The Holy Door and *Uprooted*. His autobiography *An Only Child*, 1960, is his memory of his youth and young adulthood.

Sean O'Casey (1880–1964) was born in Dublin. Although Irish Protestant, he lived in the worst of poverty, being the youngest of thirteen children, of whom only five survived. With only three years of formal schooling, he educated himself by reading and developed two principles that were to dominate his life and work: a vitality of language and an uncompromising social conscience. He was a member of the Irish Citizen Army and the Gaelic League and learned the Irish language. He left politics in disillusionment and turned to drama. His plays include *The Shadow of the Gunman*, 1923; *Juno and the Paycock*, 1924; *The Plough and the Stars*, 1926 and a six volume autobiography, *I Knock at the Door*, 1939. *The Plough and the Stars* caused riots in Dublin when it was produced at the Abbey Theatre. It concerned the Easter Rising of 1916 and Irish patriots thought it belittled these Irish heroes.

After this the Abbey Theatre rejected his plays so he moved to England, married an Irish actress and remained in England.

Edna O'Brien was born in 1932 in County Clare. Her books were banned in Ireland because of the way she portrayed women. She now lives in London and is a full-time writer. Her autobiography, *The Country Girls*, consists of tales and sketches from her childhood. She received a strict convent education and is ever concerned with the enslavement of women. Her novel *The Lonely Girl*, 1962, was made into the movie, *The Girl With Green Eyes*. She has also written short stories. She received the Kingsley Amis First Novel Award in 1962 and the Yorkshire Post Novel Award in 1971.

Flann O'Brien (1911–1966) was born in Strabane, Co. Tyrone, in Northern Ireland. He was a columnist for the *Irish Times* newspaper for 26 years. He is particularly known for his novel *At-Swim-Two-Birds*, which is a blend of folklore, legend, humor and poetry. He also wrote *The Hard Life*, 1961; *The Dalkey Archive*, 1964, which was adapted as a play; and *The Third Policeman*.

Samuel Beckett (1906–1989) was born in a suburb of Dublin, educated at the Portoro Royal School in Enniskillen and graduated from Trinity College, Dublin, in 1923. After studying in Paris he returned to Ireland and taught French for a year. He then began to wander and found himself in Paris in 1937 as a member of a

SEAN
O'CASEY

EDNA
O'BRIEN

FLANN
O'BRIEN

SAMUEL
BECKETT

neutral nation. He joined the underground resistance group in 1941 but then found it necessary to go into hiding where he supported himself as an agricultural laborer in the unoccupied zone. After the war he joined the Irish Red Cross as a volunteer in France.

He began writing in French and then translating his works himself into English. He was considered a comic writer who expressed the despair of the human condition. His literature reflected the Absurd, the meaninglessness of human existence in the modern world. He won the Nobel Prize for Literature in 1969. Among his works are *More Prickles Than Kicks*, 1934; the trilogy with *Molloy, Malone Dies* and the *Unnameable;* and the play *Waiting for Godot*.

SEAMUS
HEANEY

Seamus Heaney (1939–) was born in County Londonderry in Northern Ireland. He won the Nobel Prize for Literature in 1995. He was praised by the Swedish Academy for his poetry and "works of lyrical beauty and ethical depth, which exalt everyday miracles and the living past." His major works are "North," "Death of a Naturalist," "Field Work," "Sweeney Astray" and "Station Island."

OTHERS

OTHER MODERN AUTHORS include Colm Toibin, who wrote *The Heather Blazing* and Walter Macken, who wrote a well researched trilogy, *Seek the Fair Land, The Silent People* and *The Scorching Wind*. The literature of modern Ireland is extensive. A more recent author who writes of the 'people' is Roddy Doyle, whose works include *The Commitments, Snapper* and *Paddy Clark, Ha! Ha! Ha!* for which he won the Booker Award.

The Arts

During the **Stone Age** in Ireland the artistic endeavors were limited only by the material and tools – stone. Architecturally there were the passage graves, notably Newgrange which combines the corbel roof with the astrological alignment of the entry to the sacred center during the winter solstice. On these passage graves there are also designs carved or pocked out by chipping at the stone. These include spiral drawing, chevrons, triangles and patterns which use the shape of the stone.

From the period known as **Ancient Ireland** no great architectural monuments remain. However, due to the preservative qualities of the bogs and the undisturbed presence of vast areas of bog, many artifacts and relics from these years have been discovered. They include early gold ornaments such as neck pieces and bracelets and bronze tools and weapons. The majority of finer hoards are now in the National Museum of Ireland.

The Irish were always concerned with life after death and the age of Christianity continued to encourage that interest. The early **Christian era's** structures were mostly destroyed by the Vikings. But the learning and illustrations of manuscripts from these learned monasteries remain and are on exhibit at the Library at Trinity College, Dublin. The art of these early manuscripts should not be missed; and the **Book of Kells** is the most outstanding example. The kings of Ireland supported these monasteries with their worldly goods and these gifts – even the actual existence of these institutions – were the expression of their beliefs. Palaces and magnificent dwellings were not the means by which these kings displayed their power and wealth.

At the time of the landing of the Normans, the Church in Ireland had reached toward Europe and the resulting variations and changes in the Irish religious structures were profound. After the introduction of the simplified Cistercian monasteries, the Gothic and more decorative influences reached Ireland. These were usually modified with the ancient Celtic styles of the Irish stonemason, often to create decoration within the monasteries which was uniquely Irish. The wealth was redistributed to the Anglo-Normans who, although they built defensive castles, continued to immortalize themselves within the churches. Ireland became quite anglicized in its artistic styles.

The **National Gallery of Ireland** is a wonder. Although there was support for creating a permanent collection of art during the 18th century, construction was finally begun in 1859 and required five years to complete. It had a modest beginning but has continued to expand and grow throughout the years. The gallery has continued to purchase but has also received gifts from generous benefactors.

The gallery has an incredibly good collection, with paintings from the Italian, German, Dutch, Flemish, Spanish, French and British Schools. Many old friends may be found and the scope is excellent. It also hosts a newly discovered Caravaggio, on loan, which is an exciting story in itself.

Irish art is interesting and reflects the different styles learned in Europe. However, it is also a great cultural and historical marker for the visitor to Ireland. The portraits are mostly of the Protestant Ascendency or of English planters who were establishing their aristocracy and prestige. The landscapes reflect the idyllic. However, in some prints, watercolors and landscapes there are drawings of the 18th century architecture.

Art may also be a political statement and not art for art's sake. Leaders are depicted in impressive poses to portray wisdom or power. At the same time the Irish common people were often portrayed as less than they were to justify their lower status within the society. Often they are dressed in rags and are barefoot although one must look carefully to see them. Many of these issues can be evaluated and understood from the art.

The influence of Impressionism and twentieth century art movements is also present among the Irish artists.

The **Hugh Lane Municipal Gallery of Modern Art** includes some excellent Irish artists, and the **Irish Museum of Modern Art** at **Royal Hospital at Kilmainham** presents 20th century Irish art as well as theatrical and musical performances. The Kilmainham Hospital is itself an interesting structure. The **Beit Art Collection** is located at Russborough House, Co. Wicklow. The collection was gathered by Alfred Beit, a cofounder of the De Beers Diamond Mining Company in South Africa.

13. *Modern Ireland*

The Prelude to Independence

The development of the organizations and political parties in Ireland reflect several major themes: **Land Reform, Home Rule** and the formation of an independent **Irish Republic**.

The majority of the Irish were farmer tenants who managed to subsist on small tracts with potatoes as their primary food. They had no rights of tenancy or rent control. The potato famine of 1845 destroyed all the potatoes and therefore their food supply. The British government did not respond well to this crisis, whereupon nearly a million died or emigrated. The Irish no longer accepted their status and nurtured the development of political awareness and its feasibility to make changes. Through the efforts of the **Land League**, some measure of **Land Reform** was achieved. Rents were set at more tolerable levels, the possibility of eviction was minimized and tenancy was secured. For some this new-found security was sufficient.

From this emerged the desire for **Home Rule**. This goal envisioned an Irish parliament which maintained control over all domestic affairs. It was this issue that aroused the violent opposition of the Protestants in Ulster. On the Irish side was the **Irish Parliamentary Party** formed by **Charles Stewart Parnell,** who worked well in integrating the various factions into a cohesive force. Eventually he was ousted as the party leader after a personal scandal which destroyed the effectiveness of his efforts. Home Rule was defeated by the efforts of the conservatives in Britain and the Ulster Unionist Council.

The legislation for **Home Rule** was approved at Westminster just prior to the outbreak of WWI. This did not meet with unanimous approval and preparations for a civil war were in the making with the Ulster Unionist Council arming the Ulster Volunteers and the formation of the Irish Volunteers by a group of Fenians. With the onset of the war, home rule and civil war were postponed. At the close of the war, new ideas and political groupings emerged.

The formation of an **Irish Republic** totally free of Britain had been a longtime dream of many Irish. These were and are the Republicans. Ireland was recognized as an independent republic in 1949. For a review of specific events dating from WWI to independence, I recommend you start with an encyclopedia. Ireland experienced much trauma and its present state of well-being is a tribute to its leaders and its people.

The Leaders

THEOBALD
WOLFE TONE

One of the early republicans was **Wolfe Tone** (1763–1798). He was the son of a coachman and a Protestant who had studied the law. The United Irishmen of Belfast was a radical debating group whose members were Scottish Presbyterians strongly influenced by events in France. In 1791 Wolfe Tone helped to change this group into the Society of the United Irishmen, a Protestant group of radical republicans who worked for reform, suffrage and Catholic emancipation. They succeeded in forcing the Irish parliament to pass the Catholic Relief Act in 1793. Their influence was greatly enhanced by the British crackdown on all radical organizations, especially those with affiliation with the French.

Wolfe Tone went to America and France in search of support. His plan for the French invasion of Ireland was favorably received by the Directory in Paris, whereupon he set sail for Ireland with a fleet of 43 ships and 4000 men. The invasion force was beset by an Atlantic storm, foundered, was scattered and the invasion did not occur.

In 1797, Wolfe again took plans for his invasion to Napoleon Bonaparte, who was not interested.

Although an attempt to unify many separate elements was unsuccessful, the United Irishmen launched a rebellion in 1798. Many rebels were killed in its suppression. Tone was captured during a small French sortie on Lough Swilly, Co. Donegal. During his trial he continued to proclaim his contempt of England and his continued passion to bring about the separation of England and Ireland. On the morning of the day he was to be hanged, he slit his throat and died the following week.

In 1800, the Irish parliament was suppressed and Ireland was thenceforward represented at Westminster with 100 seats in the House of Commons and a total of 32 seats in the Upper House. This Act of Union did not include Catholic emancipation.

DANIEL
O'CONNELL

Daniel O'Connell (1775–1847) was called the "Great Liberator." He was born in Kerry and educated at Catholic College in France. He left France with the coming of the French Revolution, studied law in London and was called to the Irish bar in 1798. He had joined the United Irishmen, but did not participate in the rebellion of 1798. He educated the Irish in politics – the power of public demonstrations within the law.

In 1823 he helped to found the Catholic Association, which was successful in introducing new candidates for election to Westminster – even though it was not legal for them to sit in Parliament. Daring to vote for these candidates also required courage to withstand the threats of reprisal. With the Emancipation Act in 1829, it finally became legal for a Catholic to sit in Parliament and to hold high office. Daniel O'Connell represented County Clare.

While at Westminster he was a commanding and respected presence and supported the Whigs in the hope of their support for his reform measures. This did not happen. In 1839 he founded the Repeal Association for the repeal of the Act of Union of 1800. He challenged the government with mass meetings. The people traveled great distances and were passionate in their support. Under threat of military interference he canceled a meeting scheduled in Clontarf in 1843. He believed that physical force should not be used in the struggle for independence. He wanted to continue his crusade, as he always had, within the limits of the law.

Following the events at Clontarf, he was arrested for sedition and conspiracy. He was released after three months. His great stamina, strength and health declined. He was not able to respond to the appeals for him to continue his campaign. He died in 1847 at his home, Derrynane, Caherdaniel. This was his childhood home and country residence throughout his career. The oldest part of the house no longer survives, although most of what is there today was built at his direction. It is now a museum commemorating the Great Liberator.

Charles Stewart Parnell (1846–1891), an Irish Nationalist, was a member of the Anglo-Irish Protestant landowning class. His family were anti-British in sentiment. He was educated in England but returned to Ireland in 1869 and joined the newly formed Home Rule League which wanted an Irish parliament with full control over domestic affairs. He was elected to Parliament in 1876 from Meath.

Parnell is described as grim and autocratic. He was able to develop a unified, disciplined, populist political party, the Irish Parliamentary Party in 1880, which unified the various factions and gained the support of Catholic merchants, lawyers, journalists and shopkeepers. In 1885 his party won four-fifths of the Irish representatives to the House of Commons, and they agreed to vote according to party directives. He integrated the Irish Fenians (Irish Republican Brotherhood) and gained the support of the Catholic church to pursue Home Rule and the Irish Land League, which was a national network supported by the farmers. It worked to protect them from eviction and secure tenure. As a member of the House of Commons, Parnell used obstructionist tactics to attain his goals. This resulted in the passage of Gladstone's land acts in the early '80s. Although they did not include all that Parnell desired, he accepted it as a basis for settlement.

As the Land Acts worked to secure fair rents, tenure and sale of land to the Irish farmers, the Orange Order and the Ulster Unionists formed an alliance with the Tories in Westminster. They feared redistribution of land and loss of power and worked against Home Rule.

Parnell was jailed at Kilmainham Gaol, which assured him continuing support and popularity. As leader of the Irish Parliamentary Party, he was an active participant in Parliament by unseating the Tories and restoring Gladstone to power. His influence and prestige ended when he was named in a divorce proceeding as a co-respondent. He was ousted as party leader, a great setback to the cause of Home Rule.

His house at **Avondale Forest Park,** Rathdrum, Co. Wicklow is open to the public and contains memorabilia of Parnell and period pieces. The estate was his birthplace and family home and used by Parnell during his lifetime.

PATRICK
HENRY
PEARSE
Patrick Henry Pearse (1879–1916) was a poet, playwright and educator who became president of the Gaelic League, an organization dedicated to the preservation of the Gaelic language. He published stories from the old Irish manuscripts and founded St. Enda's College as a bilingual college. It is prophetic that the motto of St. Enda's College is "I care not if I live but a day and a night, so long as my deeds live after me."

When the Irish Volunteers were formed in response to the Ulster Volunteers, he became a member of the provisional committee. He then became a member of the supreme council of the Irish Republican Brotherhood. With the outbreak of WWI, he opposed any support of Great Britain during the war. It is said that "he reveled in the wartime lie that the shedding of blood was a 'cleansing and sanctifying thing'" and felt that these sacrificed heroes would unify the great rebellion to achieve the independence of Ireland.

Pearse helped to plan the Easter Rising, a plan that would maximize the loss of life, to create martyrs to liberate Ireland. The revolt was easily crushed and he was tried and executed by a firing squad. The rebellion was poorly supported. He spent his last days at Kilmainham Gaol. The Easter Rising would have remained unheralded except for the overreaction of the government at Dublin Castle. The martial law which followed with thousands of arrests and deportation to Britain roused public opinion and support.

Pearse's Cottage, Rosmuc in Connemara, Co. Galway is the thatched summer home of Pearse. The cottage is opened to the public and is maintained in the style in which he lived. **St. Enda's College,** Rathfarnham, Co. Dublin, holds the Pearse Museum. It was to this 18th century mansion that he moved his school in 1910. The house was bequeathed by his mother in memory of her sons and is now under the care of the Dúchas. It has been restored and contains many original furnishings. The surrounding **National Historic Park** includes woods, lake and stream and is open to be enjoyed.

Michael Collins (1890–1922) was the hero of the struggle for Independence. His leadership and organizational talents made him a beloved hero during the Anglo-Irish War (1919–1921).

He was employed as a British civil servant from 1905 to 1916 when he returned to Ireland. He joined the Easter Rising, was arrested and held in detention for the remainder of the year. In December 1918 he was one of the 27 Sinn Fein delegates elected to the Dail (Irish Assembly). When it convened in Dublin and declared for the republic, its elected president, Eamon de Valera, and vice president, Arthur Griffith, were both in prison. Michael Collins became the minister for home affairs and shouldered much of the responsibility. He arranged for the escape of De Valera from a London prison and became minister of finance.

He became director of intelligence for the Irish Republican Army and was the chief planner and coordinator of the revolutionary movement; the British placed a price on his head of £10,000. His team was loyal and daring.

There have been many books written about Michael Collins. One of his team, Batt O'Conner, wrote of the day to day experiences and dangers that he faced in *With Michael Collins Through the Fight for Irish Independence*. He told about the raids on the Sinn Fein headquarters at No. 6 Harcourt Street where he had an office. It was a close call as Collins was able to pass himself off as an unimportant assistant clerk and thereby leave the building unmolested. They did not stay long in one place.

Realizing that avenues of escape were essential, they made arrangements with a nearby hotel. The proprietors were not supporters of the Sinn Fein but were against violence and chivalrous toward the oppressed so they agreed that a skylight in their building would be left unlatched. These preparations bore fruit, for when No. 76 fell to the police Collins was able to make his escape through the skylight. Although there was a hazardous drop, he managed to escape injury and joined the spectators on the street to watch the progress of the raid.

After the truce of 1921, Michael Collins and Arthur Griffith were sent to London by De Valera to negotiate the treaty. He signed the treaty in the belief that it was the best that could be achieved. The terms of the treaty stipulated:

1. Dominion status
2. Partition of Ireland
3. Members of Parliament take an oath to the crown
4. Britain maintain naval bases

Since De Valera and other republicans did not accept the treaty, a provisional government was formed with Arthur Griffith as president and Michael Collins as chairman. Effective administration was obstructed by the republicans and the IRA. Civil War broke out with the IRA seizing the Four Courts in Dublin. Collins became commander of the army and became head of the government. Ten days later he was shot to death from ambush.

In Clonakilty, Co. Cork, the **Cork Regional Museum** contains material on the War of Independence and Michael Collins, who was born at Sam's Cross several miles north.

EAMON
DE VALERA

Eamon De Valera was a great patriot with the vision and ability to guide Ireland to its present state of well-being. Although born in the United States in 1882, he was sent to his maternal relatives in county Limerick. He was brought up in a laborer's cottage, educated in the local schools, Blackrock College in Dublin and the Royal University. He became a teacher of mathematics and a strong supporter of the revival of the Gaelic language.

In 1908 he joined the Gaelic League; in 1913 he joined the Irish Volunteers; and in 1916 he commanded one of the four battalions in the Easter Rising. Having been born in the United States, he escaped execution but was sentenced to penal servitude. He was released, arrested and deported to England.

In 1917 he became President of the Sinn Fein; in the election of 1918 he was elected to the Dail (Irish Assembly) and declared the President of the Dail in 1919 while still in prison in London. After his escape from prison, he went to the United States to raise money. He opposed the 1921 treaty because it accepted the exclusion of Northern Ireland and demanded the oath of allegiance to the crown. When the Dail ratified the treaty, he supported the republican resistance, after which he was imprisoned until 1924. In 1926 he severed connections with the IRA, resigned from the Sinn Fein and formed the Fianna Fail, which could not sit in the Dail as they refused to sign the oath of allegiance.

In 1927 De Valera persuaded the members of the Fianna Fail to sign the oath of allegiance. Once seated in the Dail they demanded the abolition of the oath of allegiance, the governor general, the Senead and the land purchase annuities payable to Great Britain. In 1932 the Cosgrave government was defeated and De Valera and the Fianna Fail were victors. He severed connections with Great Britain and withheld the payment of annuities, and economic war followed. In 1937 he declared the Irish Free State a sovereign state while conceding voluntary allegiance to the crown and the **Constitution** was written.

Eamon De Valera was president of the Council of the League of Nations in 1932 and of its assembly in 1938. During the following years Ireland was faced with increased emigration, rising prices and a primitive agricultural system. In 1955 Ireland joined the United Nations. In 1973 Ireland became a member of the EC (European Community), which has led to agricultural prosperity and access to community funds for development projects.

Eamon De Valera died in 1975. The **De Valera Museum** and **De Valera Cottage** in Bruree, Co. Limerick, are located in the town where he spent his early childhood. The cottage was typical of those built for farm laborers in the late 19th century. The museum is housed in the school which contains his books and desk and other early farm tools.

Women Patriots

MAUD GONNE
MACBRIDE

Maud Gonne (1866–1953) was a patriot who was one of the founders of the Sinn Fein and founded the Daughters of Ireland. She is frequently mentioned in poems by W. B. Yeats, who had a permanent attachment for her.

CONSTANCE
MARKIEVICZ

Constance Gore-Booth Markievicz was born in 1868. She was an artist and a patriot. Her family's home was Lissadell House in Co. Sligo. She was condemned to death for her part in the Easter Rising but was reprieved two years later. She was the first woman elected to the House of Commons in Westminster but did not take her seat. She became Minister of Labour for the First Dail in 1919. She died in 1927.

The Political Parties

Throughout Irish history, the Irish have worked to rid Ireland of British control. They were not successful as there was no unity or sustained purpose. Support for these attempts came from the aristocracy, not the people.

Daniel O'Connell changed that and introduced political agitation for the right to vote. He strongly felt that all progress should be made through the legal system and not through violence. He believed the success of the movements toward independence was in the coalitions and the working unity which brought the people together.

THE FENIANS

AFTER THE effective suppression of the rebellion and the death of Tone, the Act of Union was passed in 1800 and the Irish Parliament no longer existed. The Fenians evolved from the original supporters of the republican values of Theobald Wolfe Tone and the United Irishmen in 1798 to become the Irish Republican Brotherhood in 1858. They were totally committed to force. Many have used this group to achieve their goals through violence and then splintered off when other methods of success became possible.

In 1880 Charles Stewart Parnell was able to integrate the Irish Republican Brotherhood, the Irish National League and the Catholic church to form the Irish Parliamentary Party. After his death the Fenian cult emulated Parnell and the Gaelic Cultural Revival became popular. The Gaelic National League and Gaelic Athletic Association were formed. These came under the control of the Fenians. It was a Fenian who formed the Irish Land League in 1882 to bring needed land reform. In 1905, Arthur Griffith splintered from the Fenians to form the Sinn Fein. Michael Collins and Eamon De Valera were members of the Sinn Fein until Eamon De Valera broke off to form the Fianna Fail.

It was also from the Irish Republican Brotherhood that the Irish Republican Army, or IRA, was formed and the Easter Rising occurred.

THE SINN FEIN was formed by Arthur Griffith in 1905 with the idea of achieving their goals through passive resistance. After the Easter Rising, it became the rallying point for the nationalists and republicans who were opposed to the Treaty of 1921. When the treaty was signed, Eamon De Valera set up a separate provisional government separating from the Sinn Fein. He formed the Fianna Fail and most of the members of the Sinn Fein joined him.

SINN FEIN

IN 1923 William T. Cosgrave founded the Cumann na nGaedheal party to govern the new Irish state on the basis of the Treaty of 1921. In 1933 it joined with others to become the Fine Gael, which promoted a broader sense of Irish nationalism. It encouraged enterprise and the ideal of reconciliation with the people of Northern Ireland. It was also committed to the development and unification of the European Economic Community.

FINE GAEL

FIANNA FAIL was founded by Eamon De Valera in 1926. His aims were to secure the independence of Ireland as a republic, restore the Irish language and develop a national life in accordance with Irish traditions and ideals. Its achievements are impressive: consolidation of Irish independence, recovery of the ports retained by the British in the Treaty of 1921, the present Constitution voted by referendum in 1937, neutrality during WWII, and many economic achievements.

FIANNA FAIL

THE LABOUR PARTY was founded in 1912 and is the oldest political party in Ireland. It represents 50% of all trade union members in the state and has taken part in many coalition governments.

LABOUR PARTY

THE PROGRESSIVE DEMOCRATIC PARTY was established in 1985 as a modern liberal party. It advocates a gradual and peaceful solution to Northern Ireland and supports movement towards greater unification and interdependency of the European Community.

PROGRESSIVE DEMOCRATS

Government

Every citizen over the age of eighteen years is eligible to vote, while every citizen who has reached the age of twenty-one is eligible for membership in the Dail. The citizens of Ireland participate in the governmental process by voting on the following four: the election of the President, referendums on proposed constitutional amendments, elections of local authorities and parliamentary elections.

Voting is by secret ballot and is based on a proportional representation system in which a voter marks his three choices in the order of preference. In the single transfer system, the voter allows his '2' choice to be used in place of his '1' choice if '1' does not need his vote to reach the necessary quota or has no chance of being elected, etc. When the number of surviving candidates equals the number of vacancies, these candidates are declared elected.

The national parliament or **Oireachtas** consists of the President, Dail Eireann and Seanad Eireann. "The sole and exclusive power of making laws for the State is hereby vested in the Oireachtas".[27] All laws passed by the parliament must conform to the constitution.

The President is elected every seven years and may stand for two terms. He is the head of the state and is the guardian of the constitution.

The members of the Dail represent constituencies, which are revised when necessary after each census. At the present time one member represents not less then 20,000 nor more than 30,000 persons. The Dail approves the appointment of the **Taoiseach** (Prime Minister) by the President.

The Seanad has 60 members of whom 11 are nominated and 49 are elected. The 11 are nominated by the Taoiseach. The 60 members are elected as follows: 3 by the National University of Ireland; 3 by the University of Dublin and 43 by panels of candidates. These panels of candidates are formed from persons having knowledge and practical experience in the following: 1. national language and culture, literature, art, education and other like professional interests; 2. agriculture and fisheries; 3. labour (organized and unorganized); 4. industry and commerce; and 5. public administration and social services.

The government is the executive branch of this parliamentarian democracy. There shall be from 7 to 15 members who are nominated by the Dail and appointed by the President. The head of government is the Taoiseach, who keeps the President informed on all matters of policy. The remaining members of the government must be members of the Parliament although not more than two are to be from the Seanad.

The Council of State aids and counsels the President and consists of the following members: the Taoiseach, Tanaiste (an emergency Prime Minister), the Chief Justice, the President of the High Court, the Chairman of the Dial Eire, the Chairman of the Seined Eire and the Attorney General.

The national flag of Ireland is a tricolor of green, white and orange. It was introduced in 1848 by Thomas Francis Meager as an emblem for the Young Ireland movement. The green represents the Gaelic and Anglo-Norman elements of the population while the orange represents the Protestant planters. According to Meager, "The white in the center signifies a lasting truce between the 'Orange' and the 'Green.'"

Information on the constitution of Ireland with its amendments can be obtained from the Embassy of Ireland in Washington, DC. The purpose of this brief synopsis is to give you a general knowledge of the land you are visiting. I find it helpful for reading the newspapers.

Oireachtas – **The National Parliament or Legislature**
Seanad Eireann – **The Senate in the National Parliament**
Dail Eireann – **The House of Representatives in the National Parliament**
Taoiseach – **Prime Minister**
Tanaiste – **Backup Prime Minister**

International Relations

Ireland has incorporated into its constitution its affirmation of the ideal of peace and cooperation among nations which is based on international justice and morality. It has been a positive and contributing member to this ideal.

Ireland is an active participant in the United Nations and twice served on the Security Council, is a founding member of the Council of Europe and an active participant in the Conference of Security and Cooperation in Europe. Ireland joined the European Community in 1973 and its commitment to membership was established with the referendum of 1972 in which 83% of those who voted approved the necessary amendment to the constitution. More information is available through the Embassy of Ireland in Washington, DC.

Northern Ireland

Northern Ireland responded to the issues of Home Rule and Land Reform with vehemence. The formation of the Orange Order and the Ulster Volunteer Force and an alliance with the Conservatives at Westminster defeated Home Rule in the House of Lords. By the Treaty of 1921 partition of Ireland was planned and supported by the people of Northern Ireland who voted to remain a part of the United Kingdom.

Lower Lough Erne

St. Patrick's Anglican Cathedral, Armagh

14. *Sites in Northern Ireland*

T HE SITES LISTED for Northern Ireland are not inclusive. I have selected a handful of sites that reflect the development and culture of the Irish or are those which are significant or easily reached from Ireland. The whole of this land mass is scenically beautiful and will be enjoyable. Further exploration of Northern Ireland is recommended and to date, the checkpoints are no longer active. The North has a different ambience.

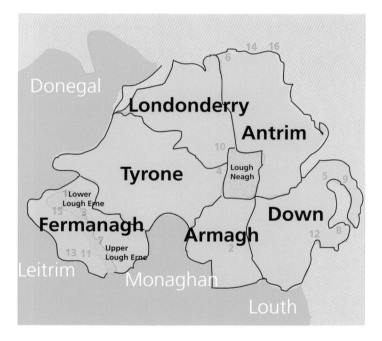

(1) *Janus Figure* is an ancient stone double idol from the early Iron Age. The two figures are back to back. It is located in a small preserved cemetery in a lovely setting which also has some other interesting stones. This is signposted and is located on Boa Island on the north shore of Lower Lough Erne by A47. **County Fermanagh**

(2) *Navan Fort* (see p. 63), also known as Emain Macha, was the religious and political center of Ulster. At the site there is an

ANCIENT
IRELAND

interpretive center. It should not be missed for those who are interested in the ancient sites. It is located west of Armagh by A28. **County Armagh**

EARLY
CHRISTIAN

(3) *White Island* is located on the eastern shore of Lower Lough Erne by B82. There is a ferry on weekends during July and August. This site includes the remains of a 12th century church with a Romanesque doorway and eight 9th century stone figures along the north wall. Their origin is not known. These figures are squat and have large faces. One figure holds a bell and crosier, another a sword and shield, while another holds two small animals by the neck. One warrior has been removed to the Ulster Museum in Belfast. **County Fermanagh**

(4) *Arboe Cross* is located on the western shore of Lough Neagh. It is carved with scenes of the Scriptures and marks the site of an ancient monastery. It is reached by B73. **County Tyrone**

CASTLES

(5) *Carrickfergus Castle* is located on the north shore of Lough Belfast. It stands on a rocky promontory. This Anglo-Norman structure is the largest and best preserved of all the early castles of this type. **County Down**

(6) *Dunluce Castle* is on a rock separated from the mainland by a deep divide. The earliest ruins date from the 14th century and additions were added in the 16th and 17th centuries. Entry was by a drawbridge from the 16th century gate house. **County Antrim**

(7) *Castle Coole* is an early 19th century neoclassic house which was restored in the 20th century. There is a center block which is flanked by wings and is an adaptation of the Palladio style. The pediment, columns and symmetry are true classical Greek. The house is sumptuously decorated and is set in a park which created the desired romantic setting of the period. It is located southeast of Enniskillen on the Belfast to Enniskillen road, A4. **County Fermanagh**

(8) *Castle Ward* is a house divided. The Viscount and his wife had different tastes. The front is his preference with classic Greek style while the back is early Gothic which was her style. The decor and the style of the interior are likewise divided according to the use of the rooms. The castle is located west of Strangford on the Downpatrick road, A25. **County Down**

(9) *Mount Stewart* is primarily a 19th century grand neoclassic mansion with rounded bays at the corners. Lord Castlereagh was the foreign secretary of Great Britain and attended the Congress of Vienna in 1814. The outstanding feature of this house is its grounds which were created in the 20th century. It is located south of Newtownards by A20. **County Down**

(10) *Springhill* is a tall slate roofed house with curving bay window additions at each end. The building is flanked by low outbuildings that were used for staff, stables, kitchen, etc. This layout was defensible and convenient in troubled times and inclement weather. It is located in the village of Moneymore near Cookstown on the Moneymore to Coagh road, N18. **County Londonderry**

(11) *Florence Court* is a vast Palladian mansion with a dramatic view. The center block was built in the mid-18th century while the wings and pavilion were added several decades later. In 1955 the main building was gutted by fire although the rococo plaster ceiling of the dining room was saved. The house has been restored and the grounds include a pleasure garden and forest park. **County Fermanagh**

Mount Stewart Gardens

(9) *Mount Stewart Gardens*. Each area of the formal gardens is a separate room – each with a different theme. One, the Dodo Terrace, was created for the Ark Club in London. The statuary of this terrace is full of fun and fantasy. There are also formal gardens, one of which includes a topiary harp. There is also a lake, Japanese pagoda and woodland walks. **County Down**

(12) *Seaforde Gardens* were created in the 18th century in the woodlands of the Seaforde Demesne. These include a tree and shrub nursery, Tropical Butterfly House (free flying butterflies), and walled gardens which contain a vast collection of rare trees and shrubs. The gardens also include a maze or labyrinth. **County Down**

(13) *Marble Arch Caves* tour includes a boat trip to an underground lake which opens into an area of stalagmites and stalactites which form sculptural creations called Organ, Pipes, Tusks, Streaky Bacon and others. The exhibit at the reception center explains the geological formation of these caves. They are located southwest of Enniskillen by A4 and A32. **County Fermanagh**

(14) *Giant's Causeway* is located on the north shore of County Antrim. The Interpretive Center and entry is north of Bushmills by A2 and B146. From the center a shuttle bus provides transport

Giant's
Causeway

to and from the site. According to Irish legend these were built by the giant Finn McCool so that the Scottish giant could come to Ireland for a test of strength. It sank below the sea after the Scot returned home defeated. There is a long stretch of interesting formations which lend themselves to a day's hike. **County Antrim**

(15) *Cliffs of Magho Viewpoint* are reached by A46 from Beleek. The drive is through the Lough Navar Forest. The expansive view from the great height is worth the trip. **County Fermanagh**

(16) *Carrick-a-rede Rope Bridge* is not for the aged or weak of heart or spirit. This rope bridge with wooden planks is used by fishermen and is replaced each spring. It is not recommended in high winds and is 80 feet above the rocks and water below. **County Antrim**

View from
Cliffs of
Magho

I R I S H   H E R I T A G E

A Thumbnail Sketch

This chapter gives a simplified overview of the history of Ireland.

You might read it first as an introduction to the book, at the end

as a summation or as a reference while you read the remainder of

the text.

Each section, Stone Age, Ancient Ireland, Early Christianity

— 1100, The Monasteries, Anglo-Norman Invasion, 18th Century

— Independence, is color-coded and is presented chronologically.

As an example, after reading the section about the Stone Age in

this chapter, one can turn to the separate chapter on the Stone

Age, Chapter 6, for greater depth and detail.

15. *Irish Heritage*

Before Recorded History

THE IRISH are an ancient people. According to archeological evidence man has existed continuously in Ireland since 7500 BC. The artifacts tell us where they lived, how they lived and about their tools, but very little about where they came from, how their society was organized, or what happened to them.

Although these ancients had no written language, there was a tradition of oral history. The responsibility for maintaining this tradition usually was designated to a particular group called the seers, druids or magicians and it was thus passed down from generation to generation. As with most stories, these were embellished and modified with each telling. No matter, for it is from these modifications that we learn.

According to these legends of the **Mythological Cycle,** the **Stone Age** inhabitants were the Formorians and the Fir Bolgs. It is thought that the Formorians were originally from the Scandinavian countries while the Fir Bolgs were colonizers from the continent about 2000 BC. The Fir Bolgs were the victors and reigned for thirty seven years.[28]

The Tuatha De Danaan arrived in Ireland "in a great fleet of ships to take the land from the Fir Bolgs." They established their cult center on the border of the Boyne River at Newgrange. They built the passage tombs and according to legend were organized and skilled. Peace and the beauties of the land were enjoyed until the rule had passed to three brothers who quarreled among themselves about the land and wealth they had inherited from their father.

Into this unrest arrived the Milesians from Spain, perhaps as early as the 14th century BC. Their leader Ith marveled at the beauty and richness of the land and cautioned them to live in peace since the land was rich and abundant and sufficient for all. The three brothers, who were convinced that Ith was covetous of their land, plotted, and ambushed Ith. His death angered the Milesians who gathered together a great army among the Gaels in Spain and returned to Ireland to avenge the death of Ith. There was a great battle which the Milesians won. Mil is considered the ancestor of the Gaels. They divided Ireland into provinces: Ulster,

Leinster, Munster, Connacht and Tara. Each province had its own king, chiefs and champions but the high king lived at Tara. The Tuatha De Danaan, although they had been defeated, did not leave Ireland. They went underground to live in the mounds and earthworks or sidhes. "From time to time, down through the ages, these mysterious, imperishable people entered the world of mortals. Sometimes they fell in love with human beings and at other times they held humans in thrall with their beauty and their haunting music. But their kingdom was that Happy Otherworld under the earth and they always went back there to the Land of the Ever Young."[29]

It was probably the Milesians who introduced the technology necessary for the development of the **Bronze Age (Ancient Ireland).**

The Celts, the Gauls of France and southern Europe, were the next colonizers in Ireland. They were skilled craftsmen and it is with them that the **Iron Age (Ancient Ireland)** evolved. The Celts were a pleasure-loving people whose greatest pleasure was war. Each tribe had its own king, aristocracy and freemen farmers. The tribes competed for dominance. The druids were their priests whose duties included religion, legal matters, oral history and poetry. They came to Ireland in small colonies from the Continent and settled along the coast and rivers of Ireland. They brought with them a culture which prevailed and blended with that of the Milesians.

Much has been written about the histories of the Irish kings. The three most published are the tales from the Ulster Cycle, the Fenian Cycle and the Cycle of the Kings. These refer to a time in Ireland from about 700 BC to 450 AD.

The Period of Written History

THE **Christian** period began in 432 AD with the arrival of St. Patrick as a missionary and includes the structure and culture of the Irish Kings. (Although St. Patrick was not the first Christian missionary to reach Ireland, he was the most effective.) It extends to 1170 AD with the arrival of the Anglo-Normans.

The Irish converted totally and peacefully to Christianity. The Celts were pagans and had practiced human and animal sacrifices. Slavery was a normal practice. At this time people believed the warning in the Book of Revelations that the world was going to come to an end in the year 1000 AD. Therefore, the people of Ireland were receptive to a leader as devoted to them as Patrick and to a God who was forgiving.

The church and the kings were undeniably intertwined and created a scholarship and devotion which was well-known and respected in Europe. Many monasteries were established in Ireland. Some were started by monks seeking isolation and remained isolated hermitages. Others expanded and became great schools of learning and scholarship not only for the Irish but also for the scholars of Europe who sought refuge from their own turmoil of war and invasion to study in Greek and Latin.

Kingships and Christianity

WITH THE ADVANCE of monastic Christianity, the position of the kings remained important. They converted to Christianity and supported it with great vigor. However, that is not to suggest that the warrior and independent character of the Irish changed with the coming of Christianity.

The social and religious structure of Ireland brought about its greatness and its demise. Ireland was still divided into five states. The social structure became more intricate with three levels of kings: local king; great king who was overlord of a number of local kings; and king of great kings, or provincial king. The provincial king had the real power, although he was not a supreme judge or lawgiver, but "the representative and leader of his people in war and in relations with other tribes." The kings received the support of the monasteries and churches and in return, the monasteries received protection. Each kingdom had its lords, high freemen, low freemen, cottiers, landless men, hereditary serfs and slaves. The high king at Tara was primarily a nominal title except in matters of genealogy and law.

Wealth and status improved with service, conquest and plunder. Loyal followers and supporters were granted land and position. As the number of holdings increased, their size diminished. The temper of the period is well perceived in the Cycle of the Kings when upheaval and battle were common. The provincial boundaries varied and flowed according to the abilities of the king and the alliances he was able to forge.

Into this melee arrived the Vikings in 793 AD. The first were Norwegian Norsemen who burned and pillaged the monasteries in search of wealth – the gold, silver and jewels used in the Christian rituals. By 823 they had rounded the whole of the Irish coastline. From 830 to 845 the raids were more intense and were perpetuated by the Norsemen of Denmark. They wintered in

Dublin in 841–842, set up defensive positions and settled along the coast. These were the founders and citizens of Dublin, Waterford, Youghal, Wexford and Cork. They became a factor in the dynastic struggles for land and leadership. These were the Ostmen who wielded great power with their navies and control of the ports.

For centuries the kingship of Ireland or the office of high king at Tara had been held by the descendants of the Ui Neill clan, as in Niall of the Nine Hostages. They claimed in their legends and genealogies to be true kings at Tara. By the 11th century there was a shift of strength and power. With his great armies, tight control over the petty kingdoms and the support of the Ostmen, Brian Boru, king of Munster (975–1014), gained control of the whole of Ireland in 1011. He paid twenty ounces in gold to have himself declared 'Emperor of Ireland' in the Book of Armagh. His victory was short-lived. The Ostmen of Dublin distrusted his power and realigned themselves with Leinster. After a very bloody battle, Brian defeated them but was killed at the Battle of Clontarf in 1014. This was the nearest attempt at creating a real kingdom of Ireland. After this break with tradition the rules changed. The "kingship of Ireland" was a prize for anyone to seek and the stability of the old system was gone.

There were two great warrior kings after Brian Boru: Muirchertach O'Brien, king of Munster (1086–1119) and Turlough O'Connor, king of Connacht (1106–1156). The stakes were great and the battles continued. These kings maintained great armies and navies and were often away on the battlefield. Royal officers managed the kings' estates and more land was given to those who were loyal or fought well. The provinces became more fragmented and the delicate balance of the past was lost.

Without the influence of the high king at Tara to mediate in matters of law, the provincial kings made laws and imposed taxes. They were arrogant and high-handed. Upon the death of Turlough O'Connor, king of Connacht, all control rested with the power of alliances rather than custom or loyalty. In this way Dermot MacMurrough, king of Leinster, was driven out of Ireland. He went to England to Henry II for help.

While these battles were going on, there was upheaval in another area of life for the Irish: a reformation within the church. The monasteries had been founded by the clan chiefs and kings of the provinces. The church was old-fashioned, very independent and had weak ties with Rome. The abbots were mostly laymen and had a great deal of power while bishops had little power. While churches were being reformed in western Europe, the Irish church hierarchy wanted to reorganize their structure to establish their influence and power. The Cistercian Order was invited to Ireland. There was continued building of churches and monasteries during the 11th and 12th centuries.

As a result of the reorganization, the church was divided into dioceses which came under the supremacy of Armagh. As the bishops took over the monastic lands, the monasteries became little more than parishes. The great monastic schools were closed and nothing replaced them.

The reformers of the church destroyed the social, economic and cultural base of Irish learning. While trying to increase their authority, the provincial kings had destroyed the stability of the Irish dynastic system.

Dublin was different from the rest of Ireland with its Viking heritage.

The Anglo-Norman Invasion

THE ANGLO-NORMAN Invasion started with a plea from Dermot MacMurrough for assistance from Henry II of England. Henry was busy with problems of his own since he had just instigated the death of Thomas à Becket, the Archbishop of Canterbury, and was trying to keep a low profile. He, however, gave his noblemen permission to go to Ireland to assist Dermot. Their aid ended with the nearly total colonization of Ireland by the British.

From 1169 to 1171, the Normans, FitzGilbert, de Clare (a.k.a. 'Strongbow'), FitzGerald, and FitzStephens conquered the southern half of Ireland. Finally, the Irish chiefs appealed to Henry II to restrain Strongbow. Henry II arrived in Ireland and received the voluntary submission of many of the Irish chiefs, who hoped that allegiance to Henry II in England would be better than the control of the Norman barons. Much of Ireland was 'claimed' by the Norman barons and Henry II, who received the blessing of the Pope in Rome for his claims in Ireland. The Pope hoped that England would bring this aloof and independent Irish church to more reasonable terms.

THIS PERIOD continued to be filled with strife. Each century had its own protagonists although the issues consistently involved the polarization of and conflicts between the Gaelic-Irish and the Anglo-Irish. The following is a severe condensation of the history of the trends.

During the **13th century** there were several ethnic factions and the balance of power continued to waver. First there were the many Irish chiefs who had been pushed back into Connacht. They battled with hired mercenaries from the western islands of Scotland, called galloglasses, against the English settlers and each other. Secondly, there were the Norman barons who married the daughters of the Irish aristocracy and formed alliances with the Irish chiefs. They spoke Irish and observed the Brehon Laws. Thirdly, there were the Ostmen or Vikings in Dublin and the other cities and fourth, there were the immigrants (also known as planters, settlers, adventurers or younger sons) from England. Henry II's son, King John, was well suited to impose structure and order in Ireland. He manipulated the many factions, and the colonization continued with the lands being divided into ever smaller holdings. DeCourcy, deBurgh, Butler and others arrived. They built temporary fortifications of wooden towers on earthen mounds which were followed by stronger fortifications.

The building of sturdy fortresses to repel attack attests to the warlike conditions of the period although, at the same time, there was a surge in the building of cathedrals and abbeys. These were founded under the auspices and protection of the Irish chieftains and the Anglo-Normans. The Cistercians and the Franciscans from Europe were most active.

There was no long-range plan to bring Ireland under the control of the English. Although all sorts of schemes were hatched and laws were passed which deprived the Irish of their land and office, there was no unity of purpose or enforcement. Landowners fell into two groups: the Gaelic Irish and the "Old English." This latter group had a great deal of influence with the monarchy and expected their rights and inheritance to be protected by the crown. They lived within the Pale, an area which encompassed what is now Dublin County. Since the crown was not willing to maintain an expensive military presence in Ireland, their defenses were not always adequate.

However, when a crisis or rebellion burst forth, the crown reacted strongly and firmly. This created a seesaw effect in the political life in Ireland for many centuries. The crown in England faced many problems of its own. When the crown was strong, the crown was in control in Ireland. When there were troubles in England, the Irish/Gaelic tradition gained strength. From the 14th to 17th century England was in a constant state of upheaval and turmoil. Society was divided and people continued to live according to their economic status.

With the **14th century** came a famine followed by the devastating Black Death, 1348–1350. The Norman towns were the hardest hit and one third of the population died. Many of the Normans left to become absentee landlords. Those who remained felt threatened and insecure and tried to protect their own interests. In 1366 Statutes of Kilkenny were passed in an attempt to segregate the Gaelic/Irish from the Anglo-Irish or the degenerate English.

"Alliance with the Irish by marriage, fosterage (the Irish custom of educating children in the families of another member of the tribe) and gossipred (a baptismal responsibility…) were forbidden as high treason and were to be punished with death.

"Any Englishman by birth or blood who took an Irish name, spoke the Irish tongue, wore the Irish dress, or adopted any Irish custom should forfeit his estates.

"No Englishman was to allow the Irish to graze cattle on his land, to grant livings to Irish clergy, or to entertain the Irish bards, pipers or storytellers."[30]

During the **15th century** England was occupied with the War of the Roses or the Cousins War. This was the time of the Geraldine Supremacy when the FitzGeralds of Kildare and Desmond were the appointed Lord Deputy and representative of Henry VII and Henry VIII. During this time there was relative stability in Ireland with England worrying about its own problems.

The Anglicized portions of the country were powerful and in control politically. More castles and tower houses were built for defense against attack from the Gaelic-Irish. The Anglo-Normans lived within the Pale which was English in law and custom. Ireland began to polarize to a greater degree. Those outside the Pale became known as Gaelic Irish and were ruled by native kings or Norman dynasts. They spoke the Gaelic language. New monasteries were founded in Gaelic Ireland, particularly the order of Franciscan Observants which received its inspiration from Europe, not England. This separation of spiritual guidance between the Pale and Gaelic Ireland would foster the coming conflict with the imposition of the Protestant Reformation in the 16th century.

The **16th century** was dominated by the matrimonial problems of Henry VIII, the Observant Friars, Old English and Elizabeth I. The separation of the church from the Roman Catholic to the Anglican Catholic caused big problems. The Observant Friars were Catholic reformers who wanted to protect the church and its spirituality against the 'greedy' aristocracy. They mobilized Catholic enthusiasm against this separation brought about by the English reformation. The Old English (Anglo-Norman-Irish aristocracy) refused to accept the Anglicized state church, and sent their sons to Catholic University on the Continent. Although they willingly gave temporal authority to Henry VIII, they could not grant him the spiritual authority which he demanded. They preferred to remain true to the religion of their ancestors and kinsmen. In 1539 Henry VIII enacted the Dissolution of the Monasteries. To demonstrate his determination and power, Henry VIII dealt with the Kildare Rebellion of 1534 by confiscating all the lands of the FitzGerald family and by putting to death all the male members of the family save an infant half-brother. Eventually the ancestral title and a portion of the family lands were returned to the surviving heir. (Note: The Rebellion was a rather feeble attempt of a young member of the family to convince Henry of the FitzGeralds' importance and power.)

Elizabeth I continued the policies of Henry VIII and was willing to use the strength of her armies to maintain her power. It was a period of great unrest and turmoil. She successfully squelched a rebellion in 1579 led by a Desmond with the result that more lands were forfeited to the crown and there was a large planting of English settlers (over 4000) in Munster. The O'Neils of Tyrone were still a problem. They sought the aid of Spain which dispatched a force to Kinsale. Elizabeth responded with a formidable army of 20,000 men and easily put down the attempt which led to the Flight of the Earls effectively removing the Irish leaders from the playing field. There was no unified support for these attempts to throw off the control of England within the ranks of the Old English or the Irish chieftains. Since they remained Catholic, they were ineligible for appointment to government office, and therefore had no influence or power.

According to legend there was a lighter touch to the history of this period. That is the tale of Grace O'Malley, about whom there are many anecdotes. She was a pirate who was brave and colorful.

Off shore in Clew Bay, is small Clare Island with the ruined tower of Grace O'Malley's Castle. "Legend says that this remarkable Irishwoman was buried on the island in an abbey which now, like her stronghold, is a ruin."

Also known as Granuaile, she was a unique character. She ruled the seaboard of Connaught at the same time as Queen Elizabeth ruled England. Her father, called the Black Oak,... "was Lord of the Isles. The clan had from the earliest days been famous for its daring deeds by sea and the old chief was accompanied on many of his piratical voyages by his daughter. When he died she was a girl of nineteen. She had a younger brother, but, she calmly set him aside and declared her intention of becoming the chief of the clan...."

"She lived in an age of piracy... Her chief attacks were against the merchant ships of Elizabeth. She became so notorious that the English Government proclaimed her an outlaw and offered what in those days was an enormous sum, £500 for her capture. Troops stationed at Galway were sent to take her castle, but after a fortnight's siege they retired, and Queen Grace was left in peace. Her first husband was O'Donnell O'Flaherty 'of the wars'".... A record of her about this time is contained in a manuscript preserved in the Dublin archives."...'

"When O'Flaherty died she chose as her second husband a powerful Anglo-Norman named Sir Richard Bourke but after a year declared the marriage ended....In 1593 she offered her fleet of three galleys and 200 men in the service of England." She visited England and was greeted by the queen although they did not seem to have much empathy, one for the other. She arranged that her son who had Saxon blood would receive a title. He was created the Viscount of Mayo and the present earls of Mayo are descendants.

On her return she was obliged to put in at Howth harbour due to a storm. "She advanced to the castle and found the doors shut, the inmates at dinner and their hospitality refused to her..." She returned to shore and saw a beautiful child, who was heir to Howth, playing in the grounds. She "deliberately stole the child and bore off her prize to Connaught." She would not give him up until she obtained as ransom, "the promise that forever at mealtimes the doors of the castle be thrown wide open and hospitality extended to all wayfarers who should demand it. This custom is still observed there."[31]

There are several accounts of the meeting of the two Queens, Queen Elizabeth and Queen Grace. There are too many variations to determine the actual truth of the meeting.

The **17th century** was a grim one for Ireland. The Catholic church suffered a tortuous existence as did the Gaelic Irish people. The reigns of James I and Charles I were marked by corruption and poor judgment. These monarchs also had to face the dilemma of loyalty. The crown was sovereign and the Catholics had not accepted that sovereignty.

The influx of Planters increased the migration from Britain to Ireland by 100,000 by 1640. To assure a safe and supportive region, the planters in Ulster were bound with the obligation of building defensible buildings and introducing ten British Protestant families as servitors on each unit of 1000 acres. These new planters were pleased with their new status and built fine houses. A wave of Englishness spread through Ireland. Other Irish proprietors also adapted English ways to show their loyalty to the Crown.

The two separate societies, which were based, not on cultural differences but, on religious differences, continued to develop in Ireland.

Since the Catholic landowners in Ulster were not allowed to hold office in the government, they decided to resort to force to achieve recognition. In 1641 the stored up bitterness against the Protestants who had taken all the land erupted and 2000 Protestant settlers were killed and many more were driven from their homes. Again, the Irish landowners and the Old English throughout Ireland did not consolidate or prepare for a retaliatory attack from the English. Since Charles I was having a great deal of difficulty with his own Civil War, it was an opportunity missed.

As a belated response to this attack on the Protestants, in 1649 Oliver Cromwell came with his army of 20,000 and avenged the massacre of the Protestants. He entered Ireland in the spirit of a religious war. His wide path of destruction of monasteries, cathedrals and all things Catholic was devastating. Those Catholic proprietors who survived were bundled northwest across the Shannon River. All their lands were confiscated. Oliver Cromwell died in 1658. His son Richard ruled ineffectively for two years.

In 1660 came the Restoration of the Stuarts and they ruled ineptly for a quarter of a century. In Ireland the restoration of the land to the Catholic landowners was insignificant. This period, however, gave a significant breathing space for the Catholic priests to return from their refuge in France and to reestablish Catholicism as the religion of the people.

James II's reign was short and William of Orange and his wife, Mary (daughter of James II), accepted the English throne. Unfortunately for Ireland, Catholic James II did not give up easily and mustered an army from his Irish subjects and the French. But the issue was not the restoration of the Stuarts to the throne, the issue was the ownership of the land. The Williamite campaign commenced in 1690.

William defeated James II. This led to another confiscation of property owned by those Catholics who had supported James II. They now owned less than 10% of the land. It also led to the introduction of the penal laws which further restricted their power. Many of the Irish Catholic aristocracy fled to Europe.

The close of the 17th century which ended with the defeat of James II at the Battle of the Boyne was not only "the struggle of a Stuart king to regain the throne of his fathers. It is the struggle of Britain and her Protestant allies to oppose the ascendency in Europe of Catholic France. It is the struggle of the Protestant Anglo-Scots and the Catholic Irish for the leadership of Ireland."[32] The six grim events of this conflict were the Siege of Derry, April 1689; Battle of the Boyne, July 1690; 1st Siege of Limerick, September 1690; Siege of Athlone, June 1691; Battle of Aughrim, July 1691 and the 2nd Siege of Limerick, September 1691. This struggle left James II and the Catholic Irish defeated.

The gallant efforts of the town of Limerick and the heroism of Patrick Sarsfield led to the Treaty of Limerick. The peace included full civil and religious liberty for the Irish and all Irish soldiers who fought with James were to be given a free passage to France. King William offered the soldiers of the Irish forces service in the English ranks. Approximately one thousand joined the English army, two thousand decided to go home and eleven thousand left for the Continent. Those who left were called the "Flying Geese" and they served throughout the world in foreign armies. After they left, the Treaty of Limerick was broken by Parliament and all chance of an amicable peace was lost.

By the end of the 17th century, the social and economic structure was similar to that of Europe. Agriculture ruled the economy for the majority and established the boundaries of the social and economic classes.

The very poor rented small holdings. They paid their rents through cottage industries, weaving and spinning of linen and woolen goods. Their landlords were often tenants themselves to an overlord or head landlord. These were the landowners who wielded the wealth and political power in Ireland. They were primarily first generation English settlers, settlers with a boon from Queen Elizabeth or James I, Scottish planters from Ulster and the Anglo-Norman descendants who had accommodated themselves to England. Their religion was Protestant. They also controlled

Ireland's exports, which were the textiles of the cottage industries and barreled meat. The export ports gained importance and influence.

18th Century Through Independence

THE POLITICS of England during these periods directly influenced the state of affairs in Ireland. The eighteenth century brought the House of Hanover to the throne and thus began the Georgian Era. George I was a German prince who did not speak English. He realized that he was merely the means of stopping the succession of the Catholic Stuarts. He left the governing to Robert Walpole, a Whig, who developed the present form of government with a cabinet of one party responsible to the parliament, with Parliament responsible to the electorate. The Stuart supporters, also known as Jacobites or Tories, continued to push for the return of the Catholic Stuarts. During the second half of the century, the English were involved in wars on the Continent in which they suffered severe reverses. They also suffered the loss of the American colonies. George III (sometimes mad) was at the helm followed by his dissipated son, George IV.

The continued struggles of the Stuarts to regain the throne contributed to a fear of Irish Catholics by the Protestant Ascendency. They feared that should England be returned to the Catholic Stuarts, they would be subject to resettlement or loss of their properties and position in Ireland.

A broad view of Irish history in the eighteenth and nineteenth centuries is a generalization of the perils of social class: the underclass beset by poverty and insecurity turn to Catholicism and nationalism vs. the dominance of the aristocracy. However, these undercurrents cover a long passage of time. The daily events in Ireland muddled along.

The Protestant Ascendency ruled without opposition. The Irish forces and their leaders, the Flying Geese, were on the Continent. The economy was so weak for the Gaelic Irish that many emigrated and often it was necessary for them to send money to their families in Ireland to assure their survival. Who were the Protestant Ascendency? Why were they so harsh with the Irish Catholics who were destitute and unorganized?

The Protestant Ascendency included those Catholic landowners who had taken the oath of loyalty and changed their religious affiliation when so commanded by Henry VIII and Elizabeth in order to keep their land, the English and Scottish planters and others who had emigrated from England. These represented about 25% of the population. Their cultural and political center was Dublin although their authority was limited and most decisions were made in London. They were not in an enviable position for they feared the strength of the Catholic Irish and feared the ambivalent politics of London. Their insecurity is evidenced by the passage of the Penal Laws.

In 1801, the Act of Union joined Ireland to England with the suppression of the Irish Parliament in Dublin. During the nineteenth century, the successes in the Napoleonic Wars were dependent upon the brilliance of the English military leaders such as the Duke of Wellington and Lord Nelson and not the skill and leadership of the monarchs. After George IV came mild William IV, who was then succeeded by the fruitful Victoria.

The story of these centuries is best seen through the architecture in the cities, towns and villages in Ireland. Dublin became the cosmopolitan center. A successful career in the British Army brought travel in Europe. The travelers brought back to Ireland ideas of building styles and booty with which to furnish their grand homes. War also provided an improved economy which led to a great surge of grand architectural buildings. The major trade and leading export was linen. Factories employed the Irish.

Not only did the Irish suffer from political and social suppression, they were also victims of the Great Potato Famine in 1845–1849 when a blight ruined the potato crop for several years in the northwest. Many emigrated to Europe, Canada and America, but the toll of the dead from starvation and disease was vast. There was little help to relieve the suffering even though the blight was limited to the northwest and the west. Some 800,000 people died of starvation, cholera and typhus. There is a presentation of this era at Strokestown Park House, Co. Roscommon, and at Cobh, the Queenstown Story, Co. Cork. One million Irish emigrated to the United States, Canada and England.

Modern Ireland

THROUGHOUT this period are historical figures and organizations whose contributions help us to focus on the political environment in Ireland. The problems between what is now Northern Ireland and the Republic of Ireland have their roots in past centuries. The political, economic and religious atmosphere is not within the province of this book, although these dynamics contributed greatly to the successes and failures of the movement for independence in the South. During the early years, economic opportunity and security were the primary factors about which most Irish were concerned. The ability to survive was paramount to their lives. Others had a dream or a vision of a new independent Ireland and strove for this dream to become a reality. Those of note included Robert Emmett, Theobald Wolfe Tone, Daniel O'Connell, Charles Stewart Parnell, Eamon De Valera and Michael Collins. Organizations of note were the Irish Republican Brotherhood, Sinn Fein and the Irish Republican Army. It is through them that a conclusion was reached with the establishment of the Irish Free State.

The government and its structure must be understood in order to have a feel for the climate of Ireland. It is an independent constitutional democracy with total religious freedom. The progress and successes of history during the twentieth century have been sustained with determination and the assistance of relatives who had emigrated. Trade sanctions were imposed by the English as retribution. The Irish neutrality during WWII also caused economic hardship. Finally with the creation of the European Community and its economic support, Ireland has preserved its historical monuments and developed the structures necessary for their thriving tourist industry.

Many things in Ireland remained unchanged through the years, such as the love of horses and competition; the ancient crafts of literature and theater; an appreciation of sports and the land; and above all, their fine talent for humor and hospitality.

16. COUNTIES OF IRELAND

Carlow

THE RIVER BARROW passes through Carlow and has been a major line of travel and communication since the Stone Age. The county is under extensive cultivation and is located in the province of Leinster.

STONE AGE

1. Brownshill Portal Tomb is a massive stone weighing one hundred tons. It is located one mile east of Carlow town by R726 on the ridge of a hill overlooking the Barrow River valley.

CHRISTIAN

2. St. Mullin's Monastic site, of which only one cross and a small oratory remain, also includes remnants of a round tower. The plan of this monastery is located in the library at Trinity College, Dublin on a document from the 8th or 9th century. It is reached by R729 north of New Ross.

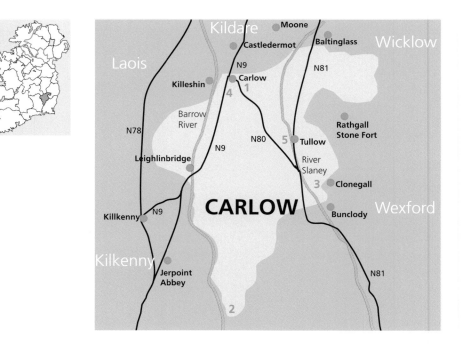

3. Huntington Castle, Clonegal, began as a tower house in the 17th century. It has been modified and added to throughout the years and now includes a Temple of Isis, dark vaulted basements and a holy well. It is located east of the Slaney River and north of Bunclody and is open on Sunday afternoon by appointment.

CASTLES

4. Carlow Court House exhibits the neoclassic architectural style which was inspired by Rome.

CASTLE/ HOUSES

4. Railroad Station, Carlow, is an excellent example of the Gothic Victorian style with all the turrets and towers as well as the textures of brick and stone.

5. Altamount Gardens, Tullow, is a Garden Domaine in which there are formal areas around the house with woodlands, bog garden and arboretum on the shores of the River Slaney. It is located five miles south of Tullow on the Tullow to Bunclody road (N80).

GARDENS

IT IS IN the county of Carlow where the Dinn Rig of the Cycle of the Kings was located. Although it is not signposted, it was the ancient center of power of Leinster or the Lagin. In the many tales of the Plunder of Dinn Rig several main themes dominate. Cobhtach had slain his brother, the king, and his son, Ailill. Labraid Loingsech, son of Ailill, was banished from "Ireland" for fear he would avenge the deaths of his father and grandfather. Labraid departed for Munster, fell in love and wooed successfully the king of Munster's daughter, Moriath. He returned later to Leinster with an army and Craiphtine's music, which lulled the soldiers of the fort to sleep. The fort was captured and all were slain whereupon Labraid built a house of iron. He planned a great feast for King Cobhtach and his petty kings. He confined them to the house of iron and set it ablaze. The Lagin, or Leinstermen are descended from Labraid.

MYTHOLOGY

CARLOW

Cavan

Cavan is a county in the province of Ulster. The central portion is covered with many lakes of which the largest is Lough Oughter. The eastern mountains are composed of shale and slate. Peat bogs and infertile land prevail. The area was part of the kingdom of Breifne which long resisted colonization by the Anglo-Normans. The Shannon-Erne Waterway en route from Carrick-on-Shannon to Enniskillin passes through the county. There is much good freshwater fishing and pony trekking.

STONE AGE

1. Cohaw Court Tomb has two court/tomb units which are placed back to back with no entry from one to the other. It dates from 3000 BC and is southwest of Cootehill on R192.

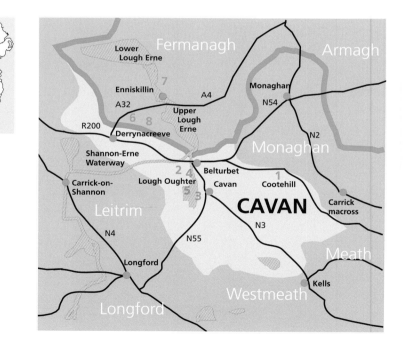

CAVAN

*2. **Drumlane Church** and **Round Tower** are located east of R201 between Killashandra and Belturbet.

*3. **Kilmore Cathedral** is located off the road on R198 southwest of Cavan. It has a 12th century Romanesque door.

EARLY
CHRISTIAN

*4. **Clogh Oughter** is a round castle on a small island which is an ancient crannog in Lough Oughter. It has four stories and often served as a prison. The island is at the northeast end of Lough Oughter.

CASTLES

*5. **Killykeen Forest Park**

*6. **Marble Arch Caves** and **Preserve** are just over the border into Fermanagh and southwest of Enniskillen. This is the same area as:

*7. **Coole Castle** and

*8. **Florence Court,** which are in County Fermanagh in Northern Ireland.

OTHER SITES

ALTHOUGH the mythological sites are not marked on most maps, according to Daragh Smyth, *A Guide to Irish Mythology,* near Ballymagauran in Cavan, the Plain of Prostration (Mag Slecht) was an ancient ceremonial site for the corn god, Crom Cruach. On this plain there were twelve stone idols embossed in silver, except for the one of Crom, which was embossed in gold. It was at Samain or October 31 that people gathered on the plain and made their animal and human sacrifices. When St. Patrick overthrew Crom, a large hole was dug in which was placed the stone of Crom. The Killycluggin Stone in the National Museum in Dublin is thought to be the stone idol of Crom. The stone head of Conn, a god/king of the Otherworld, was found in a passage grave at Corleck Hill, and is now at the National Museum and referred to as the triple-headed god of Corleck.

MYTHOLOGY

CAVAN

Clare

CLARE, in the province of Munster, is bordered by Galway Bay, the Atlantic Ocean, the Shannon Waterways and County Galway.

Much of the underlying countryside is limestone, which causes the poor drainage that created peat bogs. In the west is the Burren, a limestone plateau with little vegetation. The Atlantic Ocean's erosion has created high cliffs such as the Cliffs of Moher. Central Clare is more fertile and well drained with crops and pasture.

In County Clare there are almost 200 castles and 150 ancient churches as well as an enormous number of megalithic tombs and stone forts. The Burren is beautiful with an otherworldly quality.

STONE AGE

1. Poulnabrone, the most photographed portal tomb found in the Burren, is located on the east side of R480. If traveling north on R476, bear right at Leamaneh Castle.

ANCIENT IRELAND

2. Turlough Hill includes a hill fort with hut sites (south from N67 at Bealaclugga).

3. Caherconnell Fort and **Cahercommaun Stone Fort** (northeast of Killinaboy) and **Cahermacnaghten Stone Fort** (east of N57 between Lisdoonvarna and Ballyvaughan) are all located within the Burren.

4. Craggaunowen Bronze Age Project is an excellent re-creation of early life and living conditions in Ireland during this age. There is a crannog with several circular dwellings as well as actors and actresses to greet you in the dress, language and style of the people. There is also a reconstructed souterrain, road and cooking area. It is interesting that the actual boat used in the reenactment (1978 by Tim Severin) of St. Brendon's voyage to the New World in the 5th century is here at Craggaunowen. This was written up in the *National Geographic*, December 1977. It is due south of Moymore by several tertiary roads.

EARLY CHRISTIAN

5. Scattery Island has ruins of a 6th century monastic settlement on an island near the mouth of the Shannon River. There is an impressive round tower which is in a fair state of preservation. The door is at the ground level which minimized its role as a defensive structure against Viking attacks.[33] The Bell-Shrine of

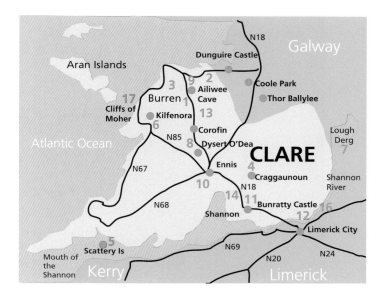

St. Seanan from Scattery Island is now in the National Museum. The ruins have undergone restoration and alterations. Access is from Cappagh Pier, Merchant's Quay, Kilrush, on the southern coast of the Loop Peninsula by N68 southwest of Ennis.

6. *Kilfenora High Crosses* and **Cathedral** are in the Burren on R481 south of Kilfenora on the road to Ennistimon.

7. *Holy Island,* Lough Derg, was a monastic settlement of the 7th century. There are extensive ruins of several churches as well as a Romanesque doorway and an 80 foot round tower. It is a wonderful place to visit on a beautiful day. It may be reached by boat from Mountshannon or Tuamgraney. The only inhabitants are some curious grazing cattle.

8. *Dysert O'Dea* is the site of an original monastery founded by St. Tola in the early 8th century. There are now the remains of an 11th century church with a Romanesque doorway (a copy of which is in the National Museum of Ireland), round tower, St. Tolas's cross and in the yard a rough shaped cross marking an unknown grave. This doorway has had extensive restoration. It is north of Ennis by R476 and a side road to the west.

Holy Island

197

Cistercian

9. Corcomroe Abbey is the relatively well preserved remains of a 12th century Cistercian abbey north of Bealaclugg by N67 (Bell Harbor).

10. In and about Ennis:

Augustinian

- **Killone Abbey** was a 12th century Augustinian nunnery located several miles south of Ennis by N68 and side roads.

Franciscan

- **Quin Abbey** is a 15th century Franciscan friary built on the remains of a 13th century square Norman castle with round bastions. There is a well preserved Franciscan cloister with dormitories on the first floor. It is on R469 southeast of Ennis.

- **Ennis Franciscan Friary,** Ennis, was built by the Franciscans in the 13th century with a 15th century addition of a square tower. This is a Dúchas site with parking available.

15th century

- **Knappogue Castle,** Quin, is a 15th century restored Tower House now used for medieval banquets. It is southeast of Ennis by R469.

11. Bunratty Castle and Folk Park was built in the 15th century. The large square keep has a high entry arch between the two corner towers. It has been completely restored and offers medieval banqueting and entertainment. It is northwest of Limerick city beside N18.

8. Dysert O'Dea Castle has been restored. It is a typical tower house with castellations and a murder hole. It is located northwest of Ennis by R476 and back roads.

16th century

9. Dunguire Castle, Kinvarra, has a tower house with bawn and is located on the shore in a picturesque setting. It is on N67 and is used for medieval banquets.

17th century

12. Cratloe Woods House is an Irish longhouse, a style which lasted from the middle ages to the 18th century. It is five miles NW of Limerick.

13. Leamaneh Castle is located at the crossing of R480 and R476. Only the shell of this once grand house remains. The elegant gateway is now at Dromoland Castle Hotel and the surrounding walled gardens, fishpond and summer house are no longer there.

It was built in 1639 by Conor O'Brien who married "Red Mary." Conor was killed by the troops of Cromwell after which Mary decided that the best way to secure her infant son's heritage was to marry one of the enemy officers, which she did. She later threw him to his death from an upper story window.[34] There are many stories about her that substantiate her name.

14. Dromoland Castle, Newmarket-on-Fergus, is a 19th century Gothic-style castle set in a lovely park beside a small lake. It is now a hotel located north of town on N18.

15. Mount Ievers Court, Sixmilebridge, is a tall 18th century house in a park. The house is three stories over a basement with a tall steep roof and tall chimney stacks. This adaptation was influenced by the Dutch although it has features typical of the Irish 18th century architecture. It may be seen by appointment.

16. Mount Shannon, Castleconnell, is now a ruin of a neoclassic house with a porte cochère.

17. Cliffs of Moher rise 600 feet above the Atlantic and extend for five miles. Take R478 from Lehinch to Lisdoonvarna. There is a visitor center along the route with information on the plants and animals of the area.

18. Aillwee Cave, Ballyvaughan, is on R480 north of the area of portal tombs. Tours of the cave are available.

19. Clare Heritage Center, Corrofin, offers exhibits of 19th century life as well as extensive genealogical records for those who emigrated after the great famines.

20. Burren Display Center, Kilfenora, offers insight and information for touring and hiking. Because of the limestone bedrock and underground rivers it is important to stay on the marked trails.

GRIAN WAS THE sun goddess associated with Clare and several lakes are named after her. According to the Ossianic poem, "Lay of Oisin in Tir na nOg," Oisin tells St. Patrick about his trip to the Otherworld, a small and beautiful city marked by white breaking waves between Lahinch and Liscannor.

Sheila na Gigs are sculptures of nude figures or stone fetishes representing a woman who grants fertility. There is one on a parapet of the bridge at Clonlara known as the Witches Stone which dates from the 16th century. These are also found in Britain and France.

Cork

CORK IS A county in the province of Munster whose southern and western coasts are bound by the Atlantic Ocean. It is the largest county in Ireland and consists of rich farmland.

The peninsulas which reach into the Atlantic are picturesque. The land belonged to the Desmonds although the city of Cork was founded by the Norse. Sir Walter Raleigh was granted a large estate here by Elizabeth I, much of which was later bought by Richard Boyle, the colorful Earl of Cork.

The ports in Cork have long played important roles in the history and activity of the county.

Throughout County Cork there are many ancient monuments which include standing stones, pillar and Ogham stones, ring forts, gallery graves, stone circles and cairns. Due to the topography and fertility of this region, it was always settled. Its position along the exposed southern coast made these settlements vulnerable to attacks from invaders. The beauty of the countryside created a desire to build, and the natural ports added to its prosperity. There is a wealth of sites in County Cork including over 100 castles in various states of repair.

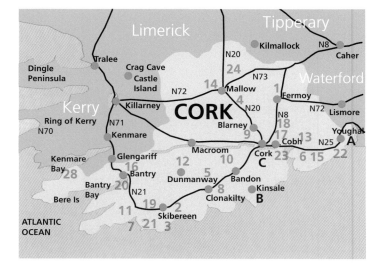

1. _Labbacallee Gallery Grave_ is on the Fermoy to Glanworth road, R512.

2. _Dromberg Stone Circle_ consists of fourteen evenly spaced stones which form a circle of 30 feet in diameter. In the center was discovered a container with the remains of a youth. The rays of the setting sun on the winter solstice go across the circle due east. Take the Rosscarbery to Glandore road R597. It is signposted although there is a walk through the fields. There is also a Fulachta Foadh, cooking place, on the grounds.

3. _Knockdrum Fort,_ Castletownshend, is a prehistoric fort with three souterrains as well as a cross and an inscribed pillar stone and is located on the Cork coast southeast of Skibbereen by R596.

4. _St. Senan's Abbey,_ Iniscarra, has the remains of a 6th century church on the Cork to Macroom road, R618.

5. _Kinneigh Round Tower,_ near Enniskean, is from the 11th century. It is unusual as the lower section of the tower is hexagonal and there are six stories inside. It is near Enniskean on the Bandon to Dunmanway road R586.

6. _Cloyne Cathedral_ (restored) and **_Round Tower_** (10th century) is found by R629 south of Midleton.

7. _Franciscan Abbey,_ Sherkin Island, was founded in the 15th century and is at the south end of R595.

8. _Timoleague Abbey_ or **_Friary,_** Timoleague, was founded in the 14th century although most of the present building dates from the 16th century. Some of the buildings are well preserved but not easily identifiable as to their purpose.[35] It is on the Clonakilty to Kinsale road, R600.

15th Century

9. _Blarney Castle,_ Blarney, is in a fair state of preservation and presents an opportunity to see the layout of a typical square tower house with the living quarters on the upper levels. Most tourists come to kiss the Blarney Stone which is inside the parapet at the top of the castle. You must lie down on your back, extend your upper body downward and then reach across the opening of the machicolation to kiss the Blarney Stone on the outside wall. There is a sturdy grate below your head, and handles and you are held securely by an attendant. It is good fun and your picture is taken for you which you may purchase at the concession booth. They are reliable about mailing it to you. You are then endowed with the gift of gab or, as some reports suggest, you are excellent at making plausible excuses.

10. Kilcrea Castle and **Abbey** are near Ballincollig, west of Cork by N22.

11. Leam Con, Schull, also called Black Castle, is reached by R592 to Castle Point.

16th Century

12. Ballynacarriga Castle, near Dunmanway, has window carvings and a view. It is west of Bandon by R586.

13. Barryscourt Castle is located in Carrigtohill and although it is still being restored, it is open. This is a typical tower house in good repair with gabled roof, projecting towers, and a surrounding bawn wall. The interior shows the structure of the tower houses with the arched ceiling.

17th Century

14. Kanturk Castle, Kanturk, is rectangular in shape with four large towers at each corner. It is in quite good repair considering it was never completed and has never had a roof. The first story has narrow slits while the upper stories have mullioned windows. This represented a breakthrough in building a castle house rather than a castle fortification. It is on the Newmarket to Mallow road.

15. Ightermurragh Castle, Ladybridge, is rectangular with projecting square towers in the center of the front and back. It has string courses, mullioned windows, external chimneys topped with stacks, and machicolations on corbels over the front door. It can be seen from the road on the left. Go north from Ladybridge at the town center. It is about a kilometer down a dirt lane which can be muddy.

CASTLE/
HOUSES

16. Bantry House, Bantry, is 18th century with Italian-style terraced gardens and a spectacular view of Bantry Bay. Accommodations are available. It is on N71 in Bantry.

17. Riverstown House, Riverstown is a plain late 17th century house with an interior which was renovated in the mid-18th century by the famous Francini brothers. The dining room walls are paneled with classical figures and allegorical scenes in stucco. The exterior remains bare and unadorned while the inside is elaborately decorated. It is northeast of Cork by N8.

Bantry House

9. Blarney House, Gardens and Rock Close was built in the 19th century on the grounds of Blarney Castle. It is northwest of Cork City, next to Blarney Castle, and reached by R617.

18. Dunkathel, Glanmire, is 18th century and is 3.5 miles north of Cork on the Glanmire Road (N8).

GARDENS

8. Timoleague Castle Gardens, Bandon, is reached by R600 on the Kinsale to Clonakilty road.

19. Anne's Grove Gardens, Castletownroche, is by N72 on the Fermoy to Mallow road.

20. Ilnacullin, Garinish Island, Glengariff, is by R572 with a ferry to the island.

21. Creagh Gardens, Creagh, by R595 is on the Skibbereem to Baltimore road.

22. Kinoith, Ballymaloe, is on the Cork to Youghal road, N25, and is signposted at Castlemartyr.

23. Fota Island Arboretum has unusual trees from Chile, China and Japan as well as a Lebanese cedar and magnolias. The house on the Fota Estate is closed and the Wildlife Park is under scrutiny as the land has been sold for development. Its future is precarious and viewing of the arboretum may be short term. It is located southeast of Cork on the Cobh road.

24. Doneraile Wildlife Park

25. Royal Gunpowder Mills, Ballincollig

26. Jameson Heritage Centre, Midleton

27. Cobh, Queenstown Story, offers an excellent portrayal of the port of Cobh and the emigration of so many Irish during the years of the famine. It is from Cork that the Lusitania sailed on its fatal journey. R624 is the coastal road around Great Island on which Cobh is located. It is east of Cork.

28. Beara Peninsula is one of beauty and interest. There are many antiquities. It is partly in County Cork and partly in County Kerry. An illustrated map of the area is available at an Irish Tourist Board.

A. *Cork City*

THE ORIGINAL city was founded by the Norse as a trading center. This walled city on the island of the River Lee was burned and raided several times before the arrival of the Anglo-Normans. It was held by the English for many centuries and later became the center for resistance to military repression. The natural harbor played a key role in yachting and shipping.

- **Grand Parade** is bordered by bowed 18th century townhouses.
- **St. Fin Barre's Cathedral,** the Anglican Cathedral in ornate Gothic design, was completed in the late 19th century on the site of an early monastery. The Michelin guide describes it as exuberant.
- **Shandon Bells** are located in St. Anne's on the north side of the River. The church is interesting in structure with a set of bells that may be played by the tourist. There are several tunes available, and to peal the bells with an Irish tune over the city is fun.
- **Cork Public Museum** attractively presents the history of Cork since prehistoric times.

B. *Kinsale City*

THIS ATTRACTIVE and old city is on the estuary of the Bandon River. In 1600 (during the reign of Elizabeth I) the town was occupied by a Spanish force which had come to assist the Irish. The English armies successfully besieged the town, after which the Spanish departed. Kinsale declared for Cromwell and remained for many years a totally English town.

- **St. Multose Church** has evolved through the centuries on the same site.

- **Desmond Castle** is a 16th century tower house which was used as a prison for American seamen during the American Revolution. It is also known as the French prison.

- **Charles Fort** was built in the 17th century. It is star-shaped and interesting to visit.

C. *Youghal City*

YOUGHAL is a seaport town on the banks of the Blackwater estuary which was first occupied by the Vikings in the 10th century. It was later settled by the Anglo-Normans and remained a strategic though vulnerable port. The English fortified it and those town walls still exist, in part. It is said that Sir Walter Raleigh introduced both tobacco and potato plants into Ireland in the 16th century while he was mayor of Youghal.

- **St. Mary's Collegiate Church** is 13th century but has undergone large scale restoration. There is a vast commemorative monument to the Earl of Cork with his three wives and sixteen children which is representative of the art in this period of the successful landowners. He was later fined for his illegal dealings in acquiring his land and wealth.

- **Town Walls** were built in the 13th century and are well preserved.

- **Myrtle Grove** was Sir Walter Raleigh's house.

Donegal

THIS IS the most northwestern county of Ireland and province of Ulster. The coast is rugged and the land is dominated by mountains and river valleys. The climate is mild and wet in the winter. This ancient land was Tyrconnell and called the kingdom of Ailech. Grianan of Aileagh was its capital.

This area contains some of the most beautiful scenic drives which include plantings and forestation as well as relics from the past.

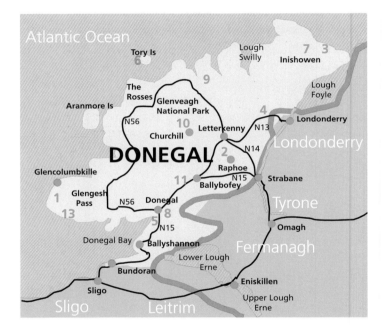

STONE AGE

1. Glenmalin Cairn consists of 64 stones and is located by R263 between Carrick and Malin Beg.

2. Beltany Circle consists of sixty stones in a circle with a single upright stone on the outside. It is thought that this ring was used by the celtic pagans to celebrate a May Day festival as early as 2000 BC. It is due south of Raphoe on what is known as Tops Hill.

3. Bocan Stone Circle is located on the Inishowen Peninsula.

4. Grianan of Aileagh is a reconstruction of a 1700 BC stone fort which crowns the hilltop. The original was the royal seat of the O'Neill sept which was destroyed in 1101 AD by Brian Boru, King of Munster, in his push to rule all of Ireland. There is an information center and restaurant at the beginning of the narrow road leading to the fort. It is located south on N13 on the Letterkenny to Derry road.

5. Ard Fothadh, also known as McGonigle's Fort, is 2 miles NW of Ballintra.

Donegal was the birthplace of St. Columb or Columba and there are many areas which commemorate him and his life.

6. Tory Island includes ruins of a church, a round tower and a cross. It is located approximately ten miles northwest off the northwest coast of the county.

7. Inishowen Peninsula has crosses and grave slabs, which date from the 7th century. Among these are Carrowmore high crosses and the Clona church and high cross. From the 8th century are the Carndonagh high crosses. There is also the slab at Fahan.

8. Donegal Abbey, Donegal, contains ruins of a 15th century Franciscan friary which is located on the banks of the river.

16th Century

9. Doe Castle, Creeslough, was a four story castle of the 16th century with a massive bawn wall and all the features of a wonderful medieval castle. It is protected on three sides by the sea and on the fourth side by a ditch cut into the rock. This was one of the castles to offer help to the Spaniards after the Armada. Its history is similar to that of many old castles in Ireland which changed hands many times. It was fought over by various Irish chiefs, the armies of Cromwell, the Stuart kings and the English. There have been many alterations and repairs but it still has the aura of a medieval castle. It is on the shore of the inlet from Sheep Haven and may be approached by tertiary road from either R245 or N56.

17th Century

8. Donegal Castle, Donegal, was constructed in the 17th century as a tower house but was destroyed by the owner himself to prevent English occupation. An English planter took over the property, repaired it and added windows and gables to the tower house. Then a gabled Jacobean manor house was built in the courtyard.

The chimney has extraordinary stonework. There is a gate tower at the entrance. It has recently been restored.

10. Glenveagh Castle, Churchill, is a large 19th century Victorian house behind a castellated facade with lovely gardens within the Glenveagh National Park. Courtesy of Dúchas: The Heritage Service

10. Glenveagh Castle Gardens, Churchill, are outside of Churchill and northwest of Letterkenny by R250 and R251.

11. Ardamona Woodland Garden, Lough Eske, has gardens that are mostly devoted to woodlands and an incredible view of the lake. Accommodations are available.

12. Glengesh Pass is well photographed, lovely and a long drive.

13. Cliffs of Bunglass are an extremely dramatic sight with a sheer drop to the sea below. This is not a short or easy excursion.

14. Glenclumbkille Folk Village consists of period cabins to show the life and culture of the area during the past three centuries. In the surrounding area are also megaliths and pattern stations. On June 9, pilgrims make a one-day pilgrimage to visit the 15 stations throughout the valley. The builders of the megalithic tombs and the pilgrims in the past probably came by sea.

15. In and about Letterkenny: Churchill, is located northwest of Letterkenny and is the center of several interesting historical sites in the area. The Columcille Heritage Center presents an exhibit on his life; St. Columcille's Oratory; Glebe House and Gallery which holds the collection of the artist Derek Hill as well as other Irish artists. Nearby is Doon Well and Rock, known for its curative powers, which is west of Kilmacrenan. **Glenveagh National Park** and its visitor center provide access and information to the park.

16. The Flight of the Earls Exhibit is in Rathmullan which is north of Letterkenny. The Catholic Earls of Tyrone and Tyrconnell were soundly defeated by the troops of Elizabeth at Kinsale. They fled to the Continent, and their lands were confiscated and opened to Scot settlers. The Earls were unsuccessfully aided by the Spanish.

17. Newmills is located three miles west of Letterkenny. This old mill complex has been restored. The upper mill was for the making of linen and much of the old machinery is still there. The lower mill was used for grinding barley and oats.

IN THE ANCIENT mythology the Tuatha De Danaan were defeated and went underground to the Otherworld. One of their mounds, Sid of Mullachshee, was near Ballyshannon. It has also been written that Partholon and his Fomorians arrived in Donegal Bay and settled near Ballyshannon about three hundred years after the Flood. It was also on Tory Island that Balor of the One Eye imprisoned his daughter to prevent her from bearing a child because a druid had predicted that Balor's grandson would slay him. This grandson was Lug, who did slay Balor.

Dublin

THE COUNTY of Dublin is one of the smallest and has the greatest population. The city of Dublin, on the banks of the Liffey and Poddle Rivers, was founded by the Vikings during the 9th century. Excavation of the remains of their settlement has been carried out along the Quay.

The Anglo-Normans established their presence with the building of Dublin Castle. Some of the original structure can be seen. Dublin was British in character and sympathy and was considered the hub of the Pale. The Pale was the area in which English law was observed and enforced. Much of the county is now a series of suburbs of Dublin City.

The land in the north is low and rolling while the south is more mountainous. There are remnants of prehistoric hill forts and dolmens.

1. Lusk Round Tower is 6th century and is north of Dublin City by N1 to R128.

2. St. Doulough's Church is a 12th century church with a 14th century tower. A small subterranean chamber covers St. Catherine's well. It is near Portmarnock by R107.

Norman

3. Dublin Castle, Dublin, has very little left of the original castle which was built in the early 13th century on the site of a Viking town. The additions have disguised many of the features although the restoration process has identified, by color, the reconstructed parts. It was rectangular in shape with four circular towers at each of the corners. A fire in 1684 did much damage after which the old walls were demolished and the present buildings and clock tower on the north side of the Upper Yard were built.

13th century

4. Swords Castle and round Tower, Swords, is a five-sided structure enclosing a courtyard built in 1200. It is north of Dublin city by N1.

14th century

5. Malahide Castle exhibits many interesting features in the wonderful setting of the Talbot Gardens. There are the 14th century tower/house; the 15th century great hall where the Talbot cousins breakfasted together on the morning before they were killed in battle fighting for James II; and the 18th century reception rooms with plaster work which reflect another era. It is north of the Dublin by N1 and R106.

6. Ardigillan Castle, Balbriggan, is a 17th to 18th century country manor house of Georgian/Victorian style which has been purchased by the Dublin County Council. The Park, Rose Garden, Walled Garden, Ice House and some of the rooms on the ground floor are open to visitors. It is between Balbriggan and Skerries, north of Dublin.

7. Ayesha Castle, Killiney, is a 19th century Victorian castle with round tower and turrets. The castle was gutted by fire in 1924 but it has been restored. Situated in acreage which includes gardens and woodlands, it is 12 km from Dublin on the Victoria Road.

8. Newbridge House, Donabate, is an 18th century classical mansion with some extraordinary plaster work and is north of Dublin by N1 and R126 to Newbridge and Donabate.

9. Fernhill Gardens, Sandyford, extend over 40 acres overlooking Dublin Bay and include all types of gardens from woodland with spectacular rhododendrons (May / June) to a laurel lawn. It is on the slope of Three Rock Mountain south of Dublin on the Enniskerry road.

10. Howth Castle Gardens, Howth, are approached by way of the Deer Park Hotel and Golf Course. It is a rhododendron garden planted on a cliff face. A rigorous climb to the top offers an interesting view. May and June are the months for these shrubs and the variety of colors is spectacular.

5. Talbot Botanical Gardens, Malahide Castle, Mahilde, is north of Dublin by N1 and R106.

11. The Shackleton Garden, Beechpark, Clonsilia

12. Fairfield Lodge, Monkstown Avenue, Monkstown, is on the south coastal road along the Dublin Harbor, R118.

13. Knockree Garden, * Glenamuck Road, Carrickmines, is a natural garden set in the foothills of the Dublin Mountains with a special collection of rhododendrons.

14. Primrose Hill, Lucan

15. James Joyce Martello Tower, Sandycove, was built in the 19th century as a defense against a Napoleonic invasion. It is now the site of a James Joyce museum.

16. St. Enda's, Rathfarnham, an 18th century mansion of classical design, is now a museum to honor Patrick and Willie Pearse who were both executed for their parts in the Easter Rising 1916.

*Indicates limited access or access by appointment

COUNTY GALWAY is located in the western part of Ireland in the province of Connaught. The region to the west, called Connemara, has lowlands with peat bogs, lakes and uplands. The scenery is often haunting. The remaining lowlands are used for crops and pasture.

The descendants of the Anglo-Norman deBrugh ruled Connaught and were known as the tribes of Galway. Elizabeth I and Cromwell redistributed the land. In Norman times Galway was a flourishing and important seaport.

Aran Islands are a rugged group of islands off the coast of Galway which have an ancient history extending at least to the Bronze Age. Gaelic is the normal speech. They are well worth a visit with the natural beauty of a rugged landscape. There are forty-eight sites listed by the Dúchas on these three islands.

1. Aran Islands have excellent examples of stone forts which are located on the precipice of steep cliffs looking out to sea and would have been easily defended. Any time spent in the islands at leisure would be enjoyable as this is one of the places where Gaelic culture lives. Access to the Aran Islands is by plane or boat from Galway City Docks, Rossaveel or Doolin in County Clare. *Inishmore* – Dun Aengus, Dun Doocaherm and several other smaller area forts *Inishmaan* – Dun Conor and Dun Moher

ANCIENT
IRELAND

GALWAY

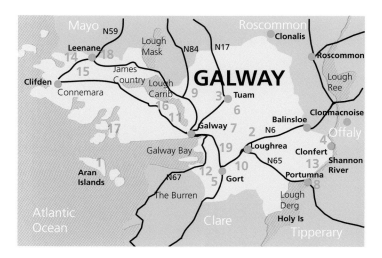

*2. **Turoe Stone*** is an early standing stone which is one of the best examples of the La Tène design. This is a rounded granite boulder decorated with curvilinear designs in the celtic style of ornament. It is reached by a series of small back roads west of Bullaun (N350) and north of Loughcrea.

*3. **High Cross*** of Tuam is from the 12th century and is now located indoors at St. Mary's Cathedral in Tuam.

*4. **Clonfert Cathedral*** (see p. 101) has a unique doorway which demonstrates the height of the Irish-Romanesque style. The entry has no undecorated space and utilizes decoration of every conceivable sort, architectural features and sculpture of not only animals and dragons but also natural human heads. It is due south of Shannon Bridge although reached by back roads from R356.

*5. **Kilmacduagh Monastery*** is particularly known for its leaning round tower and is in an excellent state of preservation. The site also includes O'Heyne's church, 13th century. Take a back road from R460 southwest of Gort.

Cistercian

*6. **Knockmoy Abbey*** was a Cistercian house dating from the 12th century. It lies on the northern bank of the Abbert River and is well off the beaten path, which adds to its charm. Knockmoy Village is just north of N63.

Dominican

*7. **Athenry Friary*** was a Norman stronghold which is now an agricultural village. These are ruins of a Dominican friary.

*8. **Portumna Priory*** was first a Cistercian chapel which was granted to the Dominicans in the mid-15th century and is located in Portumna Forest Park on the shore of Lough Derg.

Franciscan

*9. **Ross Abbey,*** founded by the Franciscans in the 14th century, was greatly expanded during the end of the 15th century. It is an extensive ruin now undergoing restoration. The view from the tower is excellent. It is north of Headford by R334.

7. Athenry Castle is a three-story keep surrounded by a wall with two towers. It is in Athenry by R348.

16th Century

10. Thoor Ballylee is a tower house which was owned and used by W. B. Yeats as a summer home. It is in excellent repair and is a memorial to him. It is northeast of Gort by N66 and some back roads.

11. Aughnanure Castle, Killarone, is on the eastern shore of Lough Corrib and south of Oughterard. The original castle was of the 13th century, but the ruins are from a six-story Irish tower house which was built in the 16th century by O'Flaherty. It has all the typical castle features – crenellations with a machicolation on each side, gun loops, a murder hole to defend the entrance and a garderobe. The inner bawn has an elegant corbeled roof angle turret. It is reached by N59 on the road from Oughterard and Moycullen.

Courtesy of Dúchas: The Heritage Service

12. Dunguire Castle, Kinvarra, has a tower house with bawn and is located on the shore in a picturesque setting. It is on N67 and is used for medieval banquets.

17th Century

13. Derryhivenny Castle is a truly fortified four-story tower house built in 1643 with a bawn and projecting turrets. North of Portumna by R355, it is signposted in a field and off the road.

8. Portumna Castle, Portumna, burned in the 19th century although the shell of this amazing structure is worth the visit. There is a painting of this house by James O'Connor at Westport House, Westport, Co. Mayo. It is within the grounds of Portumna Forest Park on the shore of Lough Derg.

14. Kylemore Abbey is a 19th century neo-Gothic mansion which is now a Benedictine boarding school. In structure the church is a miniature Gothic cathedral situated in a storybook setting. It is on N59 between Letterfrack and Leenane and is well signposted.

CASTLE/
HOUSES

15. Dan O'Hara Homestead site includes a megalithic tomb or dolmen with a huge capstone, a reconstruction of a prehistoric crannog (lake dwelling) from 1500BC, and the O'Hara farm. It is reached by N59 in the Twelve Pins area, Connemara.

16. Hill of Doon has a wonderful scenic view of the Lough Corrib and is reached by taking R345 between Maum and Corr na Mona. There are many scenic overlooks in this area.

17. Patrick Pearse's Cottage, Rosmuc, is a three-room thatched cottage on the shore of Lough Ariikagh which Patrick built to spend his summer holidays and devote time to the study of the Gaelic language. It is south of Gortmore by R336.

18. Leenane Cultural Center concentrates on the sheep and wool industry.

19. Coole Park is outside of Gort on the Galway road. The original house, the home of Lady Gregory, was demolished in 1950 but the park is now a National Forest and Wildlife Park. Lady Gregory was prominent in the founding of the Abbey Theatre as well as being a close friend of W. B. Yeats.

Aughrim Interpretive Center was the creation of Martin Joyce. He gathered the information through artifacts, letters and records to relate the story of the Battle of Aughrim. This is a comprehensive and intelligent rendering of the battle in a dramatic way.

IN MYTHOLOGY, this area was the site of battles and legend. It is believed that the Plain of Moytura, the site of two battles between the Fir Bolgs and the Tuatha De Daanan, was due east of Cong. The Marble Hill megalithic tombs are located west of Portumna.

Kerry

KERRY SITS to the southwest and is bordered by the Atlantic Ocean. There are fingers or peninsulas which reach out to the sea that are mountainous. Clouds and frequent precipitation hover about this area. The bays between are narrow and very picturesque. It has been inhabited by and served many: the ancient settlers, monks who wished solitude, and Vikings, English and Spanish who sought a port. The sea, moderate climate and mountains make this a hauntingly beautiful part of Ireland.

1. Ardfert Cathedral, Ardfert, is northwest of Tralee by R551. The earliest part of this structure is the west end with its Romanesque doorway and blind arcading which has been totally restored. Nearby is an Ogham stone and two other later small churches or temples. St. Brendon was born in Ardfert.

2. Rattoo Church and Round Tower is in Ballyduff which is west of Listowel.

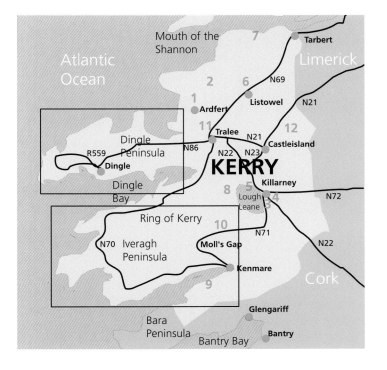

MONASTERIES *Franciscan*

3. Muckross Abbey, Killarney, is a well preserved ruin of a 15th century Franciscan friary with the long hall. There was a later addition of the tower halfway along its length and an exceptional cloister. The abbey is located off of the Muckross road within Killarney National Park. It is a delightful setting.

4. Inisfallen Abbey, Ross Island, has a Romanesque doorway. This is reached by pathway or boat from Ross Castle.

CASTLES *15th Century*

5. Ross Castle, Killarney National Park, has been totally restored. The castle includes a rectangular keep, crenellated parapets and garderobes. There is an exhibition center with an explanation of the structure. It is south of Killarney by N71, Ross Road to Knockreer Demesne and is on the shore of Lough Leane.

17th Century

6. Listowel Castle, Listowel, is in the center of town.

7. Carrigafoyle Castle is on the south shore of the River Shannon west of Tarbert. It was used during one of the civil wars in which the Irish and the Spanish held out against the English. Although it is a ruin, the structure and setting are interesting.

CASTLE/
HOUSE

3. Muckross House, Killarney, was built in the mid-19th century to entertain Queen Victoria. It was then bought by the Guinness brewing family and let out for hunting and fishing parties. Later an American purchased it as a wedding gift for his daughter. She died quite young after which the house and 11,000 acres were given to the Irish nation. There is a tour and a number of craft work areas. It is situated on the Killarney to Kenmare road.

GARDENS

3. Muckross Gardens are on the grounds of Muckross House.

8. Hotel Dunloe Castle Gardens, Beaufort, is on a side road. Take R562 west from Killarney.

9. Derreen Gardens, Lauragh, are a subtropical jungle encompassing the 90 acre peninsula near Kenmare and north of Lauragh. There are a vast variety of plants and vistas of mountains and the sea. Take R571 west from Kenmare to Lauragh.

10. Killarney National Park scenic drives include magnificent views of the three lakes, Moll's Gap and the Torc Waterfall. There is an information center where the flora and fauna of the area are described.

11. Kerry the Kingdom, Tralee, portrays the history of Kerry.

12. Crag Cave is located northeast of Castleisland.

The Dingle Peninsula

THE DINGLE PENINSULA is one of great beauty. The active seaport of Dingle coupled with the Gaelic influence and agricultural scenery has made travel in Dingle a real delight. There are preserved Iron Age forts as well as many early Christian monuments. The peak of Mount Brandon was a destination for pilgrims, and it is thought that the many beehive huts may have been used by them en route to the peak. Offshore are the Blaskett Islands. The land is often shrouded in cloud and fog which lends a haunting beauty to the verdant green fields. In following R559 west of Dingle and making the circle the following sights are found en route.

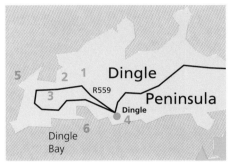

1. Gallerus Oratory of the 9th century is an excellent example of a corbelled roof and looks like an upside down boat made entirely of stone. The doorway has a double lintel above from which two stones project and each is pierced with a round hole suggesting that the entrance may have had a wooden door. It is reached by the ring road on the Dingle Peninsula and should be signposted.

2. Reask Stone, 8th to 10th century, has an etched design and cross marking an early monastic site. It is near the ring road.

3. Kilmalkedar Church, Dingle, is 12th century Romanesque in design. There are Ogham 'alphabet' stones in the area. It is by dirt road from the ring road and very difficult to find.

4. Beehive huts of great number and in excellent repair and **Dunbeg Fort** are on the south side of the peninsula beside the ring road. The stone walls were thick and typically on the edge of the cliff, so much has already been eroded into the sea.

5. Blaskett Island Interpretive Center, Dunquin, is where the essence of the Gaelic language, art and culture of the islands is beautifully demonstrated. From nearby Slea Head there is a view of the islands that is well worth the trek to the top. The Blaskett Islands are no longer inhabited and the ecology is being preserved.

6. Ogham Stones are also found on the small peninsula southwest of Dingle Harbor.

Ring of Kerry

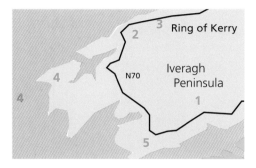

THE RING OF KERRY is the road, N70, which follows the coast of the Iveragh Peninsula. The area is mountainous and there are wonderful 'gaps' through the mountains. There are also monuments from Ancient Ireland and the monastic era of Christianity.

1. Staigue Fort is in the hills by a narrow side road (well worth the detour) north of Castlecove, N70.

2. Cahergall Fort, a large stone fort, has drystone buildings, a beehive hut and other interesting features. It is north of Cahersiveen.

3. Leacanabuaile Fort, 3 miles from Cahersiveen, is from the 9th or 10th century and includes four clay huts and two chambers on the terraced rampart.

4. Skellig Islands are 9 miles from shore. At Valentia Island is an exhibit, Skellig Experience, which includes an audiovisual presentation on early monasticism. This island monastery was founded in the 7th century by St. Finian and dedicated to St. Michael, the patron saint of high places. It rests on a terrace 600 feet above sea level. The ruins contain the church, two oratories and six beehive cells which use the corbel principle in building. In these huts a handful of monks lived their lonely existence. The oratories are rectangular in floor plan and have a small window and low doorway.[36] The access to Valentia Island is by road from Portmagee from N70 to R565. There is also a day trip by boat from Knightstown Harbor. Due to erosion and the importance of this archeological site, landing on the island is restricted.

5. Derrynane National Historic Park, Caherdaniel, is the ancestral home of Daniel O'Connell, an important figure in Irish history. It is now a museum. The present house was planned by him in the early 19th century.

Kildare

COUNTY KILDARE is located in the province of Leinster just west of County Dublin. Much of the land is farmland. The Grand and Royal Canals pass through and the Rivers Liffey and Barrow are also significant waterways. The Bog of Allen limited the use of the land although the Curragh has nurtured famous horse breeding farms.

There are monuments of Ancient Ireland here as well as many early Christian ruins. Many castles were built during the Norman times and by the 16th and 17th centuries it was within The Pale. The Kildares controlled the government in Dublin during this period.

1. Punchestown Standing Stone is dated from the Bronze Age and is 20 feet tall. It is located southeast of Naas by R411.

2. Ardscull Motte is 4 miles from Athy, N78.

Meath
N6
N4
Royal Canal
N3
Maynooth
6
KILDARE 9 8 Celbridge
N4
14
Grand Canal
Bog of Allen
11
Tullamore
R.Lifey
15
Offaly
Grand Canal
12 N7
16
Dublin
7
Naas
1
5 Newbridge
Emo Court
Kildare
Blessington
10 13
N9
N7 Tully
Reservoir
The Curragh N8
Portlaoise
2
4 Wicklow
Athy
Moone N81
Laois
N9
River Barrow
3
Baltinglas
Carlow
Carlow

3. Castledermot includes the monastic remains of two 9th century granite high crosses with scenes from both the Old and New Testaments. The depiction of the crucifixion and Adam and Eve are both clearly seen. The base on which the cross rests has the typical early spiral designs. This was an isolated hermitage of St. Dermot and his grave is thought to be marked by "a hump-backed cross-decorated stone unique to Ireland."[37] Nearby is a later round tower and Romanesque door fragment. There is also evidence of a Franciscan friary.

4. Moone Cross (see p. 85) is a hidden treasure. You must go over a stile and through a field to find the cross within the walls of a church ruin. It was moved here to protect the sculpture from the weather. It is off of N9 and northeast of Carlow town. It is sign-posted but the signs are not conspicuous.

5. Kildare Cathedral, Kildare is under ongoing reconstruction incorporating portions of the 13th century structure. A special feature is the 16th century burial tomb with an effigy of Bishop Wellesley.

13th Century

6. Maynooth Castle consists only of a keep from the original castle which was built by Gerald Fitzmaurice, an Anglo-Norman knight. In the 15th and 16th centuries, there was a magnificent library of manuscripts here. Maynooth is west of Dublin by N4 and the keep is at the entrance of St. Patrick's College, which is south of N4 by R405.

17th Century

7. Jigginstown House, Naas, is a 17th century, never-finished brick palace of great dimension. According to deBreffny and ffolliott, it was built for Charles 1, who never came to Ireland. It is located on the outskirts of Naas by R446.

8. Castletown House (see p. 127), Celbridge, is reached by R403 and a tour of this grand house is worthwhile.

9. The saloon at Carton House* has some wonderful stucco.

10. Moore Abbey, Monastervin, is an enormous fifteen-bay Gothic revival house which was built in the 18th century. It is a modification of the Palladian style and now a hospital of the Sisters of Charity.

11. Lodge Park Walled Garden,* Straffan, is divided into sections and was a working garden for the house, which included fruit, vegetables and flowers.

12. Coolcarrigan Gardens,* Naas, continues to be developed. There are wonderful rhododendrons and azaleas with a myriad of spring bulbs, Victorian greenhouses, lawns, a wooded area and a lake. It is reached by R407 toward Clane.

13. Tully Japanese Gardens, Tully, is on the grounds of the Irish National Stud south of Kildare by R415.

13. Irish National Stud, Tully, is south of Kildare by R415. This area, called The Curragh, is famous for the breeding of horses. The lands belonged to the Sarsfields, of Siege of Limerick fame, until 1900 when they were sold. Horse breeding was successfully introduced and it became the British National Stud Company. In 1943 it was given to the Irish government and is now the Irish National Stud Company. This is a MUST. The grounds are beautiful and meticulously maintained while the breeding of excellent horses continues. Special features are the Sun Chariot Yard, Foaling Unit and Stallion Boxes.

Stallion boxes at the Irish National Stud

14. Celbridge Abbey Grounds, Celbridge, were planted by Vanessa, daughter of the Lord Mayor of Dublin, for Jonathan Swift.

15. Lullymore Peat Center is located in the midst of the Bog of Allen by R414 west of Roberstown.

16. The Hill of Allen is a good place to view the Bog of Allen and is reached by R145 north of Kildare.

THE HILL of Allen was the site of the famous fortress of the Fianna at Almu, and the Fenian, or Ossianic, Cycle was enacted here.

*Indicates limited access or access by appointment

Kilkenny

T HE COUNTY of Kilkenny is in the province of Leinster. The area is excellent for agriculture with three major rivers and a mild climate. The area has long been inhabited by the Irish, the Anglo-Normans and early monastic Christians.

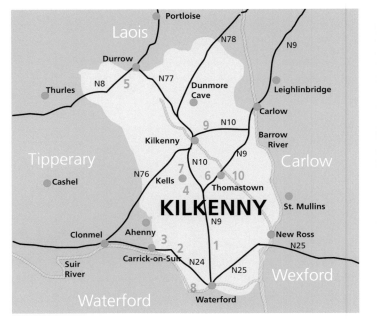

<table>
<tr><td>STONE AGE</td><td>

1. Kilmogue Megalithic Tombs, Harristown, is one of the largest dolmens. It is located northwest of Mullinvar by N9 on the Waterford to Kilkenny road.

2. Knockroe Portal Tomb has decorated stones, and on the day of the Winter Solstice, the setting sun reaches the horizon in a direct line with the passage.

</td></tr>
</table>

STONE AGE

1. Kilmogue Megalithic Tombs, Harristown, is one of the largest dolmens. It is located northwest of Mullinvar by N9 on the Waterford to Kilkenny road.

2. Knockroe Portal Tomb has decorated stones, and on the day of the Winter Solstice, the setting sun reaches the horizon in a direct line with the passage.

EARLY
CHRISTIAN

3. Kilkieran High Crosses stand alone with no written history to explain which monastery they were associated with. The surfaces are decorated with closely meshed interlacing ornaments, panels with spirals and animals and large rounded studs or bosses. It is reached by back roads and perseverance and R694 north of Carrick-on-Suir.

4. Kilree Round Tower and **Crosses** are located due south of Kells.

5. *Ferlagh Round Tower* is located by N8 on the Johnstown to Durrow road.

MONASTERIES

Cistercian

6. *Jerpoint Abbey* is a classic representative of a 12th century Cistercian abbey. The remains of the wall divide the nave into two parts, one for the monks and the other for the lay brothers. There are stout Romanesque pillars in the cloister which are decorated with secular and religious sculpture. This is a Dúchas site with excellent guides and literature. Typically, the tower and a murder hole over the entrance to discourage unwelcome visitors or enemies were added later. It is reached by the Waterford to Carlow road, N9, and is near Thomastown.

Augustinian

7. *Kells Priory* is a fortified priory with tall well-preserved walls interspersed with defensive towers. The church is not well-preserved although there are some interesting features such as the stone waterways. It is on the Callan to Stonyford road.

Norman

CASTLES

8. *Granagh (Granny) Castle* is a 12th century castle on the banks of Carrick-on-Suir south of Kilmacow. It has three round turrets and part of the curtain wall rising out of the river.

13th Century

Kilkenny Castle (see p. 226), Kilkenny

16th Century

9. *Clara Castle* is a well-preserved tower house of the 16th century. It may not be open to the public, but inquiries can be made. It is north of N10 and about five miles east northeast of Kilkenny.

17th Century

Rothe House (see p. 226), Kilkenny

10. *Mount Juliet,* Thomastown, is now a hotel with access only to hotel guests. The stucco work done by provincial stuccodores is rich in detail.

CASTLE/ HOUSES

10. *Mount Juliet Gardens,* Thomastown, has an 18th century park land, walled gardens, lawns and rose garden. Admission upon request.

GARDENS

10. Kilfane Glen and Waterfall, Thomastown, is a woodland garden.

11. Dunmore Cave is signposted on N72, north of Kilkenny.

KILKENNY WAS the ancient capital of the kingdom of Ossory. There are many buildings which reflect the various phases through which it has passed. In the middle of the 17th century, the Confederations of Kilkenny, representing the native Irish and the Catholic Anglo-Normans, installed an independent Irish parliament. Cromwell's forces attacked and they surrendered.

- **Black Abbey,** founded in the 13th century, is a medieval Franciscan church which is still in use.

- **St. John's Priory** is 13th century with excellent mullioned windows.

- **Kilkenny Castle** stands on the banks of the Nore River and had been a residence since the 13th century. It was presented to the nation in 1967. The first fort, which was destroyed, was built by Strongbow, an early Anglo-Norman Earl of Pembroke. Then a four-sided stone castle with towers at each corner was erected by his successor, William Marshall, from which three towers remain. It became quite elegant during a period of prosperity in the late 17th century, when it was modified to a chateau. In the 19th century it was rebuilt into a great country house in its present form.

- **Rothe House** is a stone house which was built at the end of the 16th century by a prosperous local Irish Catholic merchant. As his family grew to include twelve children, he added two more houses with courtyards. Peter Rothe, who inherited the house from his father, was among those transported to Connaught by Cromwell.

- **Cityscope** or **Shee's Almshouse** is a stone house built at the end of the 16th century by Sir Richard Shee that remained in the ownership of the family for over three centuries. In the late 19th century it was used by the Ladies' Charitable Association and now houses the Cityscope exhibition of 17th-century Kilkenny.

Effigy of Piers Butler and his wife Margaret

- **St. Canice's Cathedral** is thought to be built on the site of the 6th century monastery founded here by St. Canice. The present building, 13th century Gothic, has been restored several times and is under restoration now. There are some interesting tombs, for example, the effigies of Piers Butler and his wife Margaret. The Round Tower has wooden steps which may possibly be climbed to give a wonderful view of the surrounding area.

L AOIS COUNTY is south of the Slieve Bloom mountains. Nearly all of the total surface was covered by blanket bog. Four-fifths is improved land where the peat has been harvested. The Rivers Barrow and Nore provide rich river valleys. Historical monuments date from the Christian era.

1. *Killeshin Church* has a 12th century Irish-Romanesque west doorway made of red sandstone. Both bearded and clean-shaven human heads with hair blossoming out into foliage or animals decorate the doorway. The arches are carved with zigzag, floral, animal and cross-diaper patterns. There is a bearded head at the top of the outermost arch.[38] Located by R430, on the Carlow to Abbeyleix road.

2. *Timahoe Round Tower,* Timahoe, is nearly 30 meters tall and includes a rebuilt conical cap. The Romanesque-style doorway dates the tower to the 12th century. The doorway, 5 meters above the ground, stands out in relief from the wall surface and is decorated with the typical bearded heads and capitals. Close to the tower are the remains of a large early church.[39] It is southwest of Portlaoise by R426.

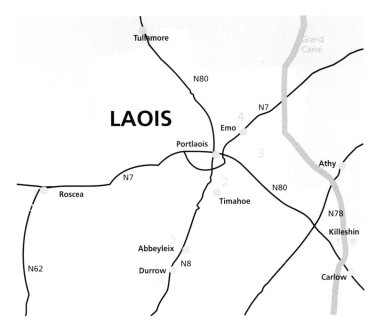

CASTLES

3. Rock of Dunamase rises up over the surrounding country and is topped with the ruins of a clan fortress which is now under restoration. It is north of N80 on the Portlaoise to Carlow road. Although it can be seen from the road, access by tertiary roads can be tricky.

CASTLE/
HOUSES

4. Emo Court and Gardens, Emo, is an elegant 19th century house which is open by appointment. It is in the classical style which includes, among other features, a dome, portico, columns and balustrade. The gardens are open daily. It is on R422 north of N7 on the Portlaoise to Kildare road.

Emo Court

GARDENS

5. Abbey Leix Gardens, Abbeyleix, are on the Abbeyleix to Durrow road.

6. Heywood Gardens, Ballinakill, is an 18th century park situated south of Abbeyleix.

Leitrim

L EITRIM is in the province of Connaught. The southern part has many small lakes and is bordered on the west by the Shannon River. Through this area is the Shannon-Erne waterway which is excellent for cruising. The lakes and streams also offer good sport fishing. North of Lough Allen are plateaus divided by deep valleys.

This was the stronghold of the ancient kingdom of Breifne, the county of the O'Rourkes.

Carrick-on-Shannon is the center for the Shannon Navigation, the system of locks for the inland waterways. The land is only suitable for pasture. A new waterway links the Shannon with Lough Erne. With the great expanse of dangerous bogs, waterways were the early means of transportation, communication and settlements.

1. *Tullyskecherny Megalithic Tombs* are south of Manorhamilton on back roads. STONE AGE

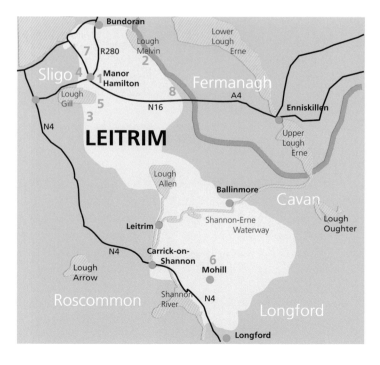

2. *Black Pig's Dyke* is the evidence of an ancient earthwork boundary separating Ulster and Connacht. It runs by R281 between Rossinver and Killyclopher.

3. *Creevelea Abbey,* Dromahair, was founded in the 16th century. There are interesting carved pillars of St. Francis. Take R287, as it is just southeast of Lough Gill.

Parke's Castle

16th Century

4. *Parke's Castle,* Fivemile Bourne, is located on the northern shore of Lough Gill. This is a restored planter's house. The foundation of an original Irish tower house was unearthed during the restoration. Planter Robert Parker started with a small tower that is now the entrance. He lost possession temporarily during the Cromwellian wars, after which he enlarged the dwelling.

17th Century

5. *Hamilton Castle* consists of ruins located east of Lough Gill.

6. *Lough Rynn Estate and Gardens* are located west of Mohill on N4. This 19th century house is the site of much Irish lore which includes a Druid's Hill, a neolithic burial mound and on the lake shore the ruin of a 16th century castle, Reynolds Castle. There are ornamental gardens and nature trails.

7. *Glencar Waterfall* is located on N16 northwest of Sligo just after you pass into Co. Leitrim.

8. *Laghty Barr,* Glenfarne, is also known as Sean MacDermott Cottage. He was one of the signatories of the Proclamation of the Irish Republic. He died at the hands of a firing squad. This thatched farmhouse was his birthplace.

COUNTY LIMERICK is in the province of Munster. It is bounded on the north by the Shannon River. The eastern portion is in the Golden Vale which is renowned for its rich pastures and dairy products. To the south are rolling hills and the peat bogs of yore. There are many ancient and early Christian monuments.

1. Great Stone Circle is due south of Limerick by R512. It is not that easy to find as there are many roads that are not on the map or signposted.

STONE AGE

1. Lough Gur Interpretive Center is due south of Limerick by R512. The center has information and the buildings are in the style of the early dwellings. Many of the sites are in the surrounding area and are not only in cow pastures but are difficult to find. There is no commercial tourism in this area.

ANCIENT IRELAND

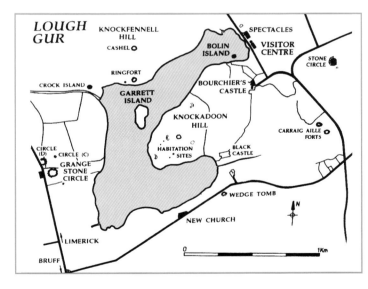

Photograph of site marker

2. Killuta Oratory is located along N69 between Kildimo and Askeaton.

EARLY CHRISTIAN

3. Clonkeen Church is a small, typical 12th century Irish-Romanesque church. The doorway has a hood with incised decoration of chevrons, beads, dentils and animal heads at each end. Carved heads also decorate the top of the arch. The arch is supported by almost full octagonal pillars with bulbous capitals and decorated, square bases. There is a 12th century round-headed window.[40] It is near R506 which goes south from N7 several miles east of Limerick City.

Cistercian

4. Monasteranenagh Abbey, Monaster, is south of Limerick near Holy Cross and Croom on back roads beside the River Camoge. It is not an easy find but worth the time. There are the ruins of a 13th century Cistercian abbey. It is in the transitional style with the pointed arches although one set of windows is totally Romanesque.

Dominican

5. Kilmallock Dominican Friary, Kilmallock, is a well-preserved ruin in a field with some spectacular windows. The collegiate church is near the friary and its tower is part of an ancient round tower. It is reached by a path from the main road at Blossom's Gate, the last of the five gates which gave access to the medieval town of Kilmallock.

Franciscan

6. Askeaton Friary, Askeaton, is a 14th or 15th century Franciscan ruin with a well preserved cloister showing a carving of St. Francis with the stigmata. It is located north of Askeaton by N69.

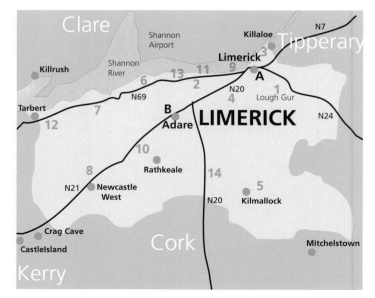

7. Shamid Castle is located off of R521, on the Foynes to Ardagh road. These are the meager remains of an early Norman fortress with a polygonal keep and a curtain wall. **King John's Castle,** Limerick (see p. 234), is described in the section on the City of Limerick.

13th Century

8. Desmond Banquet Hall, Newcastle West, has been restored. This castle was square in shape with a round tower at each corner and included a peel tower and probably two halls. The two halls, peel tower and a part of the curtain wall are all that now survive. There were three Desmond castles so this is often referred to as Newcastle West or the Desmond Banquet Hall. It is southwest of Limerick by N21.

14th Century

9. Carrigogunnell Castle, Mungret, has the remains of a large 14th century fortress. The interior structure is exposed so that the arch of the third level, which became the floor of the fourth level, is very visible. It is located north of N69, Limerick to Askeaton road, by a side road. The castle is surrounded by some water and marsh but is no longer on the Shannon River.

15th Century

6. Askeaton Castle, Askeaton, sits on the bank of the river near the bridge in the town. It is not open nor is it under restoration at the present time. Although it is a go-by, it is one of three Desmond castles in this area. It can be confusing.

10. Castle Matrix, Rathkeale, is a 15th century Norman tower house which has long been associated with literature. The first owner was one of the earliest Norman poets who wrote in the Irish language. It is now a residence, contains a literary collection and is open for tours and tea. There was once a mill complex here.

11. Dromore Castle, Dromore, stands like an ancient ruin. It appears as a very distant story book silhouette on a hilltop on the south shore of the Shannon River west of Limerick. This 19th century ruin has an interesting history. It was built by the Earl of Limerick, who was without a grand Irish estate.

The 3rd earl was a colorful figure whose mistress was a famous actress and they were acquainted with many artists and aesthetes, among whom were Whistler and Oscar Wilde. The walls were six feet thick with a batter (outward sloping walls). Guards were posted at the entrances, not only to protect against the political unrest of the times, but also because the earl was not a beloved landlord. Since dampness remained an insurmountable problem, the house was inhabited only until 1950, at which time the interior was demolished and sold.[41] It is not open to the public but the towers are visible from the back roads from the north. It is not easy to find as there is not a close-up view. Hopefully access to the grounds will be allowed in the future.

12. Glin Castle and **Pleasure Ground** and **Walled Gardens** comprise a Georgian house which was made Gothic in the 18th century. There is an interesting collection of Irish furniture and the interior contains elaborate plaster work. It is available for hire. It is located on N69 between Tarbert and Foynes.

GARDENS

13. Ballynacourty Garden,* Ballysteen, is a garden that was designed with care and attention to detail. It is at its best in May and June.

OTHER
SITES

14. De Valera's Cottage, Bruree, is a 19th century cottage built by local authorities to house laborers and farm workers and it was here that Eamon grew up.

MYTHOLOGY

LIMERICK was the site of many battles of both the Tuatha De Danaan and the Milesians. Cormac MacAirt also fought battles here, and there is evidence of ancient Irish forts. The town of Adare was once an early 11th century religious center.

A. *Limerick City*

LIMERICK CITY was founded by the Vikings. Its strategic location at the mouth of the River Shannon has made it important historically. The Normans conquered Limerick and built many castles and extensive walls. During the 17th century it suffered much damage and was the site of the great siege of Limerick. Of interest there is the Treaty Stone which sits on the river bank opposite King John's Norman Castle.

*Indicates limited
access or access
by appointment

- **St. Mary's Cathedral** contains some early romanesque features which constitute the oldest surviving structure in Limerick. It was founded in the 12th century and is in the transitional Romanesque style. These old features are not prominent, but they are there.
- **King John's Castle,** 1200–1212, is on the banks of the River Shannon at the Thomond Bridge. It is a typical Norman fortification in design and played an important part in the siege of Limerick against William III of England. It is well restored and there is an interpretive center within the castle.

B. *Adare*

ADARE's original settlement here was built in the 11th century. The Anglo-Normans settled here after which the Earls of Kildare acquired the land. The town you visit today was built in the 19th century.

- **The Church of the Most Holy Trinity** was once a Trinitarian abbey. The monks became victims of the Dissolution of the Monasteries. All that remains of the 13th century abbey are a tower, nave and part of the original choir. These ruins were restored and enlarged in the 19th century to the building you now see.
- **The Adare Parish Church** includes the remains of an Augustinian priory of the 14th century. The nave, tower and part of the choir are part of the now restored church.
- **Adare Friary** is a 15th century ruin that was founded by the Earl of Kildare.
- **Adare Manor,** Adare, was a 19th century Neolithic limestone mansion which is now a luxury hotel with lovely grounds.

Chapel by Desmond Castle

- **Desmond Castle** is reached by way of the Adare Golf Course and a large restoration is in progress. It consists of a large square tower on the Maigre River. There is a lovely church ruin in this setting. This is also known as Adare Castle and was first built in the 13th century. Since these are on the grounds of the hotel and golf course, the grounds are exquisitely maintained and picturesque. There are views of the castle walls on the edge of the river, covered with ivy and flowering vines, a chapel with a Romanesque doorway as well as the castle towerhouse and bawn walls.

Longford

Longford is located in central Ireland and is part of the province of Leinster. It borders on Lough Ree and the River Shannon as well as other rivers and loughs in the western part of the county. The land has many bogs and some of the meadowlands are flooded in the spring.

The Royal Canal passes through Longford and there are some charming villages along this route. Cloondara, for example, is at the junction of the Royal Canal and the River Shannon. It is not only picturesque but it includes a canal basin, two locks, a bridge, a water mill and some ruins.

ANCIENT IRELAND

1. Granard Motte, Granard, appears as a large mound of earth. It was erected by the Norman invaders at the end of the 12th century to establish a base from which to hold and protect the land which had been won by the sword. The mound was flat and topped with a wooden tower which was probably used as a lookout. Attached to this was a flat, half-moon-shaped area or bailey, which was defended by a bank and ditch. Mottes were not only for defense but also for living and contained cattle and residential wooden buildings. It is southwest of the town on unmarked tertiary roads.

CASTLE/ HOUSES

2. Carrigglas Manor is a 19th century castellated Tudor Revival house with the appearance and setting for a romantic 19th century novel. While this is Oliver Goldsmith country, the son of the manor was a 'friend' of Jane Austen and thought to be the model for Mr. Darcy in *Pride and Prejudice*. The interior has been well restored with plasterwork ceilings. The stable yard was designed

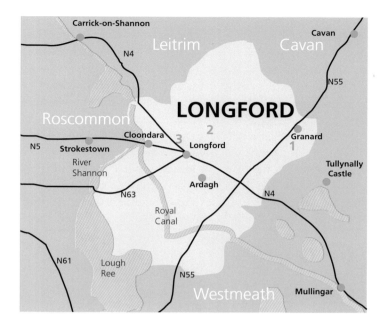

by James Gandon, who was the architect for the Four Courts and the Custom House in Dublin.[42] It is reached from Longford on R194, the Ballinalee to Granard road.

3. St Mel's Cathedral, Dublin Street, Longford City, is a 19th century Italian Renaissance structure which resembles a Greek temple. It is surmounted by a tall domed belfry. The interior has a double row of Ionic columns.

OTHER SITES

ARDAGH, which is southeast of the city of Longford, is the ancient site of the mound Bri Leith where Midir, a lesser god of the Tuatha De Danaan, lived among the people of the mounds. This is the the Midir of the "Wooing of Etain" and this sid, burial mound, fairy hill or hill of the ancient spirits, was his possession after their defeat by the Milesians.

MYTHOLOGY

237

Louth

COUNTY LOUTH is located in the northeast of Ireland and is bound on the north by Northern Ireland and the east by the Irish Sea. It is mostly lowland except for the mountain range in the Carlingford Peninsula where there is some delightful scenery.

It is through here that the early Christians on the island of Iona fled from the Vikings and here that the prestigious monasteries of Mellifont and Monasterboice were founded.

Drogheda, located in the estuary of the River Boyne, was founded by the Norse and developed into a defensive stronghold by the Anglo-Norman DeLacy in the 12th century. The original town walls have been destroyed as it has been under siege twice. Much of the population was massacred or deported by Cromwell. It also played a role in the Battle of the Boyne.

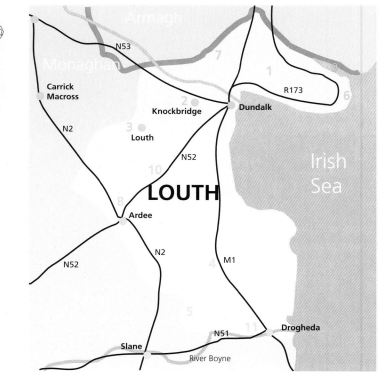

1. *Proleek Dolmen* is located from R173 on the golf course of the Ballymascanlon Hotel. They will direct you to the site. Nearby is a wedge-shaped gallery grave.

2. A large ***standing stone*** in Knockbridge, which is on R171 between Louth and Dundalk, is the one to which Cuchulainn tied himself during his last battle. "Wishing to die standing up 'feet on the ground and facing the foe'…at first his enemies were afraid to approach. But, then seeing a bird settle on his shoulder and pecking at his eyes, they realized that Cuchulainn must be dead".[43]

3. *St. Mochta's House,* Louth, is a 10th century stone oratory with a corbelled roof which has a room between the barrel-vaulted ceiling and the roof. This room was typical and was used by the monks.

4. The three ***Scriptural Crosses*** at ***Monasterboice*** make this an important site. Although there once stood a great monastery here, the crosses, round tower and shell of a church are all that remain. It is north of Drogheda and west of N1 by secondary roads.

5. Old ***Mellifont Abbey*** was the first Cistercian foundation in Ireland. The original was replaced by a huge Gothic structure, now destroyed. You can see the foundation stones of the buildings as well as the lavabo which has retained the round arches. There is a new and active Mellifont Abbey which should not be confused with the ruins of this earlier structure, which is east of N2 between Slane and Collon and back roads.

Norman

6. King John's Castle, Carlingford, is a 13th century Norman castle standing on a bluff on the north side of the harbor of Carlingford Lough. The road passes underneath the castle entrance.

Castleroche

14th Century

7. Castleroche was built in the 14th century to defend the de Verdon lands, and later became an outpost of the Pale. According to legend, the daughter of de Verdon "promised to marry the architect if she liked the completed building, but when he came to claim her, she had him flung out of a window instead...."[44] It is located near R177 northwest of Dundalk. This ruin on a rocky outcrop is a wonderful example of a Norman-style castle.

15th Century

8. Ardee Castle, Ardee, was an early 13th century structure although the additions and restorations are of the 15th century.

9. Taafe's Castle, Carlingford, is of the 15th century overlooking the harbor with a square tower fortified with machicolations, crenellations, arrow slits and murder holes.

10. Roodstown Castle is a 15th century tower house and is located by the road north of Ardee, N52.

17th Century

11. Beaulieu House is located on the River Boyne near Drogheda and is open by appointment only. It is an excellent example of classical architecture.

MYTHOLOGY

COUNTY LOUTH is located between the two great ancient capitals of Navan Fort, Armagh, and Tara and was the site of many ancient battles. It is here where Cuchulainn died after his battle with Fer Diad. Near death, but wishing to die standing, he tied himself to a pillar stone which can be seen at Knockbridge.

Mayo

MAYO IS WITHIN the province of Connaught in western Ireland. The coastal region, which borders the Atlantic Ocean, is wild and broken with many cliffs. There are many rivers and lakes with the largest expanse of bog in Ireland. Near Bangor in the northwest there is a peat-powered generating station.

The area has many Neolithic monuments and was significant in early Christianity with St. Patrick's presence. There are many monastic ruins and few castles.

1. The Ceide Fields, Ballycastle, are reached by R314 on the Ballycastle to Belmullet road.

STONE AGE

2. Carbad More Court Tomb is a double court cairn located off R314, near the Carrowmore to Kilcummin road.

3. Doonamo Fort is a stone fort on top of cliffs overlooking the Atlantic Ocean off R313 and west of Benmullet. This is a rugged and beautiful coast.

ANCIENT IRELAND

Atlantic Ocean

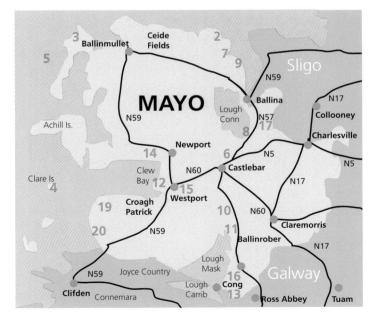

4. Clare Island includes the ruins of St. Bridget's Church as well as a castle that is purported to be where the famous Grace O'Malley is buried.

5. Inishglora Island contains 5th century monastic ruins. This is a small island off the coast of Mullet Peninsula and is ideal for those with great curiosity and a sense of adventure, weather permitting. It was founded by St. Brendan, a seafaring monk who set sail with thirteen others and discovered the New World. Inquiries may be made in Belmullet for transport by boat.

6. Turlough Round Tower is located by N5 on the Castlebar to Swinford road.

MONASTERIES   *Franciscan*

7. Moyne Franciscan Abbey was built in the 15th century although the six-story narrow tower was added later. Leave Ballina by R314 and take a back road east just short of Killala. There is a short walk though a cow pasture. The road which connects Rosserk Abbey and Moyne Abbey is called the Western Way.

8. Strade Franciscan Friary, later Dominican, is 13th century with a 15th century tomb front which is intricately and finely carved. It is located by N58 on the Castlebar to Foxford road.

9. Rosserk Franciscan Friary is often photographed as it is situated on the shore of Killala Bay. There is a piscina through which the water was poured after the celebration of Mass. It has two eye-like openings which give a view to the sea outside. There are some interesting carvings which should not be missed. Leave Ballina by R314 and take a back road east.

Augustinian

10. Ballintubber Abbey is a 13th century Augustinian house still in use. It is the only royal abbey in Ireland to maintain continuous use. Restoration is in progress as are plans to excavate a buried ancient boat. The nave is original and there are some delightful carvings on the arches. The guides are enthusiastic, informative and very proud with interesting tales of its history and efforts of preservation. It is located east of N84 near Newtown.

11. Burriscarra Abbey built in the 13th century is located south of Ballintubber by back roads on the shore of Lough Carra.

12. Murrisk Abbey is an Augustinian friary of the 15th century which was founded by the O'Malleys. The ruins of this crenellated church are located by R335 on the Westport to Louisburgh road. It sits on the shore of Murrisk Peninsula.

13. Cong Abbey, Cong, was a 12th century Augustinian monastery of which only the chancel remains. Its importance is recognized by its possession of the Cross of Cong which was created to house the "first relic of the True Cross"[45] now in the National Museum of Ireland. The abbey is located where R345 and R346 join in Cong by the banks of the river. It is also near the exit of Ashford Castle.

Typical fortified early tower house

CASTLES

16th Century

14. Rockfleet Castle is also known as Carrigahowley. It is a 15th or 16th century tower house, a four-story structure with a corner turret. It is associated with Grace O'Malley and is off N58 on the north shore of Clew Bay and west of Newport.

CASTLE/HOUSES

15. Westport House, Westport, is an excellent example of the neo-classical style in architecture as well as having an interesting genealogy. This was the site of an ancient O'Malley castle (complete with the present-day dungeons) and was built by Colonel John Browne and his wife, who was a direct descendant of Grace O'Malley. He was a Jacobite in the siege of Limerick. The house had three different architects with three different styles. One is the typical Palladian central block facade with seven bays and some distinctive windows. Another is neoclassical with columns and pediment. The house is in good repair and there are many extras: model railway, dungeons, amusement arcade, secondhand book shop and a 'kiddies ball pond.'

16. Ashford Castle and Gardens, Cong, was a 19th century castle-style mansion which incorporated a 13th century tower house. It is in the style of a French chateau and is now a hotel. Access to the gardens and grounds is available at the main gate for a small fee.

OTHER SITES

17. Foxford Woolen Mill Visitor Center, Foxford, is located on N57 on the Swinford to Ballina road.

18. Croagh Patrick is south of R355 on the south shore of Clew Bay. A long climb to the top is a wondrous thing, offering a wonderful view of Clew Bay on a clear day. It has long been a pilgrimage site.

19. Folk and Heritage Center, Louisburgh, traces the history of the O'Malleys and particularly the famous Grace O'Malley. It is west of Westport by R335.

20. Bunlahinch Clapper Bridge is an ancient stone bridge of thirty-seven arches built by laying flat slabs on stone piles. It is southwest of Louisburgh by back roads.

MYTHOLOGY

MAG TUIRID is the Plain of Reckoning where the battles between the Fir Bolgs and the Tuatha De Danaan were fought. The Tuatha De Danaan were finally victorious. This site is thought to be either between Cong and Neale in County Mayo or west of Lough Arrow, Co. Sligo.

The Children of Lir began their journey in Westmeath (see p. 269). After 300 years they flew to the sea of Moyle, in the north channel between Ireland and Scotland, and remained for 300 years. There they met Ebric, who wrote down their story. They were at Inis Glora when 'the boundary which was put on their enchantment' came true. They turned back into human form (900 years old) when they heard the bells chiming in honor of God. They died as humans. And their graves are together at Inis Glora with that of Fionula, their sister, in the center.

T HE COUNTY of Meath is in the province of Leinster. It has rich agricultural areas and was therefore ideal for prehistoric settlements. The great gods of the Tuatha De Danaan are buried here which indicates that it was also a great ceremonial site. The seat of the Irish Kingship, the Hill of Tara, is also in Meath. The early Christians arrived here to convert the Irish and set up seats of learning.

The Anglo-Normans also settled here, building fortifications to protect their interests and putting Meath within the Pale. The waterway of the River Boyne was important for travel, trade and battle.

Passage Tombs exhibit a high degree of development in Neolithic culture. The area has many of these tombs. The one at Newgrange was the tomb of the kings and/or gods of the Tuatha De Danaan. The art which has been found on these stones is interesting and though the meaning of the different symbols is not known, they can be appreciated.

1. Newgrange and **Knowth** are accessed only through their Interpretive Center. The center is signposted on N1 south of Drogheda and on N2 east of Slane. Dowth is a protected area and is not open to the public at this time. It is located about one mile northeast of Newgrange.

2. Fourknocks is located on a small side road between Ardcath and Naul. (Naul is located at the intersection of R122 and R108.)

3. Loughcrew has some wonderful examples of Neolithic design and is a part of Sliabh na Caillighe or Witches Hill, which includes a group of thirty chambered cairns extending over three main peaks, Cairnebane and Cairnebane East and Patrickstown. The area is reached from R154. The Dúchas offers guided tours of the interior.

4. *Hill of Tailte* is the site of the Black Fort (Rath Dubh) where one of King Tuatha's four ancient residences stood. It is west of Kells.

5. *Hill of Tara* is reached by a tertiary road from N3 and is due east of Bective Abbey. The Stone of Destiny is in the center of the Forrad Royal Seat. A new publication, *Tara: an archeological survey*, has been released, which expands on previous knowledge and uses sophisticated technology. One important conclusion stresses the fact that each succeeding generation built upon the earlier structures – incorporating beliefs as well as construction. Imagination and knowledge are the best way to view this site – filling in the gaps with mythology. The view is spectacular.

Stone of Destiny

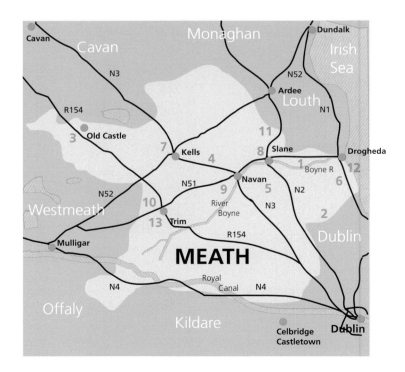

6. Duleek Monastic, which is the site of an early settlement, is located in the area of the intersection of R150 and R152.

7. Kells is famous for the Book of Kells which is now in the Library at Trinity College in Dublin. The monks from Iona sought refuge here when they fled from the Viking attack of 807. Here, the **Book of Kells,** an illuminated manuscript of the four gospels, was completed and from here stolen in 1007. It was found two months later without its gold ornament. It is fortunate that in the 11th century, gold was considered more valuable than this great manuscript. The monastery here was founded by St. Columb in the 6th century and was extensive. It suffered from raids by both the Vikings and the Irish and the reorganization of the church in the 13th century reduced the size and importance of this site. The **Cross of St. Patrick and St. Columba** in the churchyard of St. Columba's Anglican Church is badly weathered although Daniel in the Lions' Den, the Three Children in the Fiery Furnace, Cain and Abel and Adam and Eve are recognizable. A short distance from the church is **St. Columba's House** or **Oratory** with its corbelled roof. The key is easily obtained. The church is on Market Street in the town of Kells which is north of Navan R162. The guides at the church are most helpful.

8. Hill of Slane is located north of Slane by N2 and is the place where St. Patrick decided to spend Easter eve before going to Tara to convert the Irish king to Christianity. St. Patrick disregarded the law that no fire could be lit before the fire was lit at Tara. After his fire was seen by the king, he was summoned to Tara.

9. Bective Abbey, an early Cistercian abbey, is located near the Boyne River. Parts of the south arcade and transept, chapter house, part of the west wing of the domestic buildings and some of the doorways in the south wing are from the original structure. In the 15th century the building was fortified and many changes took place which include the cloister, the tower and the great hall in the south wing. Other changes occurred at a later period.[46] Although not a great deal of the original building remains, the differences in style make it an interesting exercise in deduction. It is on R161 due south of Navan and near the Boyne River.

10. St. Mary's Abbey, Trim, is across the river from Trim Castle and reached by a walking bridge. There is now only a tower to mark the site of an Augustinian community of the 12th century. There is a good view of the castle.

CASTLES

Norman

10. Trim Castle, Trim, is a 13th century Anglo-Norman castle located on the River Boyne. The walls originally enclosed three acres and was first a central keep with four projecting towers. From R161, there is an excellent view of this architecture, which is typical of the King John, or Norman, castles in Ireland during the 12th and 13th centuries. The D-shaped towers in the curtain wall, gatehouse and barbican were added later. The central keep is presently under restoration.

15th Century

10. Talbot's Castle is now a private home and is located next to St. Mary's Abbey. It once formed the west cloister of the abbey but was converted into a fortified house in 1425.

CASTLE/
HOUSES

11. Slane Castle, Slane, is presently closed due to a fire. Restoration is in progress. The wonderful stucco ceiling in the ballroom was not damaged. The castle is in the Gothic revival style and when restoration is complete, it should not be missed.

12. Annesbrook, Duleek, has a large Greek portico that is south of Duleek by R152.

GARDENS

13. Butterstream Gardens, Trim

Monaghan

MONAGHAN is one of the three counties belonging to the Republic of Ireland which make up the province of Ulster. The River Blackwater is its boundary abutting Northern Ireland. In the north is a plateau, in the west the river valley from Erne to Lough Neagh Basin. The south is hill country. The land is dominated by mounds, lakes and peat flats.

This was part of an ancient kingdom which was outside the Anglo-Norman influence until the 17th century. There are small farms for produce, cattle and dairying and the towns are market centers with monthly fairs. Fishing is excellent.

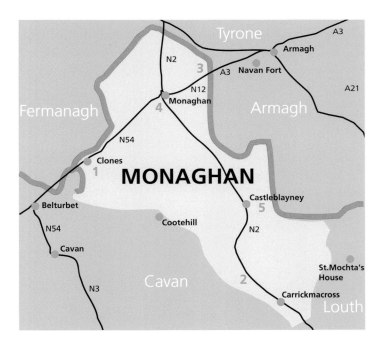

IN THE TOWN of Monaghan, there is a crannog on the lake within the grounds of St. Louis convent.

1. *Clones* was the site of a monastery founded by a local saint in 550 AD near the round tower. Nearby is a stone in the shape of a sarcophagus with a carved figure, decorated finials and hinges. This probably represents the original made of stone and wood for

ANCIENT
IRELAND

EARLY
CHRISTIAN

the reliquary of the founder. The high cross that stands in the Diamond at the center of the town is the shaft of one cross and the head of another. It displays scenes from the Old Testament and the New Testament. The cross is located on N54, the road from Monaghan to Belturbet.

CASTLES

13th Century

2. Mannan Castle was once a large motte and bailey which was encased in stone during the 13th century. It is less than 4 miles north of Carrickmacross.

CASTLE/
HOUSES

3. Castle Leslie and **Estate Gardens,** Glaslough, is of the 19th century with fine stucco work, Italian and Spanish furniture, Belgian tapestries and Persian carpets. There are also many unusual memorabilia from famous people such as Wellington's bridle, Napoleon's bed and Churchill's baby dress. There is also a ghost tour! The castle is north of Monaghan at Glaslough Village.

GARDENS

4. Rossmore Forest Park is an exceptional wooded area with rhododendrons, located south of Monaghan city by R189.

OTHER SITES

5. Lough Muckno Regional Park was once the grounds of Blaney Castle, or Hope Castle (after it was purchased by the owner of the Hope Diamond). It is a large wooded area with many nature trails.

THE WESTERN BOUNDARY of Offaly is the Shannon River. The land is primarily peat bogs which provide fuel for electrical power plants (see p. 30). Clara Bog is of international importance as it is one of the largest relatively intact bogs of its type in Ireland. Bogs, although an interesting area for birding, are soft and dangerous and access should be limited to approved tours.

1. Clonfinlough Stone has vertical striations which are natural to the stone while the semicircular markings are man-made. The significance, if any, of using the striations as part of the design is not known. The boulder is located in a field about two miles east of Clonmacnoise by back roads.

ANCIENT IRELAND

2. Clonmacnoise has a high cross of the scriptural type. Within the confines of the monastic walls are replicas of the original crosses which are now located within the center to preserve them from deterioration and weathering. This site includes ruins of chapels and churches destroyed after the Dissolution of the Monasteries in the mid-16th century. The site is dealt with in the

EARLY CHRISTIAN

OFFALY

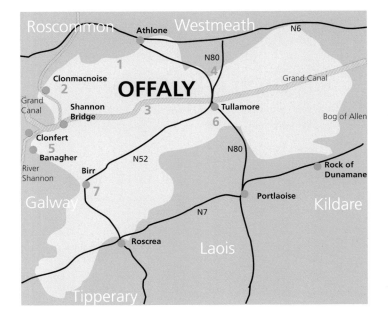

text and should not be missed. It is located on the River Shannon and reached by going north on R444 from Shannonbridge.

The Nun's Chapel near Clonmacnoise has an excellent example of an Irish-Romanesque doorway.

3. Gallen Priory and **Grave Slabs** mark the site of a monastery founded in the 5th century. The grave slabs are from 8th to 11th centuries and are located off of N62 between Cloghan and Ferbane.

4. Durrow High Cross, from the 10th century, includes the typical scenes from the Old and New Testaments. It is the site of an early monastery where the **Book of Durrow,** now in the Library at Trinity College, Dublin, was produced. This book is very important in the history of medieval art. The Durrow high cross and other grave slabs are located north of Durrow by N52. There is a short walk to the signposted site.

CASTLES

17th Century

5. Cloghan Castle, near Banagher, is a restoration of an earlier structure.

CASTLE/
HOUSES

6. Charleville Forest Castle, Tullamore, is "the finest and most spectacular early 19th century castle in Ireland, and the Gothic masterpiece of Francis Johnston."[47] It is located just south of Tullamore on the road to Birr. It has been acquired by the Charleville Heritage Trust and is being restored. This is a joint venture with the Quest Campus Foundation, which is in the process of developing an international interuniversity campus. The participants living there are delighted to offer a tour.

GARDENS

7. Birr Castle Demesne is located in Birr on the grounds of the castle. The formal and informal areas are nicely integrated and there is a small museum with a telescope which was once the largest in the world. The castle is available for hire.

OTHER SITES

The **Grand Canal** passes through Offaly from east to west, traveling through the Bog of Allen to Tullamore and through six locks. There are several aqueducts which carry your boat over some small rivers and under some humpbacked bridges. Sites along the way include fortified houses, church ruins and wonderful countryside.

The Bog of Allen on the border with Kildare is perhaps best seen from the Grand Canal.

Shannon Harbor is at the junction of the Shannon River and the Grand Canal.

The **Bog Rail Tour** from Shannonbridge offers an opportunity to see the Blackwater Bog and watch the peat being harvested by the Bord na Mona. This area supplies the electricity for the area. One tours about in the vehicle (below) to see the vast amount of acreage that is being mined for peat. The mining is a commercial operation on a huge scale. Classes on bog wildlife are also available, but must be arranged and are located in a different area.

The **Clara Bog,** a raised bog 2 km south of Clara, can be viewed from the public road. It is not safe to access the bog. For those with a great interest in the fauna and flora of the bogs, the Bord na Mona can be contacted.

Bog Rail Tour

Roscommon

ROSCOMMON is in the province of Connaught. It is bordered on the east by the Shannon waterway. Since this area was left to the Irish by Cromwell it retained the social and cultural patterns of the Irish. Three-quarters of the land is agricultural while the remainder is peat bog.

STONE AGE

1. Drumanone Portal Tomb is one of the largest in Ireland. It is west of Boyle by R294.

ANCIENT
IRELAND

2. Rathcroghan, with its earthworks and monuments, was the center of an ancient kingdom that is full of legend with few facts. It was here that Queen Maeve (see p. 47) discovered that her husband, Ailill, had a better bull for his herd of cattle. It was from here that she gathered her army to go forth to fight Cuchulainn and the Ulster warriors. The site includes the King's Cemetery (Relignaree), the pillar stone of Dathi's mound, and a large ring fort as well as round earthworks, flat-topped mounds, linear earthworks and a souterrain with Ogham stones. Some ancient Irish

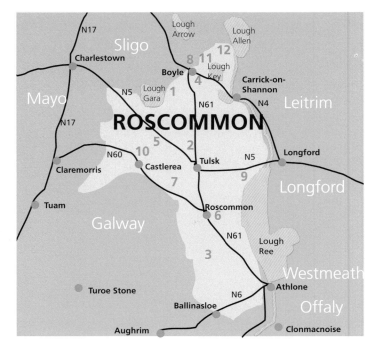

thought this was the place for entrance into the Underworld.[48] It is on N5, the Tulsk to Frenchpark road, and covers a large area which requires exploration and imagination.

3. Castlerange Stone is a rounded granite boulder decorated with curvilinear designs in the Celtic style of ornament known as La Tene. It is southwest of Roscommon by N65 on the Athleague to Roscommon road.

MONASTERIES

4. Boyle Abbey, Boyle, although a ruin, is well maintained and demonstrates the Cistercian influence as well as the transition to the Gothic style. There is a model there which shows how the abbey looked in its earlier days in the 12th century. There are also some interesting carvings of animals and figures and exquisite lancet windows. The windows of the nave have round Romanesque arches on the north and pointed arches on the south overlooking the cloister. It is an excellent example of the transitional style.

5. Clooneshanville Abbey is located by N5, west of French Park.

6. Roscommon Friary, Roscommon, is the ruin of a 13th century Dominican Friary founded by Felim O'Connor, Lord of Roscommon. His effigy includes his mail-clad warriors to support his tomb. It is south of Roscommon by N63.

13th Century

CASTLES

6. Roscommon Castle, Roscommon, is a vast square building with rounded corner bastions. The ownership of the castle changed frequently although it was mostly unoccupied until the 16th century when one part was transformed into a fortified Elizabethan manor house with mullioned windows. Although in ruins, it is an impressive site with access through a pasture and over a stile. It is a national monument and there is a caretaker. The site is to the northwest of Roscommon town by N60 to Ballymoe. This photograph does not show the expanse of the castle but demonstrates the mass and style.

14th Century

7. Ballintubber Castle is a ruin with two projecting turrets guarding the entrance gate on the east. The high walls, fortified by a polygonal tower at each corner, enclose a courtyard. After a 17th century restoration, the castle was occupied through the 19th century. It is now in ruins. Although this was an Irish royal residence of the O'Connors, it was severe in style and amenities, especially when compared with their founding of elaborate Ballintober Abbey, Co. Mayo. The O'Connors were more concerned with the salvation of their souls than with the elegance and comfort of their earthly residence.[49] It is located on the Ballymoe to Tulsk road, R367.

8. King House, Boyle, is a restored 18th century house located in the center of Boyle on N4.

9. Strokestown Park House, Strokestown, has the residential quarters in the central block while the north wing is the kitchen and the south wing is the stable with a unique vaulted ceiling. The gardens have been restored. In an outbuilding is a documentary presentation on the Great Famine of the 1840's. Strokestown is located on N5 between Tulsk and Scramoge.

10. Clonalis House, Castlerea, is a 19th century house standing on lands which have belonged to the O'Connor family for fifteen centuries. The inauguration stone of the Gaelic kingship is here, as well as a small museum which includes a copy of the last Brehon Law judgment in 1580 and the harp of Turlough O'Carolan. It is west of Castlerea on the Castlebar to Westport road.

11. Lough Key Forest Park, located two miles east of Boyle, contains the new Moylurg Tower which commands an excellent view of the surrounding area. There are boat trips to Castle Island where a 19th century folly contains traces of a MacDermot castle.

12. Carolan's Grave is located between Keadew and Ballyfarnan. The transept of the ruined church is the tombstone of Turlough Carolan, a blind harpist who wrote music and poetry including the melody of the "Star Spangled Banner."

9. Strokestown Famine Center, located in an outbuilding of Strokestown Park House (above), has a documentary presentation on the Great Famine of the 1840's. Strokestown is located on N5 between Tulsk and Scramoge.

IT IS HERE that the legendary Laegaire, king of Connacht, helped Fiachna of the Otherworld free his wife. Laegaire preferred to remain in the Otherworld at the bottom of Lough Naneane. Cruachain was the ancient site of the kings and queens of Connacht at Rathcrogan.

Sligo

S LIGO is in the province of Connacht on the west coast of Ireland. It contains much rough pasture, hills, mountains and peat bogs. Along the west coast are the Ox Mountains. In the southeast is Lough Arrow. There are many Stone Age monuments and burial sites.

William Butler Yeats's grave is here and it is on Lough Gill that the Isle of Innisfree was immortalized in his poem, "The Lake Isle of Innisfree."

1. Carrowkeel is a classic passage tomb cemetery located on a series of flat ridges overlooking Lough Arrow west of N4 and south of Castlebaldwin. It is best to leave the car there and walk the 6 km to the tombs. One of the tombs, Cairn E, has a passage tomb at one end and a court tomb at the other. There are no geometric patterns on these stones.

2. Carrowmore is the largest area of megalithic monuments in Ireland. Although many of the stones were quarried, a group of monuments (dolmens and stone circles) survive and will be preserved under the auspices of Dúchas. It is considered to be as old

or possibly older than Newgrange. It is 5km west of Sligo by R292 which skirts around Knocknarea.

3. *Knocknarea* is the largest unopened megalithic tomb in Ireland and is considered to be the dolmen of Queen Maeve's Grave. Many feel it worthwhile to hike to the top of the hill for the view. It is west of Sligo by R292.

4. *Creevykeel* is a court tomb on the east side of N15, the Sligo to Bundoran road.

5. *Heapstown Passage Grave* and ***Labby Rock*** are both located near Riverstown. The latter is an enormous portal dolmen.

6. *Magheraghanrush* (Deer Park) is in the area north of Lough Gill.

EARLY CHRISTIAN

7. *Drumcliff High Cross* and ***Tower*** are all that remain of an early monastery. It is across the road from the grave of W. B. Yeats and located beside N15 north of Sligo. The scriptural cross has an excellent stylized panel of Adam and Eve.

8. *Inismurray Island* lies off the coast between Donegal Bay and Sligo Bay. The 6th century monastery is a D-shaped enclosure surrounded by a high wall. The inside is divided into three parts: a collection of churches and beehive huts, cross-decorated slabs and cursing stones to bring bad luck to your enemies. Dotted throughout the island are prayer stations. A visit to the island is dependent upon the kindness of the wind and the tides.[50] This is under the protection of Dúchas and is in a good state of preservation. The island has long been a destination for pilgrims. Check with an Irish Tourist Board in the area for transport to the island.

MONASTERIES

9. *Sligo Abbey,* Sligo, was originally a Dominican friary founded in the 13th century. It is a delightful site with the usual high quality of Dúchas guides. Part of the abbey was founded in the 13th century (sacristy and chapter house) while the altar and other features are from the 15th century. The monument to O'Connor Don, 1624, is interesting for its iconography: "The cherub's head on the memorial symbolizes immortality, the skull death, the winged hour-glass the swift passage of time, or life running out, and the bunch of grapes redemption."[51]

10. *Ballymote Castle* was built in 1300 as a well defended fortress without a keep. There are six towers intact; it is south of Ballymote by R293.

11. *Lissadell House,* Drumcliff, is large, austere and interesting. It is in a lovely setting although not in the condition of its former years when Yeats was a frequent visitor. The most unusual member of the family was Constance, Countess Markievicz. She was condemned to death for her part in the Easter Rising but was pardoned and, later, was the first woman elected to the House of Commons in Westminster. Her active role and contributions are celebrated in the National Museum of Ireland in Dublin in the exhibition "Road to Independence." Lissadell is located west of N15. Take a secondary road at Drumcliff to the west.

THE TOWN HALL in Sligo is high Victorian with Venetian arches as at the Museum at Trinity College, Dublin. The variety of styles in the buildings in the city of Sligo makes it an interesting city to wander in.

WEST OF LOUGH ARROW, in Sligo, is considered to be Mag Tuired or the Plain of Reckoning. It was here that the Fir Bolgs first defeated the Tuatha De Danaan and later were defeated by them. The tomb of Queen Maeve, Mebd in the myths, on Knocknarea has not been excavated.

Statue of Yeats in Sligo.

Tipperary

TIPPERARY is in the province of Munster. The land is dominated by mountains, valleys and lowlands and is used for agriculture. The Golden Vale and areas to the south are very picturesque with the River Suir and the Gap of Aherlow. The west is bounded by the River Shannon and its lowlands.

The Rock of Cashel was of importance as both a royal seat and an early Christian site. This limestone outcrop has been of strategic importance.

1. Knockgraffon Motte is a large pyramid-shaped motte which is purported to have been the crowning place for the kings of Munster before the seat was transferred to Cashel. It is on the back roads north of Cahir.

2. Ahenny High Crosses are decorated with Celtic designs and embossed knobs. It is reached by R676 north of Carrick-on-Suir and a back road.

3. Rock of Cashel is also known as St. Patrick's Rock upon which is **Cormac's Chapel.** In the surrounding area are other interesting things to see: Hore Abbey, GPA Bolten Library and the Bru Boru, a national heritage center with an Irish cultural village. Cormac's Chapel is one of the most important sites in Ireland with reference to Christianity and early architecture. This chapel is perhaps the apex of Irish Romanesque architecture. It should not be missed. Not only does it display unique architectural features such as blind arcades (now covered with scaffolding), but in earlier days the large area above the vaulted ceiling of the chapel housed an extensive library. More information on this unique site is discussed in the text (see p. 69). It is located in Cashel.

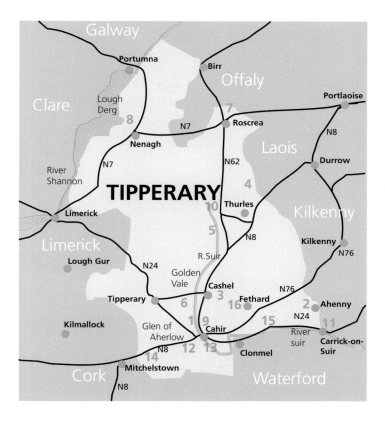

Cistercian

4. Kilcooly Abbey was a Cistercian house founded in the 12th century. It was burned in the 15th century and reconstructed. It is reached by going south from Urlingford on R690 to R689.

3. Hore Abbey, Cashel is a 13th century ruin of the last Cistercian house built in Ireland and is near the Rock of Cashel.

5. Holy Cross Abbey was originally founded in the 12th century by the Benedictines but was soon transferred to the Cistercians. The building is restored and used as a parish church. On the grounds is a replica of the Vatican gardens. It is located south of Thurles by R660.

Augustinian

6. Athassel Abbey, Golden, is the ruins of a 12th century Augustinian priory. The central tower of the main church, the nave and chancel walls are somewhat preserved. It is south of Golden on the Tipperary to Cashel road, N74.

13th Century

7. Roscrea Castle consists of a 13th century gate tower, curtain walls and two corner towers. The elegant Damer House was built within the curtain walls of the old castle. It has been restored and is now a Heritage Center.

8. Nenagh Castle, Nenagh, has a circular keep which has been restored. The walls were 16ft thick at the base and entry was by a removable ladder. It is located where N52 intersects N7.

15th Century

9. Cahir Castle, Cahir (or Caher), dates from the 15th and 16th centuries and is on a naturally protected island in the River Suir. The stout curtain walls with square and rounded bastions were not able to withstand the cannon of Queen Elizabeth, some cannon balls remain embedded. Well-restored, it offers an audiovisual presentation of the area.[52] Little remains of the original castle built on this site in the 13th century.

16th Century

10. Ballinahow Castle is a 16th century round castle or Purcell structure which is located between R503 and R498, west of Thurles.

11. Ormond Castle, Carrick-on-Suir, is an Elizabethan-style manor house built on the site of an earlier castle from which some walls and towers remain. It is also called Carrick-on-Suir Castle. This is a Butler creation which he designed and completed in the unfulfilled hope that Queen Elizabeth 1 would visit. It has some interesting features and appears to be one of the first with extensive use of mullioned windows. This would seem to reflect the more peaceful nature of the times although some evidence of earlier precautions and gun holes exists.

17th Century

12. Burncourt House, Boolakennedy, was also known as Everard's Castle, or Clogheen. It was reputed to have been set afire either by Lady Everard to prevent Cromwell from taking it or by Cromwell's troops. It was an amazing structure with "a long rectangular body flanked by four projecting square towers…twenty-six gables, seven hexagonal chimney-stacks and a great number of mullioned windows with hood-mouldings."[53] It is a mere shell of its former self that can be seen in the town of Burncourt on a country road which runs parallel to N8 (south of Cahir).

13. *Swiss Cottage,* Cahir, was built in the 19th century (completely restored 1985–89) as a fanciful realization of an idealized countryside cottage.[54] It has the appearance of a thatched roofed Swiss chalet and represents the fancies of the aristocracy, specifically Richard Butler, the 12th Lord of Cahir, who intended this as an occasional residence and a backdrop for entertaining. It is understated with disguised luxury and sits one mile south of Cahir on the banks of the Suir River. The cottage includes many architectural innovations and is a worthwhile place to visit.

7. *Damer House,* Roscrea, is an elegant town house built in the 18th century within the curtain walls of Roscrea Castle.

14. *Mitchelstown Caves,* Boolakennedy, are west of Cahir by N8. There is a guided tour of three caverns containing stalagmites and stalactites.

8. *Nenagh Heritage Center* is housed in the 19th century jail which is preserved as a museum.

15. *Tipperary Crystal* is located east of Clonmel on N24 and is open for tours.

16. *Fethard* is a small village which retains ruins of the Anglo-Norman settlement. There are also a 15th century crenellated church tower and sections of the 14th century wall with one of the three keeps of Fethard Castle.

Waterford

WATERFORD is in the province of Munster and bounded by rivers and ocean. To the west is the Blackwater River, to the north is the River Suir, to the east is the River Barrow and to the south is St. George's Channel. The west is mountainous while the east is dominated by the port of Waterford and its lowlands.

The port was founded by the Vikings and was a significant point of entry for the Anglo-Normans and the English. There is much beautiful scenery which encompasses rivers, mountains and woodland gardens.

STONE AGE

1. Knockeen Portal Tomb is located southwest of Waterford City and north of Tramore by secondary roads. It consists of two tall uprights supporting two capstones with one partially overlapping the other.

EARLY
CHRISTIAN

2. Ardmore Round Tower, Ardmore, is of the 12th century and nearly 100 ft tall with a conical cap. It is an excellent example and has the unusual feature of string courses. A good portion of the cathedral dates from this early period. There are some interesting sculptures as well as an early Ogham stone.[55] Ardmore is reached by taking R673 south off of N25 between Dungarvin and Youghal.

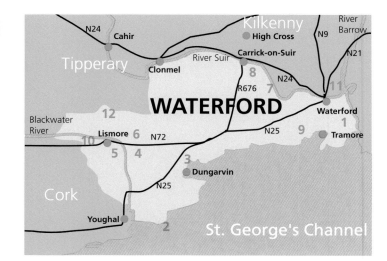

Norman

3. King John's Castle, Dungarvin, was built by King John in the late 12th century. There is a large round keep and fortified walls. There have been many modifications.

17th Century

4. Dromana Castle was an 18th century house which was demolished in 1957 to reveal the original 17th century structure. A number of rooms and the gardens are open to the public on a limited basis. In Villierstown go through the gateposts to Dromana Woods which are now managed by the Irish Forestry Service, Coillte.

5. Lismore Castle, Lismore, has been built upon since the 12th century. The present castle dates from the 19th century. The walls which surround the garden were built in the 17th century. There is a wonderful view of the castle on entering Lismore.

6. Cappoquin House, Cappoquin, is an 18th century mansion on the site of an old castle. The house burned down in 1923 but has been reproduced with great attention to detail.

5. Lismore Castle Gardens, Lismore, has an upper garden that is surrounded by walls built in the 17th century to protect the family from the turbulent troubles of the countryside. The lower garden is a Victorian pleasure garden. The architectural planning of the gardens is impressive and a visit here is most pleasant.

7. Mount Congreve, Kilmeaden, has a vast variety of the plants that grow well in Waterford. There are rhododendrons, azaleas, magnolias and camellias. Tour by appointment at magnolia blossom time is recommended.

8. Curraghmore Gardens are near Portlaw.

9. Celtworld, Tramore, is an audiovisual presentation of the myths and legends of the Celts in Ireland.

5. Lismore Heritage Town reveals the history of the town using multimedia sources. The town was one of THE centers of monastic learning in Europe. It was here that King Henry II of England received the submission of the Irish chiefs of Munster and Leinster in 1171. Shortly thereafter the monasteries were completely destroyed and Lismore's importance as a center of monastic learning and education ended. King John of England built the first castle on this site in 1185. Cromwell burned the town in 1645 and it remained in neglect until the 19th century.

10. *Ballysaggartmore,* Lismore, is an elaborate Gothic gateway and bridge to a house which was never built. Called The Towers, it can be seen after a twenty-minute hike from R688. It is an interesting demonstration of the Gothic in domestic architecture. It was a folly instigated by a rivalry between two sisters. Unfortunately, this sister's husband ran out of money. The Lismore Heritage center has some excellent literature. There is also an activity booklet for a walk on the nature trail through The Towers for the young of heart and spirit.

4. *The Hindu-Gothic Gateway,* also known as Dromana Bridge on the Dromana Drive, is located just south of Cappoquin and east of Lismore. It was inspired by George IV's interest in Eastern styles of architecture as seen in his extravaganza at Brighton and drawings of the Taj Mahal. While the owner of Dromana was on his honeymoon in 1826, the Hindu-Gothic gateway was erected of temporary materials to greet and surprise the returning bridal couple. They were so enchanted with the gateway that they had it built in durable materials. The Irish Georgian Society has restored the lodge and gateway.

Reginald Tower, Waterford

11. *Waterford* town is interesting to visit and a walking tour is available. Parts of the original city walls survive as does the Reginald Tower (photo at left) which was built as a fortress by the Vikings in the 11th century. This area is also famous for Waterford crystal. The factory which offers guided tours is located several miles south on N25. Waterford Castle is now a luxury hotel accessible by ferry to the island, Ballinakill. It has an interesting history and is built on the foundation of an old keep.

12. *Mount Melleray Abbey* is an active Trappist monastery built in the 19th century. Only the chapel is open to the public for services. It is northeast of Lismore by N72 and R669.

WESTMEATH is in the province of Leinster. With Lough Ree and the River Shannon on the west, the remainder of the land is rolling lowlands, lakes and hills. Only a small part of the county is under cultivation. Bogs are more common in the west. The Royal Canal passes through Westmeath.

1. Hill of Uisneath, marked by the Stone of Divisions, is the center of Ireland, for it was at this point that the original provinces met. It was also a site of religious significance, associated with the druids and a fire-cult; it was here on the first of May that fires were lit for Bel to protect the cattle from disease. During excavation a huge bed of ashes was found although there is no evidence of living quarters or pottery from this time. During the 3rd to 5th centuries AD it was the seat of Ireland's high kings. There are burial mounds and a fort. It is located 29 miles west of Mulligar by R390 between Ballymore and Loughanavally.

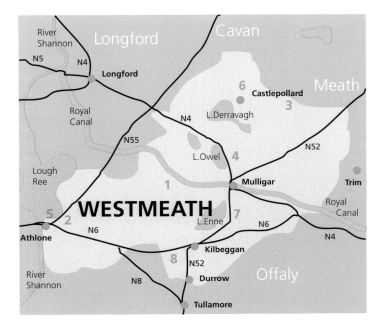

2. Twyford Cross, Bealin, is a sculptured high cross from the 9th century that is west of Athlone by R390.

3. Fore Abbey was an early church and Benedictine abbey. It was within the Pale and fortified to protect it from attack from the Irish. "Even without the 'Seven Wonders' (such as water flowing uphill) which local tradition associates with Fore, the place is wonderful in itself."[55] The abbey is under the protection and preservation of the Dúchas. It is two miles from Castlepollard by R195.

4. St. Munna's Church is a 15th century fortified church with a four-story tower. It is located west of Crookedwood by R394 from Mulligar.

13th Century

5. Athlone Castle was a 13th century Norman castle. The polygonal keep is the oldest part of the structure while the curtain wall and three fortified towers were added later. It has a commanding position on the River Shannon and the Lough Ree crossing. The upper part of the castle was altered in the 19th century. There is an exhibition center in the keep of the castle which shows the siege of Athlone following the Battle of the Boyne.

6. Tullynally Castle, Castlepollard, has 19th century Gothic enlargements added to a 17th century edifice by Francis Johnston to create a sham castle. Beyond the arched gateway is a great gray pile of turrets and crenellations which are set upon high ground sloping south to Lough Derravaragh (see "Mythology" below). Throughout the years the house has been fortified, embellished and expanded. It is located north of Mullingar and just outside of Castlepollard.

7. Belvedere, near Mulligar, is an elegant 18th century villa which is a solid gray limestone house of two stories over a basement with a long front and curved end bows. It has delicate rococo plaster work on the ceilings. There are extensive gardens. There are spicy tales of this wicked earl and his charming wife who preferred his younger brother. It is south of Mulligar by N52

6. Tullynally Castle Gardens, Castlepollard, have a woodland garden, flower garden and kitchen garden as well as a forest walk.

8. Locke's Distillery, Kilbeggan, welcomes visitors. The buildings have been restored and became a museum on the Process of Irish Pot Whiskey Distillation. Locke's was founded in the mid-18th century and closed in 1953. It was bought in 1954 by Cooley Distillery which makes its whiskey in County Louth and brings it here to mature in casks.

ON LOUGH DERRAVARAGH the Children of Lir (see p. 244) lived for their first 300 years. They had been brought to this lake by their stepmother to be killed but instead they were given a curse: to become swans for 900 years. During their 300 year stay at Lough Derravaragh they talked and sang for their friends and their father. They brought serenity to those who came to hear them – people from all over Ireland – and they were happy. When the 300 years was over, they had to follow the terms of the curse and spent the next 300 years in the north – the Sea of Mayle.

Wexford

W EXFORD is in the province of Leinster in the southeast of
Ireland. On the west are the Blackstair Mountains. Most
of the area is lowlands although the coast has wide bays with
rocky cliffs and sand dunes. Farming and cattle are the chief economic pursuits.

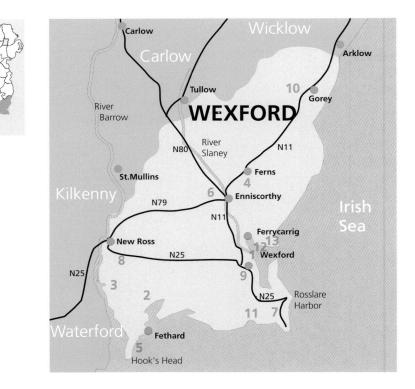

*1. **Selskar Abbey*** was founded in the 12th century and is located near Westgate in Wexford City. The outer walls and square tower are well preserved.

Cistercian

*2. **Tintern Abbey*** was a Cistercian abbey founded in 1200 by monks who came from Wales. Although the church was probably built in the early 13th century, it was altered and made into living quarters after the Dissolution of the Monasteries. These alterations have been removed and the building has been preserved and is now under the care of the Dúchas. It is between Wellington Bridge and Duncannon.

*3. **Dunbrody Abbey*** was founded in the 12th century by the monks from St. Mary's Abbey in Dublin. It is well preserved although roofless. It is beside R733, north of Arthurstown.

Augustinian

*4. **Ferns Abbey,*** Ferns, was a monastery founded in the 7th century which is now marked by an early 19th century Church of Ireland cathedral. Parts of the 13th century building are visible. The tower is an interesting feature which is square at the bottom and round at the top. It was built by Dermot MacMurrough, the king of Leinster who invited Henry II of England to invade Ireland. It is located north of Enniscorthy by N11.

Norman

*5. **Dunconnon Fort,*** Hook Island Peninsula, is a 12th century fortress that was reinforced in 1588.

13th Century

*4. **Ferns Castle*** is a 13th century castle with a rectangular keep and round towers. On the first floor is a chapel with a vaulted ceiling. It is northeast of Enniscorthy by N11.

*6. **Enniscorthy Castle,*** Enniscorthy (see p. 114)

15th Century

*7. **Rathmacnee Castle*** is a well-preserved 15th century structure located south of Wexford by R738.

*8. **J. F. Kennedy Arboretum,*** Campile, was established in memory of JFK as a scientific plant collection with over 4000 plants and new ones still being added. It is 7 miles south of New Ross by R733.

9. Johnstown Castle Demesne, Murrinstown, is a 19th century Gothic Revival castle in a wonderful setting with trees, shrubs, three lakes, ruined tower house, statue walk and walled garden with hothouses.

8. Kilmokea,* Campile, is open for admission by appointment.

10. Ram House Gardens,* Coolgreany, Gorey, are divided into small rooms allowing for greater variety in a woodland glade.

OTHER SITES **11. Tacumshin Windmill** is a 19th century three-story tower mill of 17th century design. It was reconstructed in 1952 with its original thatched roof. The mill, operational until 1936, is under the aegis of the Dúchas.

12. Wexford includes the **Westgate Heritage Center.** This 13th century gate tower is the setting for the presentation of the history of Wexford.

13. Irish National Heritage Park, Ferrycarrig, presents 9000 years of Irish history.

*Indicates limited
access or access
by appointment

Wicklow

WICKLOW is in the province of Leinster with the Wicklow Mountains the most impressive feature. The mountains, valleys, waterfalls, rocky cliffs and beaches make this one of the most scenic areas to visit. Nearly half the land is under crops or pasture but the rest is wild and inaccessible.

The Norse settled Wicklow, as did the Anglo-Normans, although the Irish remained a presence and led forays against the Pale from the protective wilderness of the Wicklow Mountains.

1. Rathgall Stone Fort is constructed with three concentric walls spaced at various distances apart. The inner wall, made of stone, may be from as late as the medieval period, while the outer two, much older, are made of earth with stone facing. The archeological finds here have been impressive. They have included 7th century BC cremated burials, a timber structure and a workshop of a Bronze Age metalsmith. The fragments of clay molds show that he was producing swords and spearheads made of bronze. This site is by R725, east of Tullow.

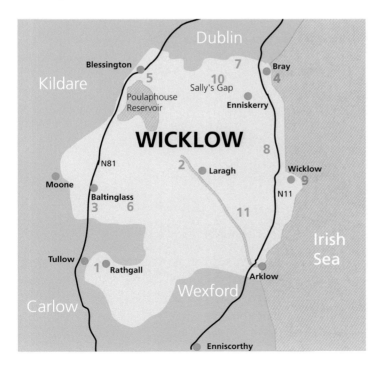

EARLY
CHRISTIAN

2. Glendalough is one of the most impressive sites in Ireland. It is not reconstructed, only preserved. This monastic site is spectacular for its location, a glen between two lakes, as well as a preserved oratory and round tower. There are also many ruins of churches from later periods showing many Romanesque-style doorways and windows. It is reached by R756 on the Hollywood to Laragh road.

MONASTERIES

Cistercian

3. Baltinglas Abbey was founded by the famous Dermot Mac-Murrough, king of Leinster, who sought the help of Henry II and ran off with the wife of the King of Brefni. She built the Nun's Chapel at Clonmacnoise. Parts of the original cloister – it is a good example of the Cistercian floor plan – have been restored. It is reached by N81 on the Blessington to Tullow road.

CASTLE/
HOUSES

4. Kilruddery House and **Gardens,** Bray, is a 19th century Elizabethan Revival manor incorporating a 17th century house. The garden is baroque on a grand scale. The house is outside of Bray on the Greystone road.

5. Russborough House, Blessington (below), now houses the Beit Art Collection and has fine examples of Francini stucco work. For his collection Mr. Beit, a cofounder of the DeBeers Diamond Mine, focused on Dutch Reform and Spanish art. Art lovers should not miss this opportunity. Take N81 south of Blessington.

6. Humewood Castle, Kiltegan, is a 19th century castellated mansion. It is reached by R747, south of Baltinglass.

Russborough House

7. Powerscourt Gardens, Enniskerry, has extensive gardens that are Italianate in design.

8. Mount Usher Gardens, Ashford, incorporates a vast collection of plants with a romantic design. The gardens wander along the Vartry River along woodland paths and groves. It is located by N11, north of Wicklow City.

9. Wicklow Gardens Festival, Wicklow, in May/June offers an opportunity to visit some small private gardens.

10. Powerscourt Waterfall is located several miles from Powers- court. The falls are at their best after several days of rain.

11. Avondale Forest Park is the national forestry training center. It includes views, trees and woodland trails. The restored neoclassical house was the birthplace of Charles Stewart Parnell. The reception and dining rooms are filled with Parnell's memorabilia.

THE SITE OF the Destruction of Da Derga's Hostel was near Bray. It begins with the Wooing of Etain and ends with Conaire breaking all his geis. He was killed by the marauders whom he had driven from the land.

1. Extensive descriptions of these gardens are available in *Irish Gardens* by Reeves-Smyth and *Gardens of Ireland* published by the Irish Tourist Board.

2. Heaney, Marie, *Over Nine Waves*, p. 3

3. Ibid., p. 50

4. Ibid., p. 33

5. Ibid., pp. 22–36

6. Ibid., pp. 155–214

7. Smyth, Daragh, *Guide to Mythology*, pp. 149–150

8. Ibid., p. 150

9. Ibid., p. 150

10. Woodman, P.C., "A Mesolithic Camp in Ireland, p. 120

11. Manning C., *Irish Field Monuments*, p. 3

12. O'Sullivan, D.Muiris, *Megalithic Art in Ireland*, p.7

13. Harbison, Potterton and Sheehy, *Irish Art and Architecture*, p. 12

14. O'Kelly, *Illustrated Guide to Lough Gur, Co.Limerick*, p. 34

15. Ibid., p. 7

16. Mallory., J.P., *Navan Fort, The Ancient Capital of Ulster*

17. Manning, C., pp. 3–4

18. *Heritage: A Visitor's Guide*, p. 63

19. Ibid., p. 103

20. Ibid., p. 64

21. *Irish Archeology Illustrated*, edited by Michael Ryan, p. 137

22. Morton, H.V., *In Search of Ireland*, p. 46

23. Ibid., p. 47

24. O'Keefe, *Barryscourt Castle and the Irish Tower-House*, p. 7

25. Harbison, p. 194

26. Yeats, W.B., *Selected Poetry*, intro. by A. Norman Jeffares, p. xv

27. "Constitution of Ireland"

28. Smyth, p. 64

29. Heaney, p. 55

30. Morton, p. 68

31. Ibid., pp. 204–207

32. Ibid., p. 149

33. *Heritage: A Visitor's Guide*, pp. 85–86

34. deBreffny and ffolloitt, *The Houses of Ireland*, p. 45

35. *Heritage: A Visitor's Guide*, p. 60

36. Harbison, pp. 67–68

37. *Heritage: A Visitor's Guide*, p. 151

38. Ibid., p. 152

39. Ibid., pp. 154–155

40. Ibid., pp. 86–87

41. deBreffny and ffolloitt, pp. 217–218

42. Irish Tourist Board, *Historic Castles and Houses and Gardens of Ireland*, p. 28

43. Smyth, p. 40

44. deBreffny and ffoloitt, p. 12

45. *Heritage: A Visitor's Guide*, pp. 100–101

46. Ibid., pp. 140–141

47. Irish Tourist Board, p. 24

48. *Heritage: A Visitor's Guide*, p. 103

49. deBreffny and ffolloitt, p. 12

50. *Heritage: A Visitor's Guide*, pp. 119–120

51. Ibid., p. 121

52. Office of Public Works, *Cahir Castle*, p. 4

53. deBreffny and ffolloitt, p. 51

54. Office of Public Works, *Swiss Cottage*, p. 5

55. *Heritage: A Visitor's Guide*, p. 47

56. Ibid., p. 155

Biel, Jorg, "Treasure from a Celtic Tomb," *National Geographic*, March 1980, vol. 157, no. 3, pp. 429–438

Boss, Ruth Isabel, *Irish Wild Flowers*, Belfast, The Appletree Press, Ltd., 1986

Conniff, Richard, "Ireland on Fast Forward," *National Geographic*, September, 1994, vol. 186, no. 3, pp. 2–36

Cross, J.R., *Peatlands: Wastelands or Heritage?*, Dublin Stationery Office, 1989

D'Arcy, Gordon, *Birds of Ireland*, Belfast, The Appletree Press, Ltd., 1986

de Breffny, Brian, and Rosemary ffolliott, *The Houses of Ireland*, London, Thames and Hudson, 1992

Delderfield, Eric R. ed., *Kings and Queens of England: Revised and Updated*, New York, Dorset Press, 1981

Dúchas: The Heritage Service, *Visitor Information for Heritage Sites*, Dublin, Ireland, 2000

Encyclopedia Britannica Eye Witness Visual Dictionaries, *The Visual Dictionary of Buildings*, New York , Dorling Kindersley, Inc., 1992

Feehan, John and Grace O'Donovan, *The Magic of Coole*, Dublin Stationery Office, 1993

Fodor's Ireland 93, New York, Fodor's Travel Publications, Inc., 1992

Foster, R.F., editor, *The Oxford Illustrated History of Ireland*, Oxford, Oxford University Press, 1993

Friendly, Alfred, "Great Book of Kells in Shining Exhibit of Ancient Irish Art," *Smithsonian*, October 1977, Vol 8, no. 7 pp. 66–75

Gilbert, Stuart, *James Joyce's Ulysses: A Study*, New York, Alfred A. Knopf, 1952

Harbison, Peter, Homan Potterton and Jeanne Sheehy, *Irish Art and Architecture: From Prehistory to the Present*, New York, Thames and Hudson, Inc., 1993

Heaney, Marie, *Over Nine Waves: A Book of Irish Legends*, London, Faber and Faber, Ltd., 1994

Hodgson, Bryan, "Irish Ways Live on in Dingle," *National Geographic*, April, 1976, vol. 149, no. 4, pp. 551–576

Hodgson, Bryan, "War and Peace in Northern Ireland," *National Geographic*, April 1981, vol. 159, no. 4, pp. 470–500

Ireland and Northern Ireland, A Visitor's Guide: Insert Map, *National Geographic*, April, 1981, vol. 160, no. 4

Irish Archeology, Illustrated, edited by Michael Ryan, Dublin, Country House, 1994

Irish Tourist Board, *Historic Castles and Houses and Gardens in Ireland*, Dublin, 1994

Joyce, James, *Dubliners*, London, Penguin Twentieth Century Classics, 1992

Judge, Joseph, "The Travail of Ireland," *National Geographic*, April 1981, vol. 159, no. 4, pp. 432–441

Keaveney, Raymond, et al., *National Gallery of Ireland*, London, Scala Publications Ltd., 1990

Kelly, Eamon P., *Early Celtic Art in Ireland*, Dublin, Town House and Country House, 1993

Kostof, Spiro, *A History of Architecture: Settings and Rituals*, New York, Oxford University Press, 1985

Levathes, Louise E., "Mysteries of the Bog," *National Geographic*, March 1987, vol. 171, no. 3, pp. 397–420

Lord Dunsany, *Ireland: A Book of Photographs*, London, Anglo-Italian Publication Limited

McGarry, Mary, *Great Folk Tales of Old Ireland*, New York, Bell Publishing Company, 1972

Mallory, J.P., *Navan Fort: The Ancient Capital of Ulster*, Belfast, Ulster Archeological Society

Meehan, Aidan, *Celtic Design: A Beginner's Manual*, Great Britian, Thames and Hudson, 1993

Michelin Green Guide: Ireland, Harrow, Michelin Tyre Public Limited, Co., 1992

Morton, H.V., *In Search of Ireland*, New York, Dodd, Mead & Co., 1930

Nuttgens, Patrick, *Simon and Schuster's Pocket Guide to Architecture*, New York, Simon and Schuster, 1991

O'Connor, Ulick, *Irish Tales and Sagas*, Dublin, Town House and Country House, 1993

Office of Public Works, Cahir Castle

Office of Public Works, St. Patrick's Rock, Cashel

O'Keefe, Tadhg, *Barryscourt Castle and the Irish Tower-House*, Kinsale, Gandon Editions, 1997

O'Kelly, M.J. &C., *Illustrated Guide to Lough Gur*, Co. Limerick, Cork, 1981

O'Sullivan, Dr. Muiris, *Megalithic Art in Ireland*, Dublin, Town House and Country House, 1993

Heritage: A Visitor's Guide, Dublin, Office of Public Works, Stationery Office, 1990

Putnam, John J., "A New Day for Ireland," *National Geographic*, April 1981, vol. 150, no. 4, pp. 442–469

Reeves-Smyth, Terrence, *Irish Gardens*, Belfast, The Appletree Press, Ltd., 1994

Reeves-Smyth, Terrence, *Irish Country Houses*, Belfast, The Appletree Press, Ltd., 1994

Reeves-Smyth, Terrence, *Irish Castles*, Belfast, The Appletree Press, Ltd., 1995

Renfrew, Colin, "Ancient Europe is Older Than We Thought," *National Geographic*, November 1977, vol. 152, no. 5, pp. 615–623

Ryan, Michael, editor, *Irish Archeology Illustrated*, Dublin, Country House, 1997

Sancha, Sheila, *The Castle Story*, New York, Harper & Row Publishers, 1984

Severin, Timothy, "The Voyage of 'Brendon'," *National Geographic*, December 1977, vol. 162, no. 6, pp. 769–797

Simms, George Otto, *Exploring the Book of Kells*, Dublin, The O'Brien Press, 1988

Smyth, Daragh, *A Guide to Mythology*, Dublin, Irish Academic Press, 1988

Synge, J. M., *The Complete Plays*, London, Methuen Drama, 1993

Wallace, Martin, *A Short History of Ireland*, Belfast, The Appletree Press, Ltd., 1986

Woodman, P.C. "A Mesolithic Camp in Ireland," *Scientific American*, August 1981, vol. 160, no.2, pp. 120–129

Yeats, W. B., *Selected Poetry*, London, Pan Books Ltd., 1990